A GOBLIN POSTMAN MAGICAL MYSTERY

WIB WILLETT

AND THE

TOMBSTONE CLUB

PATRICIA BOW

Acknowledgements

Warm thanks are due to Susan Meredith Fish and Eric Bow, who read the manuscript and offered generous encouragement as well as perceptive criticism.

Chapter 1

EVERYTHING was changed.

To start with, the tall black gate with the curling iron vines and leaves that Wib used to climb on and look through: that was gone. The part of the stone wall that used to run along Circle Road was also gone, or most of it. A stub remained, attached to the gatepost to the right of the driveway entrance.

The proper thing, he knew, would be to walk openly up the driveway to the house and knock on the front door. He thought about that a minute. *Right. And get it slammed in my face.*

So he went in along the south garden wall instead, then fought his way toward the west wall behind the house. The tidy lawn he remembered had exploded into a jungle of tall grass and wildflowers — daisies, black-eyed Susans, chicory, goldenrod, milkweed, and a dozen other kinds of plants he had no names for — all thriving despite the trees that chopped the August sunshine into chunks of black shade.

Wib was tall for twelve, but most of the plants stood taller than he did. They kept slapping him in the face and catching at his shirt with thorns. You'd think they were defending the house and he was an enemy commando.

He stumbled out into an open space at the back. On the west side of the house, and on the north, the area between the house and the garden wall was filled with vegetable and herb plots. They were thriving too, the beans emerald green and longer than his hand, the tomatoes red as stoplights. Scents of ripe cantaloupe and sage drifted on the warm breeze.

Wib remembered his mother's failed attempts at gardening inside these walls. She always said it was because she didn't have a green thumb. Somebody here sure had a green thumb.

He stopped behind a row of ten-foot-tall sunflowers, rubbed his scratched arms and whacked unsuccessfully at the smears of pollen and plant juice all over his T-shirt and chinos.

Meanwhile he studied the house. It looked almost exactly as he remembered, except brighter and cleaner. A big red-brick mansion sparkling with freshly painted white woodwork.

Not a tidy house, though. It was one of those sprawly old places with things sticking out all over: bow windows, wrap-around porch, gables covered with rounded shingles like fish scales, brick chimneys in clusters. And, the thing that always caught your eye, a turret capped with a pale blue-green copper dome that rose an extra storey above the main roof at the northwest corner. The observatory.

What he'd really come to see was a window high in the rear wall, overlooking the vegetable garden. A small, round window made of coloured glass that showed a robin on a branch. And yes, there it was, same as ever.

No, wait. He shaded his eyes with a hand and squinted. Was it the same? It had to be, it was stained glass set in lead. Even if it broke, they couldn't just...

He stared, blinked, stared again. A face was in there behind the window, a pale oval peering down at him. His breath caught. If someone had found his secret place....

If they had, the thing he'd come for was probably gone. And he'd have failed, and years of guilt and worry and hope would all be wasted. And nothing would ever be right, ever again.

He looked again and saw no face. But the stab of anxiety stayed, and rankled. *I could kick myself! Should have known!* After six years away, how could he expect to find things exactly the way he'd left them?

Behind him somebody yelped. Leaves thrashed. He turned around and saw a girl trying to climb up into the ancient silver maple that grew against the wall at the back of the garden. He remembered that tree, and its massive lower limb that rested on top of the wall and would probably one day demolish it.

The girl was swearing under her breath, but not very far under. She kept slithering down the trunk on her useless shiny sandals. A side pocket of her white shorts caught on a stub of broken branch. She freed herself, tearing the pocket; scrambled into the lowest crotch, then up into the one above that and out of sight.

Wib knew that place, he used to sit there himself. It was like sitting in a green tent, private and special. Until somebody walked close to the tree and looked up and noticed you.

An idea lit down in the gloom of his brain. A way to get inside the house, maybe.

He walked over to the tree and looked up. "Hi!"

She frowned down at him out of a triangular face: sharp at the chin and wide across the eyes, which were big, gleaming, and green as the leaves. Her hair was short and light brown and stuck up all over her head in fluffy points. She looked about his own age, twelve or so. Her red tank top and white shorts were streaked with tree dirt and crushed leaf juices. Her knees were scratched.

"Never seen you before," she said accusingly. "Who the heck are you?"

"Wib."

"Funny name."

"It's short for Wilbur."

"Even funnier."

He frowned back up at her. This conversation was not going well. "So what's yours?"

She tilted her head back and gazed down her nose at him from half-lidded eyes. "They call me... Rebecca..." she said in a throaty voice.

"Yeah, sure." This was so fake. "What's your real name?"

"That is my real name." She untilted her head and just stared, which made her look more normal. "You're new, right?"

"New to Amstey, yeah."

"Really? Where you from?"

"Toronto. We moved here yesterday."

"Cool!" She sat up straight. "Where you living now?"

"Fairview Avenue."

"Uh-oh, one of those falling-down places by the lake?"

"It's not falling down. Just needs some fixing." Here was his opportunity. "Not like this house. Must be nice living here, eh?"

"How would I know?"

"Well, you live here."

"What makes you think that?"

Patience, Wib told himself. He pointed. "You're up in that tree."

"I'm staying out of sight, *if* you don't mind. Show yourself around here and before you know it you're pulling weeds, or making baskets, or *knitting*, for Pete's sake!"

"What are you, slave labour?"

"Are you nuts? I'm in the club! *Not* my idea!" She waved furious hands fanwise.

Wib took a breath. *Patience.* "What club?"

She opened and closed her mouth, shut her eyes tight, snapped them open. Then scrambled down, ripping the other side pocket on the way. She reached back up to drag down a small colourful cloth bag on a long strap, that had gotten hooked on a stub of branch.

He had a moment to see that she was about his height, but smaller-boned. With that feathery short brown hair, she made him

4

think of a tall sparrow. Then without warning she grabbed his wrist and started running. He could have pulled free any time, but he was curious to find out where she would take him.

They ran along the wall northward. Then, skirting the herb garden, they ran along the north wall to the front, where it turned a corner and became the east wall, the stub next to the gatepost. She pulled him out onto the sidewalk and let go of his wrist.

"There!" She stabbed the air savagely. A large sign was bolted to the stub of wall: a board painted white, its neat black letters touched up with gold and green here and there.

> # THE THREE SISTERS
> 3 Circle Road
>
> Hand-crafted textiles ~ Classes
>
> Fresh baking ~ Organic produce

Some kind of shop, Wib thought.

A smaller wooden A-frame sign stood on the strip of grass between the wall and the sidewalk. It said:

> # THE TUESDAY CLUB*
> Crafts ~ Fun ~ Friendship
>
> Boys and girls 10-14
>
> 3-5 p.m. Free!
>
> *Includes all Monday Club members

Rebecca kicked the sign. "Didn't you see that?"

"No. I came in along the south wall, not this way."

"Staying out of sight, huh? Not so dumb after all." She knelt by the A-frame sign, dug a large marker out of her cloth bag and blacked out the word TUESDAY.

"Hey!"

"It's the only way I have left to express my feelings." Above the blacked-out word she printed TOMBSTONE, so that the sign now said THE TOMBSTONE CLUB.

"That doesn't make any sense."

"Sure it does." She stood up, capped the marker and stuck it in her bag, which she slung over her shoulder. "It expresses how I feel about being forced to join this stupid club. It's like being dead and buried. This is only the second day and I already hate it. You won't like it either."

"I'm not joining any club." He looked nervously toward the house.

"Good for you. So what are you doing here?"

Before he could think of an answer, the front door of the house opened and a tall, thin teenaged girl with short white hair stepped out onto the wraparound porch. She pointed at them, jerked a thumb back over her shoulder, turned on the spot and went back in.

"Who's that?"

"One of the Three Sisters. Aster Morgenstern. Talk about made-up names, that one's got to be fake."

"Why?"

"It means Star Morningstar, get it?" Rebecca stuck her hands in her ripped pockets and moped along the curving driveway, under its honour guard of big old silver maples, toward the house.

"If you hate this club so much, why don't you just go home?"

"Don't be ridiculous."

6

"It's not like school. You don't have to be here. Nobody's hand-cuffed you to the porch."

"No, but my gran or my dad would just bring me straight back. It's no use. I'm trapped!"

Chapter 2

ASTER MORGENSTERN was waiting inside the open door, one bare foot impatiently kicking the floor. Wib saw that her hair wasn't white, it was very pale blond: bleached, he figured. It was even shorter than Rebecca's. She wore low-cut tight jeans that showed her belly button ring, and a tank top with sequined green leaves on it. She looked bored, fed-up, and about eighteen.

Rebecca sailed through the doorway ahead of Wib, chin in the air. Before she'd taken two steps Aster's thin arm snapped across like a subway turnstile bar and Rebecca stopped so short she bounced back.

Aster levelled her other palm. "Hand it over."

"Uh, what?"

Aster's eyes narrowed to shining slits.

"Okay! Okay!" Rebecca fumbled in her bag and pulled out a sky-blue iPod. She slammed it into Aster's palm.

"Now go! You're late! " Aster waved them up the stairs.

Wib just had time for a glance around. Wide, high, airy front hall, white marble floor with small black triangles inlaid around the edges, glossy dark wood panelling halfway up the walls. There was a huge coat stand to their right with a full-length mirror set in its back and a low cabinet against the wall to their left. Farther in, a clock ticked on a high shelf and a graceful white staircase curved up to the floors above. All much as he remembered.

Then they were trotting up the staircase ahead of Aster. "No electronics allowed, eh?" Wib murmured.

"Yeah, stupid rule." Rebecca glanced back and added loudly,

"And Aster is so suspicious!"

At the top of the stairs they stepped out into a wide corridor. They were facing three tall windows at the front end, with arched doorways left and right. Aster waved them through the door to the left. A cardboard sign tacked up next to the door said CRAFTS ROOM.

The crafts room was a huge space with a bronze-and-crystal chandelier, unlit, hanging from a gilded plaster circle in the ceiling high above. The polished floor was inlaid in star patterns in dark and light woods, centred on a six-foot star mosaic under the chandelier. The walls were covered with gleaming pale stuff like satin, divided by two-foot strips of mirror etched with ferns and roses around their edges. All along the front wall, a row of windows reached nearly to the ceiling.

It was, in fact, a ballroom, a place where crowds of people used to come, all dressed up, to dance — which they hadn't done for more than fifty years, according to Wib's mother. He knew enough now to be sure that most houses did not have ballrooms. It was the saddest room in the house, his mother said, because it ought to be full of light and people and music, and instead it was full of dust and silence.

The chandelier didn't work. Wib had never seen it lit up. The only hint of the room's musical past was an upright piano standing in a front corner, half covered by a length of frayed blue velvet that might once have been a window drape; and, pushed into a back corner, a tangle of spindly gold-painted chairs that looked as if they would collapse if a flea sat on them.

Wib's parents had never used the room, never held dances. You'd think it would be a good place to play on a rainy day, with all that space, but Wib had never played there. He'd only wandered through, making a game of walking just on the inlaid stars and the mazelike patterns between them.

Now the silence was gone, and there were people. A mob of girls milled around four long wooden tables set up near the windows, doing things with string and yarn and beads and paper and flowers and more stuff that Wib had no wish to see any closer-up. Most of the girls were talking and some were laughing at the same time. There were no boys.

He stared with horror and took a step back toward the doorway, but Aster gripped his shoulder with a long-fingered and surprisingly strong hand and he froze. "Stay," she said, as if he were a dog. He stayed.

"Now you." Aster pointed at Rebecca, upturned that hand and crooked the finger. Rebecca followed her across the room as if on a string. Aster pushed her into the middle of a group of girls who were sitting in a circle on wooden chairs, doing something with coloured twine and feathers. Rebecca slumped onto the one empty chair. Aster handed her a tangle of twine. "Here's your project. Needs work. Ask for help if you need it." Two of the other girls sighed loudly, rolled their eyes and exchanged whispers. Rebecca started tearing at her tangled mess.

When Aster came back to Wib, she was holding a clipboard with a paper on it. "You're our first boy. That's cool."

"Uh, wait. I'm not here to join the club."

She pinned him with her eyes, which were a bright, pale blue, intense inside a frame of black lashes. Nailed like that, Wib found it hard to think. He dithered: "I, you see, I used to live here and I, um, I left something here and I, I just need to go and get it."

She stared a moment longer, then grinned. Her teeth were small and white and even but looked sharp, as if she could cut string with them. "What, let you wander around the place and take things? Not bloody likely!" She held out the clipboard. "If you wanna stay, sign up."

Wib took a steadying breath, furious at himself and at her. He glanced across the room and saw Rebecca watching him. She made a fist and stuck it up in the air. The other girls ducked their heads. Wib thought: *Right, this is pathetic.*

He looked up at Aster, who was at least six inches taller than he was and looked even taller when seen close up like this. "I don't want to be rude. But could I please speak to somebody else? Somebody, uh, older?"

She gazed down at him coldly, then smiled her sharp smile. "Older. You betcha." She whirled around and strode from the room. Before Wib had time to take more than one steadying breath, and ask himself why one bad-tempered teenager could intimidate him like this, she was back, two steps ahead of a woman in a blue denim jumper over a white T-shirt, and sturdy canvas sandals.

The woman looked around the room, smiled, and then directed the smile at Wib. He smiled back, though he hadn't meant to. "I'm Dulcey Blythe," she said, in a voice warm and rich as baked bread. Didn't look anything like Aster's sister, Wib thought. She might have been anywhere from thirty to fifty, sturdy but not plump, long gold-brown hair braided and the braids wound around her head like a crown. Her eyes were sky-blue and smiling. She smelled like baked bread, too, and something else spicy and sweet.

While Wib stared up at her, she dipped a hand into one of the big pockets of her jumper and brought out a cookie and held it out. He took it and bit in. Oatmeal, his very favourite, and better than any he'd ever eaten: crunchy and chewy and buttery and with chocolate chips and raisins and walnuts mixed in. As he chewed, and gazed, he felt this Dulcey Blythe reading him through his eyes. Reading every last thing in his mind and heart and soul.

He didn't like that. He dropped his eyes.

"So this is Wib," she said in her rich voice.

11

"Wib Willett," he supplied, looking at the hem of her sleeve.

"And you don't want to join our club?"

"No. Sorry. I, you see, why I'm here, I used to live here, in this house, years ago. I was only six when we moved away. And something got left behind. Something important. So I need to find it. That's all." He looked up hopefully. Then the hope drained away. She was shaking her head, still smiling.

"Perhaps, at some point, if we can find time, we might look for this thing with you. But right now we're far too busy, and I can't say when that will change."

"But that's not fair! You need to let me look!"

The chattering stopped. All the girls froze and stared at him, some with mouths open. You'd think he'd yelled a bad word in church, Wib thought. But he wasn't about to say sorry.

Dulcey was still smiling at him, her eyes sparkling. She didn't seem angry.

Aster smiled her different smile. "We could go get someone older yet, if that's what he needs. There's always Mrs. Doun."

A couple of the girls gasped. Dulcey clicked her tongue and said, "Now, Aster, that's uncalled-for." She looked at Wib again. "But she's right, Wib. I understand that this used to be your home, but it's ours now. If you want to stay you will join the club. I promise you won't be bored!"

Aster held out the clipboard. Wib looked at both their faces, saw no yielding in either, took the pen and wrote his name and address. It was his only choice, and not a bad choice after all, he decided. Joining this club would give him chances to move through the house, to search and find. If not today, another day.

"Okay, over here." Aster walked Wib over to a cluster of girls sitting beside a window, pointed him into a chair, and dropped a ball of bright pink yarn on his knees. Two long knitting needles were stuck through the ball. He grabbed it before it could roll off. "These are Ingrid, Venice, Zira, Maura." She stabbed the air above each head. "And Wib." She rapped his head with hard knuckles. "Teach him." She was gone.

Wib held the ball of bright pink yarn out for a look and nearly gagged. It was the exact same shade of pink as Barbie doll furniture. Was this his punishment for asking to speak to someone older?

He looked around at Ingrid, Venice, Zira, and Maura. Ingrid frowned and went back to her knitting. Venice giggled in a silly way that made him want to get up and leave. Zira smiled at him, a flash of white teeth in her dark face. Maura, small and brown-haired, and younger-looking than the others, said softly, "Do you like knitting?"

"No idea."

Venice giggled again. Ingrid said, "Typical." Zira said, "Don't worry, it's not hard."

He pulled the needles out of the ball, held up an end of the yarn and looked at it helplessly. He wished he'd never signed up. Nothing was worth this humiliation.

"Aster said we should teach him," Maura said, her soft voice unexpectedly firm. She took the yarn and needles from him and looped yarn over her fingers and in a minute, while Wib watched in fascination, she had a couple of dozen stitches lined up on one of the needles. "There, you've cast on. Now you can start."

"Um..."

"Here, take this needle in your left hand. No, like this." She gently rearranged his fingers. "Now take the other needle in your right hand. You are right-handed, aren't you? Okay. Now put the tip of the right needle through the first stitch. The other way. That's right. Now...."

He hated it. The needles kept slipping out of his fingers. The ball of yarn kept dropping to the floor and rolling away, until Zira went

13

and got a cardboard box to corral it with. Some of his stitches were so tight they would barely move along the needle, others gaped. After an hour of poking, wrapping, twisting, and pulling, he had a skewed rectangle, about two inches high, of what Maura called garter stitch.

"You're doing great," she said. "Now you can knit on your own!"

He held it up and made a face at it. "What the heck would I do with this?"

"Knit some more and make a scarf," Zira said. "Like mine." Her piece was a long strip of Dr. Seuss-style red and white stripes.

"That's right, a scarf for your mom." Maura picked up her own knitting, which was fine and smooth and blue-violet, and had small diamond-shaped holes in a regular pattern that showed they were not mistakes.

Wib shook his head. Even if he finished enough to make a scarf, it would be the ugliest scarf in Canada, possibly in the world.

He sighed and started a new row. Needle through stitch, loop yarn around, pull yarn through, slip stitch off. And again: needle through stitch... "So this is a club for boys and girls, right? Where are the boys?" He pictured a bunch of boys in a back room, cutting wood with power saws, shaping metal with blow torches, and programming computers. Why wasn't he there instead of here?

"There aren't any boys!" Ingrid snapped.

Zira said: "They're not interested. You're our token boy." Venice giggled.

"No, there's one other." Maura's needles moved so fast, they flickered. "We don't know his name."

Zira laughed. "Oh, Maura! Not this again!"

"Yes! I've seen him! I think he lives here with the Sisters. Maybe he's Dulcey's nephew. He watches us, but he doesn't mix in."

Ingrid put down her knitting. "Once and for all, there is no other boy!"

"Or if there is," Venice said in a creepy voice, "he's a g-g-ghost."

"Ghost?" Wib grinned, sceptical. His mind had already leaped to thoughts of his own prompted by the mention of this other boy. Six-year-old memories. But of course there could be no connection, not now.

Maura laughed softly. "They're being silly. There's no such things as ghosts."

"Sure there are." Ingrid was blunt. "Everybody knows this house is haunted. Has been for years and years. Just ask anybody."

Chapter 3

WIB WOULD HAVE asked more questions, but just then Dulcey walked in with a big platter of those delicious oatmeal cookies. Aster followed with a stack of glasses and a giant pitcher of a fizzy, pale purple drink that Maura said was made from elderberries. The girls all jumped up with cries of delight.

Wib was uncertain about the drink until he tasted it. Then he gulped it down. "The Sisters make all their own snacks," Maura confided. "Aren't they yummy? Some of the girls, that's the only reason they come." Wib saw Rebecca trying to stick extra cookies in her shorts pockets and looking disgusted when they kept sliding out of the rips.

AT QUARTER TO FIVE Dulcey came in, smiled around the room and announced: "Time to start wrapping it up, everyone!" Wib dropped his knitting in relief and was astounded to hear cries of protest rise around him. Another five minutes of this would have had him gnawing his hands off.

Dulcey pulled a chair up to Rebecca's group and the girls, all but one, clustered around her, holding out samples of intricately twined and beaded and be-feathered string. They were shaped into masks, bags, belts, necklaces and other things, or at least the beginnings of them. Rebecca sat with arms crossed and her work piled on her lap like the remains of a gutted chicken.

"This is wonderful!" Dulcey said. "You're well on the way to creating some lovely pieces, all of you. I'm impressed!"

"All of us except Rebecca," said one of the girls, a sneer in her voice. Some of the others laughed. Dulcey looked at them and even from yards away Wib could feel a cool stillness descend.

"But she's trying hard," the girl added, and the others nodded quickly.

Rebecca seized her tangled pile in both hands. "It's a masterpiece!" she yelled, and flung it high in the air, the ends flailing. Everybody stared at her, some glaring, some giggling. Wib frowned. Why was she being such a jerk?

Dulcey reached up, laughing, and neatly caught Rebecca's project as it dropped. She spread it over her outstretched hands, held it up, looked it over, and winked at Rebecca. "A good first effort, I'd say."

Wib supposed she was being kind. Compared to that, his own work was a thing of beauty. Rebecca's whatever-it-was was so full of irregular holes, saggy bits, shredded feathers and sticking-out ends, you'd almost think she'd done it that way on purpose. Nobody could possibly make such a....

Oh, right.

"It's a plant hanger," Rebecca said defiantly, as if she hadn't just been praised.

Maura showed Wib where to store his pink monstrosity, in a set of shelves under the windows. "And make sure you put your name on it — here's the paper for that, and the pencils and pins." As if anybody else was likely to mistake it for their own.

Then she picked up her own work and started in on it again. "I need to do another inch," she said, answering his raised eyebrows. She sat down and got at it. Her needles flew so fast they made a sound like castanets.

He was just getting the pin in the paper on his knitting when he smelled butter and cinnamon, and turned around to find Dulcey smiling past his shoulder. "Wib, you've done really well for a first-timer."

"Maura helped a lot."

"Yes, she..." Dulcey's smile faded. "Who is that?" She pointed at his knitting, not quite touching.

He picked it up and looked it over. There were a lot of holes in the wrong places. At first he didn't understand what she meant. Then he saw the holes made a pattern. A face, sort of, if you squinted and made it go blurry. A face that looked teasingly familiar. *Who is that?* A suggestion of big dark eyes, mouth half open as if to say something. But when he looked again, it was nothing but a mess of badly shaped stitches and accidental holes.

"I don't," he began, then saw that Dulcey had moved away and raised her voice. "Time to go home! I hope you'll all be back tomorrow!"

"What time is it?" Maura was still knitting madly.

"Almost five," Rebecca said, strolling up beside them, swinging her cloth bag by its strap.

Maura made her needles flash, faster and faster. Then stopped, dropped her work in her lap, heaved a big relieved sigh, and rolled the piece neatly around the needles. "There, that's done." She looked at Wib and wrinkled her nose. "I took too much time to finish today. I'll tell my mom it was to help a friend. I think she might call that a good reason, don't you?"

Wib's mouth opened and closed. She might have been talking Icelandic, for all the sense she was making. Rebecca figured it out before he did. "You mean you have to finish a certain amount every day? And your mother keeps track?"

"Well, yes." Maura kept her eyes on her knitting, while stowing it away in a quilted cloth bag. "I take it home and she puts it in a spreadsheet on her computer. How much I do, what kind of stitch, the gauge, how long it takes me. Then she plots it on a graph and we look

18

at it every evening and discuss."

"Discuss what?" Rebecca was staring.

"Whether I made the target, and if not, why not. We do that for all my projects, not just the knitting. It's all about setting goals, and self-discipline."

"I thought it was supposed to be fun," Wib said.

"Fun!" Maura laughed, not in a happy way. She looked from Wib's face to Rebecca's. "You aren't having fun, either of you. Right? I know why I'm here, but why are you?"

"I was forced," Rebecca said. Wib said nothing.

"Five sharp!" Dulcey called. Maura wheeled and scurried across the room, clutching her knitting bag. Dulcey knew everybody's name, waving goodbye to this one, lightly touching another's shoulder. Some got hugs. She seemed to know without asking who would want hugs and who wouldn't. Maura clung to her longer than the others. Then Aster shouted up the stairs: "Maura! Move it, your mother's here!" Maura pulled away and rushed out as if the club had a guard dog and it was nipping at her heels.

"Poor kid," Wib said. Rebecca didn't answer. When he looked around she was across the room, hand out, facing Aster, and Aster was reaching into her back jeans pocket and handing over a sky-blue iPod. Rebecca smirked and strutted out the door.

Wib was the last to leave the room, not by accident. Dulcey did not touch his shoulder or hold out her arms for a hug. Instead she stood, hands interlaced, and waited. Wib cleared his throat and offered a hand to shake. Dulcey shook his hand ceremoniously and with dignity. "Until we meet again," she said. Wib felt for that moment as if he was in a story, something like Agents of S.H.I.E.L.D., and he was a soldier about to go underground against a deadly enemy.

Out in the corridor he watched the last of the girls clatter down the stairs. Dulcey was moving about the ballroom, out of sight, and singing softly to herself. Aster had disappeared. He was alone. Here was his chance. He set a foot on the stairs that curved up to the third floor. Then froze as Aster ran down from above on bare feet.

She stopped in mid-step. "Where d'you think you're going?"

"Um, out."

"That way." She pointed down the stairs. He went.

Chapter 4

REBECCA'S FATHER was setting the dining table, her grandmother was cooking dinner, and Rebecca, who had failed to tiptoe upstairs in time to avoid being caught, was being cook's helper. She was toasting slices of whole wheat bread and buttering them.

When her dad, Keith, made dinner, he made one of three things: spaghetti and meatballs, breaded baked fish with coleslaw, or grilled cheese sandwiches. Boring, but you knew what to expect, and the food usually turned out all right.

It was different when Flora made dinner. Those meals were exciting, although not always in a good way. You never knew what she might come up with, especially when she was getting geared up for a contentious town council meeting. And when that happened, whatever Flora cooked, no matter how awful it was, you had to eat it. Arguing about Gran's cooking never got you anywhere and wasn't worth the aggravation.

Tonight Gran was in a relaxed and pleasant mood, and was making peas and cheese curry with raita. Also buttered toast. If she'd been feeling tip-top there would have been naan from the Indian restaurant on Gunn Street, but toast was an acceptable substitute.

Now, as always, came the questions. "So, Rowena!" Flora looked up from the simmering pot. "How was your afternoon? Was the club fun?"

"It was okay." Rebecca put on her question-deflecting voice and face. "No more deadly than yesterday."

"Make any new friends?" her dad asked hopefully, coming into the kitchen.

Rebecca concentrated on spreading butter into every corner of each piece of toast. "There was somebody new. A boy. First and only."

"Ah," said Keith. "Nice?"

Rebecca thought of Wib. Quiet, but far from meek. Brown all over, from his too-short hair to his steady caramel-brown eyes to his khaki chinos and dust-smeared T-shirt. "I don't know about nice, but he's smart. Didn't want to join the club. He said he used to live in the house, he wanted to look the place over. That's the only reason he was there."

Flora stopped stirring. "Used to live there? What's his name? How old is he?"

"Wib. He's my age, I think."

"Wib What?"

"I forget." Rebecca went to the fridge to get the bowl of raita.

"In heaven's name, lass!" Flora's Scots background always slipped more into the foreground when she was annoyed or excited or at all worked up. "Who could he be? The last time a family lived in that house was a good six years ago. Now, who were they?" She forgot she was holding a wooden spoon and nearly scratched her head with it, but remembered in time. "He'd have been a wee thing then. I don't suppose you know where he lives now?"

"He just moved here from Toronto. They're in one of those houses down on Fairview Avenue, near the fair grounds. You know, the ones the council wants to de—"

"Demolish! I hope his parents know what they're doing. We'll pay them a visit this very evening."

Keith picked up the plate of warm toast. "Wouldn't it be better to let them settle in before mounting the invasion?"

"And since when is one old woman and one young girl an invasion?"

Rebecca looked up. "What young girl?"

"It's my duty as a councillor to welcome new citizens. Besides, we can help. And we won't come empty-handed. A good thing I made a big batch of the curry." Flora was ladling it into bowls as she spoke. "Rowena, you'll come along, since the boy's your friend. Close that refrigerator."

"He's not my friend, I only just met him."

"You'll come. No argument. Carry this."

Rebecca set steaming bowls on the dining table. As she reached for toast, she put on her most winsome granddaughter face, eyes sparkling, head tilted. "We'll make a deal. You agree to call me Rebecca from now on and I'll come along."

"I'll do no such thing and you *will* come along. Now eat!"

Rebecca ate. She'd expected no different outcome, but it was always worth a try.

IT WAS THE SECOND day of unpacking, and the house was starting to look less like a recycling depot. Yesterday Wib helped his mother find and unbox the things they needed first: dust cloths, cleaners, can opener, knives and forks, soap, bed sheets, toilet paper, screw driver, hammer. Then he put together the bed frames, so they wouldn't have to sleep on the floor. This morning he put up book shelves in a small back room that his mother had decided would be the library.

Now he was shelving books. His father'd had a lot of books and his mom had never thrown a single one away, not in all the times they'd moved after leaving Amstey six years ago. He had about half of them on the shelves, more or less in the right places, and their cartons flattened. The full boxes rose up like islands in the middle of the room now, instead of continents.

He paused, a book in each hand, hearing women's voices at the kitchen door. First outside the door and then suddenly inside, louder. One was his mother's voice, light but clear. The other, more penetrating voice had an accent that he recognized after a moment as vaguely Scottish.

"MacBeth, dear, Flora MacBeth. I'm your town councillor, here to welcome you to Amstey, and I do hope this is a good time. You like peas and cheese curry, I've no doubt. Here, I'll just put this in the refrigerator. It's homemade. No, don't thank me. And this — come along in, girl! — this is my granddaughter Rowena. Your son is just her age, I believe. And you'll be?"

There was a sharp pause. Wib pictured his mother catching her breath. "I'm Sharon Willett," she said. "It's so nice of you to visit, but I'm afraid just now—"

"Willett!" A thwack, as of a hand hitting a thigh. "Of course, now I recall! You'd be Griffin's widow. Poor soul, and now you're all on your own?"

"Why no, I... Oh, here's Wib."

Wib appeared in the inner doorway, sensing his mother needed backup. "She's not on her own. She has me." His mother darted a quick grin at him.

Then he looked across the kitchen and spotted the girl, Rowena. She was standing in the doorway that opened on the drive, more out than in. She was looking around as if she had got there by accident and didn't know anyone.

Rowena? *Yeah, right.* He grinned at her but she was careful not to catch his eye.

Flora, her grandmother, was not what he would have expected, if he'd thought about it. She was not tall and slim like Rebecca (Rowena); instead she was small for a grown woman and shaped like a beer keg. Her hair was short and white, which fit his mental image of the typical grandmother (he had none himself, to compare). But she also wore baggy shorts, thick leather sandals, and an old T-shirt printed with a picture of a guy in a beret and the words CHE LIVES, which did not fit that image.

But there was something of Rebecca in her, all the same. Or something of her in Rebecca. "So you're Wib." Flora raked him up and down with a pair of sharp green eyes. "Right. You'll do." She reached behind her and grabbed Rebecca's arm. "Rowena! You and Wib here, off you go. Sharon and I have things to discuss."

Sharon smiled her politest smile. "I'd love to chat, Mrs. MacBeth—"

"Flora."

"Flora. But as you can see, we're really busy right now."

"I can see that, and I'm not here to get in your way. Quite the opposite. Go on, children, out you go!"

Wib looked at his mother, unsure if it was safe to leave her with this elderly bully. But she seemed to find something funny in the situation. She sent him that just-for-you grin and wink. "Go on, Wib. You've worked hard, you've earned a break."

Rebecca lunged across the room, grabbed his wrist, hissed in his ear: "Come on, before they change their minds!" and towed him out.

Sounds followed them down the driveway. The rusty screech of the oven door, and Flora's voice: "Now this needs scouring out and no mistake! Where's your steel wool? Good. Now, dear, tell me all about it. Where've you been and what've you been doing since poor Griffin died? What brings you back to Amstey? And what do you plan to do with this house?"

"Fix it," Sharon said.

25

Chapter 5

WIB AND REBECCA walked side by side down Fairview, hands in pockets. Rebecca still wore the dusty red top and the white shorts with the stains and rips. They turned the corner onto Churchill Avenue and passed the fairgrounds, where men shouted and machines boomed behind a chain-link fence. A banner fixed to the fence said: AMSTEY FALL FAIR - DON'T MISS IT!

"Fair starts soon," Rebecca said, pointing with her chin. "Look, they're already starting to get the rides set up. It's fun, we should go."

Wib glanced that way, but he knew an attempted diversion when he heard it. "So that's your grandmother."

"Yeah." Rebecca squinted along the street to the end, where the setting sun had turned Lake Huron into a blinding glitter.

Wib whistled softly.

Rebecca shrugged. "She's like that. Means well. By the time you get back she'll have the whole kitchen clean and your mom'll be signed up to help with the Thanksgiving food drive. Plus she'll know everything about you and your mom right down to what you eat for breakfast."

Wib smiled one-sided. Not his mom. There was more steel in her than most people guessed. "MacBeth, huh? Scotch? Is that why she talks like that?"

"Yup. Been here since 1965 but still sometimes sounds like she just got off the boat from Edinburgh."

"I thought Macbeth was somebody in a play."

"Right, Shakespeare. Killed a king." She tossed her head, as if flicking back an invisible mop of long hair. "Plenty other MacBeths around. With a capital B."

They were on the boardwalk now, Rebecca's hard-soled sandals ringing the boards like a wooden xylophone. The lake burned gold all the way to the horizon, on their left. Ahead, beyond the creek that ran into the lake and divided the town in half, rose a hill with roofs and chimneys poking out of thick trees, and a twinkling gold cross at the top.

Rebecca whirled around and walked backward in front of him. "My turn now. So you weren't lying, you really did used to live in the old Morphy house."

"Yeah, we left when I was six."

"How come?"

"Just because." Time for a diversion of his own. "You were lying, though. You said Rebecca was your real name."

"It is my real name. I gave it to myself last year. How much realer can you get?"

"Your grandmother said Rowena."

"That's why I had to change it."

"What's wrong with Rowena?"

She sighed extravagantly and spun back to walk beside him in the normal way. "Apart from Rowena is just a really dumb girly name? I guess you never read a book called *Ivanhoe*?"

"No. I had an old comic book called that, though. There was a knight on the cover."

"OK, then maybe you remember this disgustingly soft, stupid girl named Rowena that Ivanhoe had to marry, when you could tell he really should've married Rebecca, who was brave and magnificent and everybody respected her because she was a doctor. Only he couldn't because he was this stuffy Christian knight and she was Jewish and that meant they couldn't be together. It was so sad."

"What's that got to do with your name?"

27

"It's my dad. He's a Sir Walter Scott fan from way back — that's the guy that wrote *Ivanhoe* — and that's why he named me Rowena."

"Why didn't he call you Rebecca if she's the interesting one?"

"I love my dad but that's him all over. Never choose anything interesting if there's something boring to choose instead."

"So that's why you named yourself Rebecca." He looked at her encouragingly. "And are you planning to be a doctor too?"

"I dunno. It would be kind of gross, wouldn't it? All that blood and people's insides and ick." She shook her shoulders. "But maybe I will, why not? You heard about Norman Bethune, that famous Canadian doctor who went to China?"

"Yeah, sure. Go on."

"Well, I bet you didn't know the Bethunes are related to the MacBeths, way back. That's what Gran says. We could be distant cousins, me and Norman Bethune!" She spun around again and waved both hands excitedly.

"Awesome! How d'you know this?"

"Oh, my gran knows all the clan..." She broke off and stared suspiciously, still walking backward. "And I know what you're doing. Trying to sidetrack me. You didn't answer why you left that house and went away."

"We just went someplace else."

"Because your dad died?"

He shrugged. He expected her to keep at him, but she surprised him by spinning back into normal walking mode and saying nothing for a while. Maybe she was smarter than he'd thought. Smart enough to see when to back off.

They came to the place where the boardwalk ended, just short of where the creek widened and spilled out into the lake. From here, unless you wanted to swim the creek, you had to turn right, circle around the war memorial, and then walk east along Gunn Street or

River Road.

Rebecca stopped on the last board and caught his arm. "Come on, what's the mystery?"

"What mystery?"

"This thing you left behind in the old Morphy house. What is it?"

He tried to step past her. She walked backward again in front of him. They were on River Road now. "Look," he said. "You don't have to stick with me, just because your grandmother kicked us out together. You can go on home. Where's your house?"

"Up there." She waved over her shoulder at the hill that rose beyond the creek.

"Oh, the rich part of town."

"Not really. Maybe it used to be, but there aren't any really rich people left in Amstey, I don't think. Not us, for sure. Even though we live right up near the top. See the gold cross?" She turned around to point. "That's the church of St. Michael and All Angels. Right at the top of Sentinel Hill. That cross on top, that's always the very last thing to catch the sunset. And the first to catch the sunrise. Our house is just a little lower on Park Circle."

"Cool."

She grinned at him. "I know you're trying to get rid of me, and I know why."

"You read minds?"

"Maybe. Maybe I have the Sight, like Gran talks about. She thinks she has it, which I seriously doubt, because she can't read *my* mind. Anyway, you can't shake me because my quickest way home is right past the old Morphy house. So you might as well let me in on whatever it is you're plotting."

"Don't be idiotic, I'm not plotting anything."

"Sure you are. You're going to get into the Morphy house and get back that thing you're after. You'll need me to create a diversion so you can sneak in."

"But that's—"

"Good! Come on, let's do it!"

She whirled and was off, racing like a maniac over the bridge and up the hill.

Chapter 6

REBECCA WASN'T SURE Wib would come after her. It was even odds he would just watch her go. Mulish and morose and liked to do things on his own, that was written all over him. Didn't take partners.

But, nerve? The way he'd spoken up to Aster this afternoon — and better, the way he'd yelled at Dulcey? That was amazing! Though she could tell he hadn't yelled on purpose, it just broke out of him. Something was simmering inside, she could tell that too, although he kept it under a heavy lid.

So when she tore across the Hay Street bridge, she was taking a chance. She didn't look back, just raced on around the curve of Circle Road and up the hill. He might easily have shrugged her off, turned around and mooched on home.

But as she panted up the steep northward curve of Circle Road and the pale stone fence of Number 3 showed through the dark trees ahead, footsteps thudded behind her. Yes! He wasn't as fast as she was, though. By the time he caught up to her she was halfway along the curving driveway, peeking at the house from behind one of the big silver maples that lined the way. He was muttering in a fed-up kind of way, but he was there.

The sun was below the horizon now, and it was getting dark under the trees. The streetlights weren't on yet. The house was dark too, except for a skin of light on the observatory dome: the last lick of vanished sun on the pale green copper.

"Looks like nobody's home." Rebecca tried to sound disappointed instead of relieved. There would be no need for her to create a diversion, whatever that might involve. "Of course, we should've

31

thought of that. The house is just where they work. They'd live somewhere else."

"That means the place will be all locked up." He kept his voice down and so did she, although there was no way anyone in the house, if there was anyone, could hear them talking. "There'll be burglar alarms."

"In Amstey? Wib, this isn't big bad Toronto. Nothing happens here except some jerks knocking over gravestones. Most people don't even lock their doors. I guess you don't remember that from when you lived here before."

They lurked there another couple of minutes, watching the house. Nothing moved behind the windows. No lights went on. "It looks safe," Rebecca said, although she wasn't clear what that meant. Safe from what? From who? "Come on."

She stepped out from behind the tree and walked boldly up the driveway to the house. Wib matched her stride for stride. Up the porch steps, not being especially quiet. Grasp the front door handle, twist... No. It didn't budge.

"So nobody locks their doors here," Wib commented.

"I said most people. The Sisters might. Being strangers." She left the porch and circled the house clockwise, east to south to west. There was a door on the west side that she thought probably opened on the kitchen. It was locked too. Wib stuck hands in pockets and scanned the sky, all silent sarcasm.

Rebecca walked on around the turret, a squared structure that projected a foot or so from the house wall on the northwest corner. Just beyond it, on the north side, she found another door. This one swung open at a touch.

"Ha!" She grinned at Wib. He didn't smile back. He stepped inside and she followed, and the door closed behind them with a sly-sounding *snick*.

They stood close together on the landing of a narrow stairwell that burrowed down and up into darkness. There was a nose-pinching herbal smell in the air. A door on the inner side, just past the stairs, opened — Rebecca pushed it and stuck her head through — into a small room. Maybe a storeroom or pantry: she had a sense that the room was full of stuff.

She stepped in, followed by Wib. Something brushed the top of her head. She let out a squeak and cowered down.

"What?" Wib breathed.

"Something touched me!"

"Huh." She could feel him moving around, then a faint laugh. "Reach up."

Not to look like a complete coward, she stretched up an arm and touched something soft and fuzzy. Now that her eyes were used to the dark, she could see ropes of things and other irregular shapes hanging from the ceiling. Hanks of yarn, probably, and bunches of dried herbs. The nose-pinching smell grew stronger.

"So this is—"

"Sh!" Wib's hand curled around her wrist and pressed: a warning. In the wall to their left, a yellow glow outlined another closed door. A machine, somewhere beyond that door, clacked and clinked rhythmically. It sounded like something large and mostly made of wood.

And someone was singing.

There were words, but Rebecca couldn't make them out. Didn't need to, the song was taking her inside itself, into someplace warm and quiet, yet full of scent and sound and life, like a meadow under trees on a perfect June day, with the softest breeze....

The spell broke like a bubble. Wib was tugging her back to the landing. "That's Mrs. Blythe!" he whispered, closing the storeroom door behind them.

Rebecca was still half dreaming. When another sound came it took a moment for her to realize what and where it was. Footsteps, slow and heavy, on the stairs below. The dark stairs that led to the cellar.

Still gripping Rebecca's wrist, Wib reached for the knob of the door to the outside. It didn't move. That *snick* had been the sound of a lock falling into place.

There was no time to fumble for a thumb latch, and only one way left to go. Wib went first, nearly silent on sneakered feet, up the narrow stairs.

On the second floor landing they found a short corridor leading past the railed-in stairwell and the stairs to the third floor. "Where now?" Rebecca whispered, and was glad her voice was steady. She was shaking with nerves. Wib was pretending to be cool, but he was close enough that she could feel him vibrating.

"Up," he whispered back. "The... what I'm looking for.... It's in a place I know on the third floor. At least, I hope—" He froze, foot on the first step up. Someone was up there and coming down, someone with bare feet, the step quick and light.

He backed away. Then, clutching hands, they cat-footed along the short corridor to where it opened onto a wider hallway that ran from the back of the house, past the well of the main staircase, to the front. Here, they could see. The rising full moon shone brightly in through the tall eastern windows, its brilliance bouncing off polished floors and outlining arched doorways left and right. The one on the left led to the crafts room.

Rebecca glanced back. If they were lucky, Aster would keep on down the back stairs and never spot them. "We can wait till she's gone," she whispered, "then go up."

Wib started to answer, then gripped her hand tight. They froze. Was that a footstep in the short corridor back there? *Not lucky.*

34

Only one way out now. Down the main stairs, and quick! Rebecca thought of the locked front door. Maybe they'd be able to unlock it from inside.

Hands on the polished railings, they started down side by side. Then froze again. A voice drifted up from below: a soft singing.

Back up to the hallway. Arched doorways opened left and right into big rooms full of shadowy hiding places. Rebecca lunged one way and Wib the other, still tightly clutching hands, and for a moment they stretched like a rubber band.

Wib won. They lurched across the corridor and into the crafts room. Moonlight flooded in, reflecting from the mirrors and striking rainbow gleams off the lowest-hanging crystals of the chandelier.

Wib skidded across the moonlit expanse, past the craft tables and shelves, which were no hiding place at all, and into the triangular space behind the upright piano in the northeast corner. Rebecca scrambled in after him.

For a few minutes they huddled and let their nerves settle. "Foof!" said Rebecca, when her breathing had slowed to normal. "Why did we get so scared? I mean, what's to be scared of? It's just Aster and Dulcey, and Dulcey at least is nice."

"It's not just them. There's Mrs. Doun. The third sister, right? I bet that was her coming up the cellar stairs."

"With the lights off?" Rebecca thought about that, and shuddered. "Must have eyes like a bat."

"Doesn't anybody ever see her?"

"Not much. They say she's really old and hardly says a word. Probably just somebody's gran. Aster's, maybe. But it's funny how they showed up wherever we tried to go, the three of them. You'd think they were doing it on purpose."

"Well, this whole thing is a bust. We were stupid to try. How are we going to get out of here?"

Chapter 7

HOW ARE WE going to get out of here? Rebecca had been wondering that herself. "We'll have to wait until they close down and leave."

"Suppose they don't leave?"

"Then we wait until they've gone to bed. Then we sneak down and get out the back door."

"Which is locked."

"I'm sure there's just a little button thing," Rebecca said, although she wasn't sure. "Or maybe the front door. We'll be out in a jiff. They won't even know anybody was here."

They crouched and waited, while the moon rose higher and the blocks of white light on the floor grew shorter and brighter. A shaft of moonlight slid like liquid silver into their hiding place and down the back of the piano.

Rebecca had never really looked at the back of a piano before. She was surprised to see it didn't have a shiny dark finish, like the front. It wasn't finished at all. A wooden panel maybe eighteen inches high covered the upper part of the back from side to side, and vertical bars of wood bridged the open space from there to the bottom of the frame. Through the bars you could see a board with slanting ribs on it, which she guessed was part of the music-making works. Maybe, she thought, the back had to be open to let the sound out.

Rebecca could see Wib's face now, too. He looked as if he was listening.

"Something?"

He shook his head, but his face stayed intent, his eyes unfocused. Rebecca strained her ears. When you really listened, you noticed the silence wasn't truly silent: it was full of small noises. Each other's breathing, for a start. Tiny cricks and cracks from the wooden beams and floors as they cooled in the night air. Sounds from outside: a dog barking distantly, a child's high voice in some back yard, a truck horn, faint, on Highway 21 on the edge of town.

Wib stirred. "I don't think this is such a great plan, waiting. Suppose the Sisters stay up until midnight? Or later? My mom will think something's happened to me."

"Well, maybe you're right." What a relief that he'd said that. Rebecca wanted more than anything to get out of there, but no way she'd be the first to admit it. "My dad will have a fit! And my gran — she'll slaughter me! Maybe we'd better try—"

"Shh."

She listened and there was another sound, very faint, but clearly right in the room with them. A soft pattering as of small feet. Rebecca edged her head out from behind the piano. She pulled her head back in. "Just a cat."

"Cat?" Wib squeezed into the corner next to the north wall, on the right, and tried to see out that end.

Rebecca poked her head out again at the other end. The cat, which was white and fluffy, was halfway across the ballroom. It was heading directly toward their hiding place, not fast but steadily, with the purposeful panther-like pace of all cats. As it passed in and out of the oblongs of silver light on the floor, it glowed like a moon itself. Its eyes caught the light and glimmered.

Rebecca pulled her head back in again. "Might as well go," she started to say, but Wib grabbed her wrist and breathed "What the heck?" They stared at the wide board that ran across the piano's upper back, a few inches above their heads.

It was cracking. Four thin cracks had formed, plain to see in the moonlight. Cracks about ten inches long, running slantwise against the grain of the wood and criss-crossing each other at the bottom. Then another crack opened, this one straight up and down, not touching the others. "They look like..." Rebecca began, but didn't finish because it was impossible, what was happening there.

"Yeah."

They looked like letters. Capital letters ten inches high. First a W and then an I.

More cracks formed. The wood made a crickling sound as it split. Small splinters hit their upturned faces. The next group of lines made a complicated shape. It looked more than anything like a B, but all angles.

"W — I — B," Rebecca said. "WIB. That's you!"

His fingertips dug into her wrist. "Where's that cat?"

She stuck her head out again. The cat was nearer, and now it wasn't alone. Something bigger and darker stalked several yards behind it.

Rebecca ducked back in. "It's a zoo in here. Now there's another animal!"

"What? Wait, look." More cracks were forming in the back of the piano. An angular G. An E. Then a T. "Get," Rebecca whispered.

They both leaned to look out. The cat had sat down with its tail curled over its front paws. It watched with an air of detached interest as the second animal — a dog? — paced under the darkly gleaming chandelier and onward, slow and steady. Straight toward the piano. Rebecca ducked back, instinctively hiding, although that was stupid and useless now.

Wib was staring at the piano back. More letters formed, faster, splinters flying. Urgent. A squat diamond-shaped O. Then a U. Then a T.

WIB GET OUT

The ribbed board inside the piano was humming. The bars of the frame were shaking. They could hear clicking footsteps, the sound of claws on the hardwood floor. More cracks formed in the piano back, hasty, rough. They couldn't look away. First an N, then two more letters.

NOW

Wib shoved Rebecca and she rolled out from behind the piano. Wib burst out behind her and hauled her up by an elbow. The animal was six long strides away, dark as thunder and untouched by moonlight. It looked like a dog the size of a mastiff, muscular and heavy-headed. Its eyes fixed on them and gleamed.

They sidled, hands locked together, toward the arched doorway. The dog veered to follow. Out the door and into the hall they slid. Then broke and trampled to the main stairs and down. Flung themselves at the front door. Clawed feet clicked on the stairs behind them.

Wib fumbled at the lock, invisible in darkness; wrenched and pulled, and they were out. Rebecca reached back to grab the handle and slam the door. Then they leaped off the porch side by side, like a team of acrobats, and sprinted up the driveway to the street. They stopped on the sidewalk to look back, panting with terror and excitement.

Nothing followed them out. No lights went on. No angry voices called. The house looked exactly as before, dark except for that sheen on the dome.

"They couldn't have missed that," Wib said between gasps. "They'll know somebody broke in."

"We didn't break in technically, that back door wasn't locked. Anyway, they won't know who it was. We're okay. But that dog — what was that?" Rebecca knew she was babbling, but couldn't stop. "And the piano... what... how..."

Wib gazed at the house, speechless. Rebecca shook his arm.

"Wib! The piano — the piano was talking to you! It called you by name! It warned you!"

Wib closed his eyes. Rebecca could guess what he was seeing. The big, splintery letters cracking the wood. The message. WIB GET OUT NOW. "Wib?"

He opened his eyes. "It wasn't the piano."

"But..."

He shook his head. "Not the piano. Something else in the house. I think..." He took a breath, deeply in and out. "I think it was Henry."

Chapter 8

HALF AN HOUR later Rebecca was sitting cross-legged on her bed. This was her favourite place in the house. Her bedroom was on the third floor of a tall house built just a little below the top of the tallest hill in the county. Some clear days she thought she could see all the way to Michigan.

She sat now with the lights off, looking southwest over the broken glow of Amstey toward the black-and-silver gleam of Lake Huron. She was mulling over the events of this evening, all the strangeness that happened inside the old Morphy house. Dulcey's sleepy-making singing. And the message cracked into the back of the piano: WIB GET OUT NOW. And that dog.

You'd almost think the house — so innocently dark and quiet — had been waiting for her and Wib to creep in and offer themselves like pigs on a platter.

Why'm I not cowering under the covers? In one corner of herself deep down, she was nothing but a huddled, snivelling little girl named Rowena, scared of the dark.

But that was only in one corner. *I am Rebecca.* And Rebecca was bold and brave, alive with curiosity, bristling with questions. Top of the list was: Who is Henry? Next under that: What is Wib looking for?

Whatever it was, he hadn't found it; hadn't even got near it. But he was stubborn, that stuck out all over him. So that meant he'd try again. And again. And if she wasn't careful, she'd get left out.

Downstairs the front door slammed and Gran's voice rang through the house. "Keith! News!" Rebecca came down to lean in the

41

kitchen doorway and listen while Flora described her evening with Wib's mom. Keith, who had been sitting at the kitchen table drinking tea, eating cinnamon toast and reading an adventure novel called *The Black Arrow*, listened patiently with one finger in the book to keep his place.

"Willett — that's the last name." Gran was putting on the kettle for tea as she spoke.

"Sounds vaguely familiar," Keith said. "Who's the husband?"

"There isn't one. Remember Griffin Willett?"

Keith crunched toast absently, then sat up and pointed his book. "The newspaper reporter! Right? He grew up in Amstey. He was a year or two ahead of me in school."

"That's right. He travelled all over the world, but his home was here, with Sharon, and their son Wilbur. She calls the boy Wib. They lived in the old Morphy house after they were married, right up until he was killed."

Rebecca leaped forward. "Killed!"

Flora gave the kettle a shake, bullying it into boiling. "Keith, you must recall. He wrote those newspaper articles on gangs in Toronto, and won a big award for them." The kettle hurried to boil and got poured, and Flora whipped the tea with a spoon to encourage it to steep.

Rebecca hoisted herself up to sit on the counter. "But how was he killed?"

"I'm getting to that. He had a reputation — cut quite a figure. Seems there wasn't a place on Earth he was afraid to go, and not a thing he was afraid to write about. That's what killed him, of course. Criminals in Asia, I think Singapore. He got his nose in too close. Wib was only six years old, poor mite."

"Is that why they left Amstey?" Rebecca kicked her bare heels on the lower cabinet. "To get away from the sad memories?"

"No, it was to make a living. She had a child to raise alone. She sold the house and went where the jobs are. And ever since, that house has been nothing but trouble."

"Trouble! Why? Is it the ghosts?"

"Ghosts!" Flora hooted. Then she noticed where Rebecca was perched and stabbed a finger at the floor. "Off!"

Rebecca thought about making a case for sitting on the counter, then hopped down. Arguing with Gran was never worth the aggravation.

"Worse than ghosts, Rowena." Her dad smiled at her. "About a year after the Willetts left, the new owners moved out, but they couldn't unload the house. Nobody would buy it, and nobody would rent it for more than a few months—"

"Because of the ghosts?"

"Well, no, it just had a bad name. It was... well, odd. Once a house gets that reputation, it's very hard to sell." Keith knew about these things, being in real estate. He had never been much of a success at it, though, because he was always more interested in the history and architecture of houses than in selling them.

"And so the new owners defaulted on their taxes," said Flora, getting the evaporated milk out of the fridge. "And since then it's been on the town's hands. More trouble than it's worth. We were lucky to get the Three Sisters on a short-term lease."

"I'm surprised the council hasn't voted to demolish it," Keith said. "They seem to like knocking old things down, that bunch."

"It may yet come to that. But there's no call to do anything drastic so long as we can lease it out and make money on it. Must have been built amazingly well," Flora added meditatively, while stirring milk into her tea. "There's been next to no work done to maintain it, so far as we know, and yet it shows very little wear and tear. Shame to destroy a house like that."

"Agreed." Keith opened his book and peeked and then closed it again on his finger, knowing Flora was not yet done. "So why is Sharon back in Amstey?"

"She does something with computers. Got a job with that start-up company that we lured to the new industrial park." Flora ladled three spoonfuls of sugar into her tea, stirred, sipped, then casually added, "She's not remarried, although I'm sure she's had chances. Nice-looking young woman, good head on her shoulders too. And the lad's a quiet, well-behaved sort."

"Hah!" Rebecca said. Quiet, yes. Well-behaved, not so much. Which was why she liked him, of course. When Keith and Flora both looked at her, Dad with eyebrows up and Gran with eyes like skewers, she said, "Oh, nothing," and swanned out of the room.

Upstairs again, she sat on the edge of her bed near the window and looked out. The town was a carpet of shadowy trees with brightly lit streets and roads swirling through, and the highway, off to the east, a hard orange line of light that curved all the way to the south end of town and out into the dark countryside. That clot of brightness down near the lake was the fairgrounds. Wib's house had to be near there, but she couldn't pick it out.

Much nearer, half a block away down the hill, stood the Morphy house, its domed turret rising above its mass of roofs and chimneys and trees. The moon, still only partway up the eastern sky, painted half the dome silver and left the other half in shadow.

Rebecca got up and pressed her face to the window. Here was something she'd seen before, but not often, and it always fascinated her. The dome was slowly rotating on its base. That meant somebody was in there getting ready to use the telescope. The two curved shutters that covered the viewing slit were coming around to this side. They were still closed, so that the dome looked like a giant child with its hands pressed to its face, playing peek-a-boo. Maybe this time the shutters would open northward and she'd be able to see inside.

She bounced over her bed and rooted in an old toy chest at the back of her closet. Pulled out a telescope, not much more than a toy, that her dad had given her when she turned eight and graduated to this room at the top of the house. "Don't use it to look in people's houses, that's rude," he'd told her. So of course that was the first thing she did.

Now she took it to the window and focused it on the dome. "Hey! Awesome!" The dome had stopped rotating and the shutters directly faced her house. Now they were sliding apart. The gap was black; there was no light inside. Even using her spy-glass Rebecca couldn't see much, just a round gleaming thing framed in the gap. That must be the end of the telescope, the lens. Someone was in there behind it, too, but she couldn't see who.

The telescope was aimed a little above Rebecca's house; at the stars, she supposed. She kept on watching, hoping for a better view inside the dome, still not seeing much.

Then, like a pouncing cat, the telescope swung down and looked straight at her, the lens a shining eye. It saw her. It saw her seeing it. She felt it like a touch on the nose. And she had the spine-freezing feeling that the person with their eye to the far end of the telescope knew exactly what she was thinking right this minute.

Rebecca dropped her little scope on the bed, yanked the curtains closed and backed away from the window.

Chapter 9

"TAKE A HAT!" Gran shouted from the dining room, where she was pawing at planning reports and survey maps and banging with one finger at her laptop keyboard.

"Aw, Gran..."

"It's UV 8 today! Take a hat!"

"Oh, all right! I got a hat! Rebecca snatched a floppy floral-print linen object from a hook in the coats alcove, grabbed her bag with the Indian embroidery, slung the strap over her shoulder, and darted out the door before Gran could come and look to see the hat actually on her head.

She jumped down the front steps, used her sandalled toe to poke in one corner of the triangular wooden lattice that closed off the space under the steps, and flipped the hat through the gap. Squinting into the dark, she spotted a few other things that were probably hats, including the white knitted one that had been lost since last March. She pulled the lattice closed and told herself to remember to get the things and bring them in next time she got home.

Rebecca headed around the curve of Park Circle to Summit Road and Church Street and the leafy, sun-spattered route down the hill. She lilted as she walked. Last night's terrors had faded behind sleep, and it was a gorgeous bright, hot day and she was Rebecca, fearless and proud. So cool in black shorts and black-and-silver sleeveless top. She ran her fingers through her newly washed hair, fluffing it like feathers. Someday, when for heaven's sake she had some say in the colour of *her own hair*, she would dye it black, black, black!

It was way too early for the club at Three Sisters, which was good, because it would give her time to tackle Wib and work out exactly what happened last evening. He'd still be at home, probably, so that's where she'd go. But not empty-handed.

She trotted across the Church Street bridge, then strode, still lilting, along Ambrose Street with its expensive (for Amstey) shops. Crossed the tightening curves of Prince's Drive and Albert Circle, and finally reached Queen's Circle, the inner curve of the snail shell that was the street plan of the old lower town. The Town Hall stood in the centre, a massive granite pile with cars diagonally parked all around it, noses to the curb. They always made her think of piglets nursing on a gigantic sow.

Rebecca cut across the roadway to reach Padgetts' Coffee Shop, on the southwest side of Queen's Circle. *I'll come bearing gifts.* Then stopped on her toes and laughed. Funny, but maybe typical, how she hadn't spotted him until the last moment. Wib wasn't an attention-grabber. He stood quietly on the sidewalk outside Padgetts' and gazed through the big front window, past the red neon OPEN sign with its radiant outline of a steaming cup of coffee.

She snuck up behind him and slapped him on the shoulder, to make him jump. "Hey Wib!" But his reflection in the glass just grinned at hers and she realized he'd been watching her cross the road. *Phooey.*

The buttery, spicy fragrance of the world's best cinnamon buns floated in the warm air. "You remember this place?"

"Yeah. I liked it." His grin had vanished and he looked at her distantly, as if not sure he knew her, or wanted to.

Never be a quitter, Rebecca advised herself, echoing Flora. "Then come on, I'll treat." She led the way inside and walked the mirror-walled length of the narrow room to the serving counter, where they bought buns still warm from the oven.

"Mmm, don't they smell like they were baked by angels?" Re-

47

becca bit, and made more appreciative noises. "Actually, Mr. Padgett baked them. He looks like two angels rolled into one, doesn't he?" She saw Wib's face soften to a near-smile as he chewed, and decided he might be worth her effort.

There were white-enamelled iron tables and chairs inside, and some outside on the pavement, but Wib said he didn't feel like sitting. Rebecca didn't blame him. She figured his restlessness had a lot to do with the two tables full of local old people who were staring at him and exchanging murmurs and who, if he sat down, would be stopping by his table in moments, bubbling with questions. New people did come to Amstey, but not all that often.

They left the shop and set out, cinnamon buns in hand, across Queen's Circle northward. As they walked they finished their buns, licking crumbs and buttery syrup from their fingers.

"So, where to?" Rebecca asked, when her mouth was free.

"Nowhere special." Wib walked in a lackadaisical kind of way. "I would've thought after last night you'd want to stay away from me."

"No way! You're an adventure. I guess you're like your dad, right? Flora, my gran, told us all about him, your dad, last night after she came back from visiting your mom. He was famous, wasn't he? You must be proud to've had a dad like that."

"I'd rather just have my dad."

"Oh. Uh. I'm sorry."

"Forget it."

"I... I guess you still remember him."

He didn't answer, just turned his head to look into the shop windows as they walked by. *Dangerous: drop it.* "I hope your mom doesn't hate us too much," she went on carefully. "Gran really likes helping people, you know. It's not just an act to get re-elected to council. Did you know she's thinking about running for Parliament in the next election? For the New Democrats. Of course, first they have to choose her as their candidate."

"My mom doesn't hate her at all. She actually helped. A lot. She cleaned the fridge *and* the oven, and got most of the kitchen stuff unpacked, and she got the ceiling fans upstairs to work." He shot a brief smile at her sideways. "And she gave my mom a bunch of phone numbers of repair shops and other things that might be useful. She likes her. My mom, I mean, likes your gran."

"A lot of people think she's too bossy, but she always says shrinking violets never get the job done. My dad's afraid I'll grow up like her."

"Like what?"

"Bloody-minded," Rebecca said with relish. "He says I'm already showing signs of it. Like, the time last year when the Board of Trade brought this speaker in from Toronto, some big-business type who said climate change was a hoax. Gran went and heckled him and threw ripe tomatoes!" She giggled and whirled her bag on its strap.

"Really?" Wib sounded impressed, for once.

"Yes! And I was with her and I threw some too! And she had to spend a night in jail!" She whirled her bag again. "And I wanted to share her cell, but Dad took me home and after that I never got to go to meetings with Gran again."

"Bummer. But why..." Wib stopped and faced her. "I mean, what about your mom?"

"Oh. Right, you don't know." She slung the bag back on her shoulder. "My mother died of a brain aneurism when I was two. That's when Flora came to live with us and raise me. And that's why Dad wants me in that club, to learn how to play nice with kids my own age. He's afraid too much of Gran is rubbing off on me."

"That sucks! Your mom, I mean." He looked right at her, then looked away again.

"Yeah, and your dad died. So we're both half-orphans. It's like it's meant!"

"What's meant?"

"That we should work together on this mystery. This problem. No, wait. This quest!"

They had stopped in front of a store called Emerson's Hobbies, Models and Puzzles. The two of them were mirrored in the shop window, with Rebecca's image grinning excitedly while Wib's reflected face was blank, his eyes on the 3-D Tower of London puzzle but not seeing it.

He doesn't see me, either. I might as well not exist for him. Angry, she poked him on the arm and pointed. "Wib! What's that?"

"What," he muttered.

"That reflection next to yours! Omigosh! There's somebody standing right beside you! Who could it be?"

He looked at her in the window, mouth pressed flat.

"I want to help!" She jogged up and down. "To find that special thing you left behind."

"Oh, that." He shrugged. "Forget that. I have."

"You're kidding! You found it?"

"No, I mean I've decided to forget it. I'll never get past the Three Sisters. You think I want to go back in there with that huge guard dog they've got?"

Rebecca thought about that. It had never crossed her mind that the dog might have anything to do with the Three Sisters. She wasn't sure why. It just didn't seem to fit with them. She glanced at Wib and saw him watching her reflection in the window. Watching to see if she bought it.

"Ha! Nearly got me." She poked him on the arm. "Of course you're going back in. You mean to find that place on the third floor. Where you hid the thing, right?"

He scowled and looked away.

"Why don't you just tell me what it is? How can I help if you keep me in the dark?"

He whirled on her. "Did I ask you to help?"

She met his eyes. They were hard and cold as brown stones. The pit of her stomach suddenly hurt. "No. You didn't."

"Well then."

"Okay, forget it. See ya." She turned and walked away along Ambrose Street, head high and proud.

Chapter 10

WIB WATCHED her go. It was for the best. This thing he was doing... what had she called it? Quest? It was dangerous: something he
hadn't expected. He'd spent a lot of last night staring at the ceiling
and trying to decide what to do.

There was no backing off, of course. No way he would give up.
But it wouldn't be easy. The dog in the ballroom, and the splintered
message in the piano back, had told him that. He wouldn't be able to
just go and get the thing.

Two months ago, when he first learned they would be moving
back to Amstey, he'd imagined it would be simple: that the only hard
part would be getting into the house. But over the years he had forgotten a few things. Things he'd seen, or felt, or been warned about.
The old Morphy house was not safe.

Best to go alone, then, and not drag other people into it. Especially not people he sort of liked.

Only, for a moment something had flashed across Rebecca's
face, just before it went blank and she turned away. Wib had seen
that look once before.

He remembered when he'd had to say goodbye to Henry, and
Henry had cried. All right, admit it, they'd both cried. They were
younger then. And then Wib, suddenly ashamed and furious, swept it
all away, all they'd said and shared, their being friends. He'd said:
"This is stupid! Why am I doing this? You're not even real!"

Then that flash across Henry's face. Hurt: a shamed hurt that had
to be covered up. And then he was gone. Wib had never seen him
again.

Wib started along Ambrose Street at a run. When he caught sight of Rebecca crossing Gunn Street he slowed to a walk, in case she looked back. He caught up to her on the near side of the Church Street bridge. "Rebecca!"

Her shoulders stiffened but she didn't stop.

"Rebecca, wait! Please!"

She slowed and stopped on the bridge. Then turned and leaned both arms on the stone parapet, not looking at him. Wib leaned on the parapet beside her. He looked sideways at her averted face, which was still blank. Something else about that face was familiar.

She was lonely too, just like him. Like Henry had been.

"There's a reason I'm not telling you everything," he said.

"Yeah, really?" She flicked a crumb of grit into the water.

"Yeah. Did you ever do anything really bad?"

She turned her head just a little, enough to eye him sideways. "How bad?"

"Really, really bad. The kind of bad you don't want to think about."

"Um... I don't think so. I mean, not *that* bad."

"Well, try to imagine. If you ever did anything that bad, would you go around telling people about it?"

"Good point."

"So, a long time ago I did something really, really bad." He watched the stream ripple out from under the bridge and felt her eyes on him. "And I wished I could fix it. But for years there was no way I could."

"And now?" She turned right around to face him, her right arm laid along the sun-warmed parapet.

"Now maybe I can. Maybe. But the only way I can fix it is to find something I left in that house. But I don't want to talk about that, so don't ask me what or why. Okay?"

"Sure, okay. No whats, no whys." She'd warmed up, but not opened up. Of course, neither had he. "How about wheres? Like, where to now?"

"I have a plan. I'll go to the Three Sisters and say I want to help out." Not much of a plan, but all he could come up with. "If I can get them to give me chores, get used to seeing me around, it'll be easier for me to go through the house on my own."

"Could work."

"Yeah. All the same...." He cleared his throat. "I guess I could, um, use some backup."

"Uh-huh?"

He knew what was coming, and he hurried to get in ahead of her. "Please."

Her green eyes narrowed. "Say pretty please."

"No."

She laughed and linked an arm in his. He endured that for two seconds, then pulled free, scarlet heat flooding up his neck. She laughed again and swept her arms out wide. "This is gonna be so cool!"

SHE STARTED IN on him as they crossed the bridge and turned up Circle Road. "Okay, let's get this moving. Who's Henry? *What* is Henry? You can tell me that, anyway."

"I don't know."

"Oh, come on! He wrote you a message! He called you by name!"

"I really don't know. I thought I did once, but now I'm not sure."

As they walked he told her what he remembered of his life in the old Morphy house. He had a secret hiding place, a crawl space under the turret stairs on the third floor. It wasn't really secret, but the way in was hard to see. "I only discovered it by accident. Even my mother never knew it was there. Whenever I turned up all of a sudden she said I must have been invisible." The memory made him smile.

"Way cool! For a six-year-old, anyway. What'd you do in there besides hide?"

"Kept things there. Comics, cookies, stuff like that. And that was mostly where I talked with Henry."

"Talked? You mean he was actually there?" She did that walking backward trick. It made him nervous.

"He was there, but not in 3D, like a real person. He just spoke to me. Usually he'd whisper through the cracks. Like blowing a flute. And once I learned to read, he wrote to me. He did printing."

"Like that message on the piano back? Cracks in the wood?"

"Better than that, and faster." Wib half-closed his eyes and saw them again, images on the back of his eyelids. "He made shapes in the dust. Or in fog on mirrors. If there was anything liquid, water or cola, and I spilled some, he made marks with that. But using the wind for a voice was always easier."

"But you never saw him?" She kept walking backward. Any second now she was going to trip and he'd have to catch her.

"I did, but only in reflections. Mirrors, window panes, polished metal. Anything shiny."

"Spooky!" She shuddered dramatically.

"I never thought it was. I liked it when he showed up in the mirror, smiling at me. I'd know him if I saw him now."

"It sounds like—" They reached the crossing of Maple Grove lane. A car swooped down the road and Rebecca nearly stepped off the curb backward into its path. Wib grabbed her arm and yanked her back.

"Are you trying to get yourself killed? Walk normal!"

She wasn't even ruffled. "I like to see who I'm talking to." The road was clear now. They crossed and started up the last steep curve

55

of Circle Road. "Sounds like you thought he was real," she said.

"At first I thought so. I thought he was an older boy, maybe 12, who was lonely and wanted company. Later, I figured out he was pretend. Even though I never actually made him up: he was just there. Like I wanted an older brother, and one showed up."

"Lots of young kids have imaginary best friends. I had one when I was about three. Sasha. She had beautiful long golden hair." Rebecca smoothed her hands over nonexistent swaths of hair. "I guess she had long hair because Gran cut my hair short about then. It was thick and I hated having it combed, so it got like a rat's nest. Tell me more about Henry."

"There's not much more. I forgot about Henry after we moved away. At least, I thought I'd forgotten. Now I don't think he's pretend. I'm almost sure he's real."

"Because of those words cracked in the wood of the piano, that we both saw, right?" She danced a little on the pavement.

"Yeah, and because who else in that house besides Henry would want to protect me?" *Even after I hurt him, that last time.*

"But if he's real and we can't see him, then... what is he?" She stopped and he stopped and they looked at each other.

"I'll say it." Wib stuck his hands in his pockets. "He has to be a ghost. Which is a real problem for me. I don't believe in ghosts."

"A ghost who wants to protect you from what, other ghosts?"

"I guess so. He used to warn me against walking around at night. Told me what places in the house to stay away from, night or day." They started walking again.

"Did he mention the black dog?"

"No."

She hunched her shoulders and shuddered. "It's not just a regular dog, is it?"

"You figured that out, eh?"

56

"It's gotta be a ghost too. How many ghosts are in that house, anyway?"

"Dunno. A few."

"I think I might believe in ghosts. I don't actually *not* believe. I'm waiting for more evidence. But I guess this decides one thing, right? We don't go exploring there again at night."

"Fine with me."

Chapter 11

THE A-FRAME SIGN was set up again near the sidewalk outside the Morphy house. Wib frowned at it. "What's this?"

"It's a different name every day. Unfair, right? I mean, it's so sneaky!" Rebecca knelt in front of the sign. "That's how they got me signed up. Dad dragged me here on Monday and they called it the Monday Club, so I thought that meant we only had to come on Mondays. So I said okay, I guess I can stand it, two hours a week. But I was wrong! When I found out the truth it made me mad, so when I left that day, I changed it to the Morons Club." She shrugged off her embroidered bag.

Today's sign said: THE WEDNESDAY CLUB*. At the bottom ran the line: *INCLUDES ALL MONDAY AND TUESDAY CLUB MEMBERS.

Rebecca dug the marker out of her bag. "This is a cheat! We don't have to put up with this!" She drew thick black lines through WEDNESDAY and printed WEIRDOS above it. Then looked at it, thought, and tipped in an E in front of the S in WEIRDOS. "It's the Weirdoes Club!" she announced.

"Are you still trying to get thrown out?" Wib asked mildly.

"Just expressing my opinion." She capped the marker and threw it back in her bag.

"Don't you see this is a good thing? Having the club every day, that'll give me more chances to get into the house and look around."

Rebecca looked blank for a moment, then embarrassed. "Oh. You're right. Well, don't worry, this stuff isn't permanent. It washes off, see?" She licked a finger and rubbed at WEIRDOES. It didn't come off. She muttered, fished a water bottle from her bag and wet the hem of her shirt, then used that to scrub with. She scrubbed hard. The letters looked bolder and shinier and more visible than before.

"What a dirty trick!" Rebecca got up, repacked and zipped her bag, and swung it over her shoulder. "Okay, if they want to play games, I'll play."

REBECCA SAID that Dulcey usually worked in the garden this time of day, so they walked around the house to the back. They heard Dulcey before they saw her. She was humming, some soft monotonous tune that made Wib think of the drone of bees on a warm, still afternoon. All he wanted was to lie down on the cool grass and cover his eyes and sleep.

I'll fall over if I listen to any more of that.

He walked on along the vegetable rows until he came upon Dulcey, who was bending with her back to them, picking ripe tomatoes and green beans and cantaloupes and putting them into a big straw basket that sat on the ground. Her dress today was white linen sprigged with clusters of red cherries. Her hair, in its crown of braids, shone so richly gold in the sunshine that it made a glow around her head.

"Hello, you two," Dulcey said, without stopping work or turning to look. "What brings you here?"

"The club, of course," Rebecca said, a tad too jauntily.

"The Weirdoes Club?"

Rebecca shot Wib a startled look. She'd changed the sign only minutes ago. "Uh... yeah."

Dulcey straightened up, looked around, smiled, and offered them each a small tomato. Wib hesitated, uneasy but not sure why. She laughed. "It's safe to eat, I promise. We don't allow pesticides here, or anywhere near here."

The tomato was a perfect scarlet globe in his hand. He bit into it and was amazed by its rich deliciousness. Rebecca was already half-way through hers, red juice dripping down her chin. "Wow," she gurgled through the mouthful. "Straight off the vine really does make a difference!"

Then her face changed. Wib could see it sinking in. She swallowed. "You won't let pesticides anywhere *near*? How would you stop them?"

"Through firm but courteous citizen action." Dulcey added: "The club's not open yet."

Wib spoke up, he hoped convincingly. "That's the problem. Nothing to do."

Rebecca finished her tomato and wiped her chin on her wrist. "Yeah, we're bored."

"We want to make ourselves useful."

"We want to help out." Rebecca put on what she probably thought was a smile that could not be resisted.

Dulcey opened her eyes wide. "Really?"

"Absolutely!"

"Wonderful. Then you, Rebecca, can help with today's baking. And Wib, why don't you go and see if Aster could use a hand? I think you know where to find her."

Chapter 12

WIB GLANCED UP at the little round window on the third floor. No face looked out at him, but he was sure now that the picture in the stained glass was different from what it used to be. That bird was no robin. One more puzzle to solve.

He circled the house to the front, where the door stood open to let the breeze flow through. This was a gift. He'd been sent right to where he wanted to go, or near it, and nobody was around to see or stop him. He climbed the wide curved stairs to the second floor, then to the third, taking the steps by twos, then trotted along the polished hallway right to the back. A square space opened here between the washroom on his left and the closed stairwell that led up to the cupola, on his right.

This storey looked different from what he remembered. Somebody had done some redecorating. The boring beige-painted walls were now covered in wallpaper with twining grape vines all over it, and bright-feathered birds peeking through the leaves.

Wib knelt in front of the wall at the base of the stairs going up. The triangular space under the stairs had been boxed in, but not solidly. The hidden entrance to his secret space was right here, this panel about two feet to the left of the bottom step. He couldn't see how it opened. But then, he never could: that was what made it secret.

The place where the panel loosened was on the upper right. You had to feel along, pushing with your fingertips, to find where it gave, and then hit the spot hard.

Now he couldn't find the yielding spot. Must be the wallpaper. The cracks around the panel had been papered over. He would have to use his pocket knife to open the cracks: but carefully, so nobody would notice. Was there time to....

"You! Kid! What're you doing there?" Aster stood in the archway to the stairwell. He hadn't heard her come. She was wearing white shorts and some kind of loose silver-grey top. With her long bare legs and bare feet and bleached head, she looked like a ghost. Wib wished he hadn't thought of that.

"I, I've come to help you." He didn't usually stammer. Only with Aster.

"Do I look as if I need help?"

"No, but Dulcey said I should offer. So here I am." That was better: more sturdy.

"Dulcey said?" Her pale eyes glinted with what might have been laughter, or maybe malice. "All right. Come on up." She spun on one foot and vanished up the stairs, apparently not caring whether he followed or not.

The cupola was up two flights of stairs, lifted well above the attic and roof. Wib remembered the long stairs that twisted up and up forever. At least it had seemed like forever to a short-legged six-year-old.

He dimly remembered the cupola, too, when he stepped out at the top of the narrow stairs and looked around. He remembered being hoisted up in somebody's arms to look through an eyepiece.

The round chamber was smaller than he recalled, only about ten feet across. At first sight it reminded him more of the inside of an old ship than an observatory, with its inner shell and floor of pieced wood. The floor was inlaid with a smaller version of the ballroom's central star. The edges of the floor next to the walls showed a border of tiny stars, moons and planets that glimmered like the pearly insides of seashells.

A short set of shelves stood by the south wall, with a few tattered star guides in it. Aside from that, the telescope and the wooden railing that guarded the top of the stairwell were the only things in the place. There wasn't even anywhere to sit.

The telescope was a series of nested brass tubes, polished bright as gold. The brass tripod it balanced on was ornamented with spiralling vines and curling feet, but the scope itself was simple and businesslike. It pointed northeast through a long, narrow opening in the dome that made Wib think of a segment cut from an orange.

"Look." Aster pointed at the eyepiece. "Tell me what you see."

He looked. "Wow!" The view was spectacular. After a baffled moment he realized that the shape of the coastline, stretching into the distance, was familiar from maps. He pulled back and looked at Aster. "That's Georgian Bay! I can see all the way to Georgian Bay!" Something about this struck him as very strange, but he had no time to figure out why.

Aster swung the telescope to the north. Then stabbed her forefinger at a brass crank that stuck out at the base of the wall. "Turn that."

Wib turned the crank. It moved quietly and easily, although only in one direction: clockwise. As he cranked, the whole dome rotated with a whispering sound, sliding the viewing gap around.

"Okay, stop!"

Wib let go the crank. "Cool!"

"Steel ball bearings," Aster said, answering Wib's wide-eyed look. "Check this out."

This time he was looking at somebody's bedroom. You'd think it was inches away. Absolutely everything was visible, including the titles of books, a pair of torn white shorts hanging off the end of the bed, and five seeds picked from a half-eaten apple that sat on a desk. A giant poster on the wall showed the actor Donald Sutherland as Norman Bethune.

"This is Rebecca's bedroom," Aster said. "Messy, isn't it?"

Wib leaped back from the eyepiece. "That's private!"

"So is this, I suppose." She swung the telescope south. The dome rotated again, although nobody had turned the crank. "Now look."

He stood back. "Why? This isn't helping you. This is just messing around!"

She smiled thinly. "Now it's your room."

"Mine! But—" He looked, and recognized his own bedroom; but not his room in the little white house on Fairview Avenue. It was his old room in a triplex in Scarborough, on the east side of Toronto, more than two hundred kilometres away. He pulled back, looked out through the gap, saw only the sun-drenched, green-bordered streets of Amstey. Then looked in the telescope again.

Same old bedroom, but this time he saw his mother packing things into boxes. Getting ready for their move, which meant this was something that happened days, maybe weeks ago. She picked up a framed photograph from the dresser. Wib knew which one it was: the one of his dad, camera in hand, grinning his wide bright grin, dark hair tumbling over his forehead, brown eyes gleaming through his glasses. She looked at it, lightly touched the glass over the face, then laid it down on a sheet of bubble wrap and folded it in.

Wib stepped away from the telescope. "I can't possibly be seeing this." His voice shook. He shook all over.

"And yet you do see it." Aster seemed different, although he was too upset to notice how.

"It's a video. You were spying on us! You're trying to trick me! Is this what you do, you spy on people?"

She shook her head. Something shadowy and silver swirled around her. "I look and see, but only a little way. It's not for me to see the whole pattern. Look again."

He meant not to look. He meant to go straight down the stairs and out to the garden and tell Dulcey what her partner was up to, because for sure Dulcey couldn't know about this crap!

But instead he bent to the eyepiece and looked. This time he saw his mother in the kitchen of the little white house in south Amstey. She was down on her hands and knees, prying old worn vinyl tiles off the floor with a stiff-bladed tool. She worked briskly, her hands and arms strong, cracking the tiles off and flinging them with a jaunty spinning motion, like Frisbees, onto a pile in a corner.

Something dark crouched behind her in the dimness under the breakfast table. It crept out and stood up on its four legs, and Wib saw it was a black dog, heavy-headed, about the size of a mastiff. Something bright hung from a silver chain around its neck.

She didn't see the dog, didn't hear when it took a step toward her. "Mom!" Wib yelled. "Look out!" She cracked off another tile and tossed it aside. Her lips moved as if she was singing. The dog took another step toward her. "Mom!"

The scene fuzzed as if someone had twisted the lens. He backed away. Aster was watching him. Everything about her except her face was blurred. She stood in a waterfall of silver. Her eyes looked at him out of the silver blur with a strange gentleness.

He felt himself spinning, and thought he might be fainting. But he didn't fall. The Earth spun below his feet, and only he was still, as if the turret floated on the planet's surface like a magnet on a dish of mercury.

THE WORLD stopped spinning. Wib staggered and caught his balance. Then lurched to the stairs and clattered down, whirling around the bends. Then in and out of the rooms on the ground floor like a ferret, out the open front door, up the driveway to the street and down Circle Road at a sprint.

He ran all the way home, only slowing to a walk every couple of blocks, then jogging onward. By the time he reached the house he was gasping and had to press a hand to the stitch in his side.

The doors were locked — his mother hadn't lost her big-city caution — but he had his key. The house was deserted, he knew that without calling, he could hear it. But he called anyway. "Mom!" His voice echoed through the empty rooms.

He ran to the kitchen. "Mom!" Not there. Broken tiles were heaped in a corner. The stiff-bladed tool lay on the floor beside a patch of whatever she'd found underneath, as if she'd just dropped it there. As if something had surprised her. His heart was pounding so hard he could hardly breathe.

He only spotted the sticky note stuck to the table because it was neon yellow. His mother's handwriting, quick and neat and slanted, like italics, ran across it. "Wib — gone to Canadian Tire. Eat that leftover pizza in the fridge. Back soon! Love, Mom. XOXO."

Wib read it again, took a deep breath, and stuck the note back on the table. He took a red pencil from the mug of odds and ends on the windowsill and wrote OK across it in big letters. Then he picked up the scraper and started in on the tiles still stuck to the floor.

Underneath was an older kind of linoleum, not tiles but one big sheet, cream with streaks of green and black, really ugly. As he pried and ripped and flung, he thought of what he'd seen in Aster's telescope, that vision of the black dog creeping up on his mother. And the shiny thing on the chain around its neck.

After a while the work calmed him and he decided that the episode of the dog probably never really happened, not right in this kitchen. But his seeing it meant something, all the same. Was it meant to put him on his guard against danger? Was it a threat or a warning? A warning from who?

He wondered what Aster really was. A maniac with a trick telescope? A fraudster? He hoped it would turn out to be that simple.

66

Chapter 13

REBECCA WORE a large white cotton apron tied over her black shorts and black-and-silver top. She would never in a million years have pictured herself in an apron, but here she was. And it made sense after all, not to get flour and butter and sugar all over your clothes.

She had never pictured herself baking, either. I am not a domestic animal, she would have said, if the question had ever been put to her. Yet for the past hour she had been working busily and, yes, happily in the Morphy house kitchen.

It was about twice the size of their generous kitchen at home. It looked older too, because this house was older, with a flagstone floor and miles of white-painted cupboards up to the ceiling. No hanging plants, no recessed lights. The windows were small but they overlooked the garden and stood open to let the sweet-smelling breeze in and the heat of cooking out. The white curtains blew in and out like waving hands. The one new thing, a stainless steel refrigerator, looked out of place there.

But the oven fit right in, queening it over the kitchen like a domineering grandmother. It was huge, shiny and black and had half-a dozen doors and the word "Aga" on the front. It looked like you could roast Hansel, Gretel and the three little pigs in it all at once.

In the centre of the room stood a table made of pale, solid wood twice as big as the MacBeth dining table. Rebecca stood at one end of it mixing dough for ginger cookies in a sky-blue china bowl. At the other end Dulcey rolled out the pale gold dough into a thin sheet on a white cloth.

67

Then she tumbled a box of steel cookie cutters onto the table. "Here: you cut while I finish mixing that next batch." Rebecca loved this part: pressing the cutters down to make oak leaves, daisies, apples, flying doves. And trying to place the cutters so as to use as much dough as possible at one go. It was like making a jigsaw puzzle.

As they worked Dulcey told her about the spices in the cookies, not just ginger, and where in the world they come from: India, China, Madagascar, Jamaica, and how they were not just delicious, but good for the body, too.

"These are things all healers should know," Dulcey said, shaping the last of the dough into a flattened ball. "Your grandmother knows. This is her recipe."

"Gran!" Rebecca looked up. "She's not a healer, she's a politician."

"Oh, there are lots of ways to heal, and lots of things that need healing. The human body is just one." Dulcey rolled the dough thin as she spoke.

Rebecca watched, half hypnotized by the swift movements of Dulcey's hands. Then a thought struck home. *Her recipe.* "Wait. Gran came here?"

"Certainly." Dulcey was cutting out shapes now, hearts and stars and little men and women.

"I knew it!" Rebecca yanked at her apron strings. "This was a plot between my gran and my dad — and you, too! You're all trying to turn me into Rowena!"

"I'm sure that's not possible." Dulcey sent her a smile in between cuttings. "And there was no plot. It was your father who suggested you should join our club. Your grandmother came on her own to inspect us."

"I just bet!" Rebecca pictured Gran snooping into cupboards, checking the washrooms to make sure they were clean, and interrogating the Three Sisters on their fitness to supervise her precious granddaughter for half of each afternoon. Her cheeks burned.

Another thought struck home. "Did she meet all of you? Did she meet Mrs. Doun?"

Dulcey's eyes sparkled. "Yes. It was an interesting meeting. For all of us."

"And when will we meet Mrs. Doun? Wib and me and the others, I mean?"

"Soon, I think. Not today. Now, let's get these cookies into the oven! No, keep your apron on a little longer. There are dishes to do. I'll wash, you'll dry."

BY THE TIME Rebecca had put away the last mixing spoon and cleaned the kitchen table, grumbling under her breath as a matter of principle, the other girls were gathering in the end of the garden where the tomatoes and cantaloupes grew. That was where the club was to start today.

She went out of the house by the kitchen door and stopped at the edge of the garden to see who was there. Mostly it was the same bunch as yesterday, including Cecily and Emily. And Maura Norton, the one who helped Wib with his knitting yesterday.

Rebecca found Maura a little disturbing. Not annoying like Sneaky Cecily and Empress Emily. Just slightly worrying. Like there was something sad about her. Like her mother or father was really sick, maybe, and you didn't know what to say or do. And yet she looked perfectly fine, just quiet and soft and sort of beige, as if she didn't want anyone to notice her.

There were a couple of new girls too, but still no boys. No Wib either, at first. Rebecca worried that he'd quit the club; or, almost worse, that he was upstairs exploring the house without her. Then she spotted him walking around the corner of the house from the meadow. She waved at him and he waved back, but didn't smile. There was no time to talk.

Dulcey led them through the garden, pointing out the different kinds of herbs and vegetables and flowers, and talking about their uses and meanings. It was unexpectedly cool, Rebecca decided, that there was an actual language of flowers, and people used to send each other bouquets that were messages in a secret code. Red roses meant love, that was obvious, but who could have guessed that marigolds meant despair, or scarlet geraniums meant stupidity?

Of course there was a craft attached. Everybody was to carry on with what Dulcey called "fibre arts," which meant messing about with string or yarn, but they were also all going to make paper. Paper for birthday cards or invitations, or for writing letters, or origami. The flowers and herbs they picked now would be embedded in the papers.

This was about the dumbest thing Rebecca had ever heard of. "Who sends cards these days?" she muttered to Wib. "Who writes letters? When you can do it all on a Smartphone?"

Two days ago or even yesterday she would have done something obnoxious with this stupid project, hoping to get herself kicked out of the club that much sooner. But her decision to stick with Wib, who needed to be here, had changed that.

Besides, the cookie baking with Dulcey had left her feeling mellow, more willing to go along with things, so she picked a few basil leaves. She liked their smell, which made her think of spaghetti sauce. Wib grabbed some random weed out of the grass at the last minute as they trailed into the house.

THE FIRST THING Wib did, as everybody crowded into the ballroom/crafts room and milled about, was to go and look behind the piano. One glance was enough. He ducked out again and crossed the floor to Rebecca, who had been watching him. "Nothing," he said.

"What? That can't be!"

"Not a mark. There's nothing there."

"But we saw it! Both of us!"

"Right. And that dog."

"We couldn't both be loony tunes, could we?"

He shook his head. "Doubt it. It's not like we're related."

"So what's going on?

"Okay, you two!" Aster set a thin hand on a shoulder of each and steered them toward the long tables, where blenders, tubs of water and wire screens in wooden frames were waiting for them. The idea was to make a mash out of water and pulped scrap paper and other fibres, then lift some of the mash out of the tubs on the screens, and then decorate the screened mash with flower petals and bits of herbs.

At first Wib was so distracted with worry about his mother and the black dog with its silver chain, and trying to make sense of the back of the piano healing up, he hardly noticed what he was doing. Not until Aster said "Odd choice" in his ear, making him jump.

"What?" He backed away from her, nervous and suspicious.

"Odd choice of plant. Birdsfoot trefoil?"

He looked at the handful of stems he'd been shredding without noticing what they were. The leaves were small and round, the flowers small and bright yellow. Attached to them were sprays of tiny brown pods. He'd been tearing them into bits and dropping them onto his screen of greyish pulp.

He dug his heels in. "Why not birdsfoot trefoil?"

"Means revenge. In the language of plants. Who d'you want revenge on?"

"Me? Nobody!"

"Then who would want revenge on you?"

"N-nobody! Why would anybody — I never—" Stammering

71

again.

"Or on somebody close to you?"

"I, I don't understand."

She was about to say more, but broke off and suddenly turned around to stare at the next table. The girl at the end nearest to Wib, but on the opposite side, was Maura. She was dreamily shredding a spray of something that looked like cedar. The bits were falling all around, on the table and the floor, and some into her screen of pulp. Aster was glaring at her as if there was a venomous snake draped around her shoulders. Then Wib saw that Aster was actually focused on the space just past Maura's left shoulder. He didn't see anything there.

Worried, he stuck close to Aster as she stepped around the end of the table, keeping her eyes fixed on Maura. She moved like a cat stalking a bird, he thought. In passing she picked up a sprig of daisies. "You don't want that," she said, plucking the cedar-like plant from Maura's fingers and thrusting the daisies in their place. Maura flinched and looked up and around, blinking. She dropped the daisies and Wib picked them up for her. She gave him a watery smile.

Aster was moving away, holding the remaining bit of cedar by her fingertips as if it was dripping with sewage. Wib went after her. "What's wrong with it?"

"It's cypress."

"That's a tree, right? What's the matter, is it poisonous?"

"No. Irritating at worst."

"Then what—"

"Language of plants, Wib." She flashed him a razor-sharp grin. "It means death."

Dulcey arrived just then with platters of ginger cookies and pitchers of iced raspberry fizz. Aster waited until the girls were all clustered around the snacks, and then showed the bit of cypress to

72

Dulcey. "How in the name of all that's holy did this get into our garden?"

The two exchanged looks. Dulcey said, "A message?"

"Worse." They both looked across the room at Maura, who was sitting limply in her chair. "Gone now," Aster said.

"Not far. What did Rebecca choose?"

"Basil. Means hatred."

They turned together and looked at Wib, a couple of yards away. He was certain they could have kept him out of this conversation. So that must mean they meant him to hear. Dulcey said: "Hatred. Revenge. Death. Someone is sending a message."

"I don't understand," he said.

"The meaning will come clear. Until it does, be on the watch."

Chapter 14

BY FOUR O'CLOCK everybody had four or five rectangles of mash littered with plant matter laid out in front of them on lengths of cotton cloth. The paper would air-dry overnight and the next day would be ready to be pressed and, if desired, trimmed. "So if you want your paper you'll have to come back tomorrow," Aster said. "Got that?"

They spent the next hour working on their regular projects. Rebecca crouched on her chair with her feet up on the rung and focused ferociously on the mess of cotton twine, wooden beads and organically dyed feathers spread over her knees, only looking up to grab another bead or another piece of string from the table. Wib guessed that was the way she was: that once she had decided *not* to screw up, she was going at it whole hog.

He himself strained to remember how to knit and struggled to do it without adding more holes to the ones already there. He added row after row of garter stitch, apparently hard at work, but it was an act: he was really watching Maura. He thought about the cypress she had picked up, which Aster said meant death, and he watched, more and more worried, as she dreamily pulled the needle from her perfect, smooth blue-violet fabric, and slowly unravelled it. The ravelled yarn piled up beside her chair.

Ingrid poked her on the arm and demanded to know what the heck she was doing. Venice sent her anxious glances. Zira spoke quietly to her twice. At last Maura woke up, looked at her knitting and let out a little shriek. Immediately she worked the remaining piece back onto one needle, and then started knitting with a speed and intensity that made Rebecca look lazy.

"Ten inches," she muttered. "I can do it. Ten. Then eleven."

At nearly five o'clock all the girls started leaving for home in ones and twos or clusters, almost all under their own steam, without parents or caregivers to pick them up. Except Maura, whose mother always came to get her at five sharp. Wib dropped his knitting into his lap and shook his aching fingers. He gathered up his pink monstrosity and stuffed it into the shelf under the window, then walked over to where Rebecca was rebraiding one of her strands. "Finished in a sec," she said. "This bit's not right."

"You sound like Maura." Wib tipped his head in that direction. "Not having much fun."

"But at least now she's acting normal," Rebecca said. "Normal for her, anyway."

"Maura!" Aster called up from below. "Your mother's here!"

There was no answering squeak, no anxious scurry across the room. Wib looked around. Maura wasn't there. "Already gone."

Except, as they discovered when they came downstairs, Maura wasn't there, either. Maura could not be found.

MRS. NORTON was a trim, tidy woman with cropped brown hair, a flat smile and anxious eyes. When it sank in that the Three Sisters had misplaced her daughter, she tightened up all over.

"Don't sweat it," Aster said. "She probably just went home on her own."

Mrs. Norton went white. "Maura would never do that! She would never go off on her own! Someone's snatched—"

"Now, you know how unlikely that is," Dulcey said.

"But—"

"You're not to worry about a thing. We'll have her here in two shakes." Dulcey laid her strong, soft hand on Mrs. Norton's shoulder and guided her down the hall toward the kitchen. "Maura tells me

75

she's home-schooled. That's so interesting! Come and have a nice cup of tea and tell me about your teaching methods."

"Oh — well — to begin with, it's not teaching in the traditional sense." Maura's mom already sounded more relaxed. "It's a shared journey toward self-knowledge and personal strength."

"My gosh!" Rebecca said, watching them go. "That explains a lot."

"You two." Aster pointed. "You go through the house. Don't split up. I'll search the grounds." She was out the front door on the last word and gone.

Rebecca looked around the front hall. "Okay. So, where?"

Wib thought of Maura worrying at her knitting, obsessed with getting it back to the right length, so her mom wouldn't think she'd failed. *Poor kid.* "Let's try the crafts room again. She might still be there."

He was on his way up as he spoke, Rebecca at his heels. On the landing, halfway up, she caught at his hand from below. "Wait! What's that?"

"What?"

Then he saw it. There was a man-high mirror fixed to the back wall of the landing. The mirror actually only took up a small part of the space within the frame. Most of it was occupied by the image, done in leaded stained glass, of an old, white-haired man in a long robe holding a lantern high and peering into shadow, as if searching. The sections of glass that made up his robe were mirrors instead of coloured glass.

Now parts of the mirror were fogged, as if someone had just breathed on it. And someone was writing on the fogged surface, as if with a fingertip. Only there was nobody there to breathe or write.

The invisible finger wrote: *mora celar*

Wib's stomach tightened. "Henry?"

76

yes hury the mirror said.

Rebecca started backing down the stairs, clinging to the banister. Wib lingered, eyes fixed on the mirror. "Henry! But how... why..."

go go dont let him get her

"Him? Who?"

A blast of wind burst in from nowhere and pushed him down the stairs with a hundred small hands. He lost his footing twice but grabbed the banister and made it to the bottom with only a few bruises. The wind died.

Rebecca stood gasping, clutching the newel post. "You think... it... he... meant Maura?"

"Yeah, I..." He wanted to go back and talk to the mirror, and he wanted to get as far away from there as he possibly could, both at the same time.

"And... celar?"

"I think that means cellar. He wasn't very good at spelling."

Rebecca darted away along the central hallway. Wib followed, his head whirling. They detoured through a dim room with a big complicated-looking wooden machine in the centre, then through a door and into the small room hung with skeins of yarn and dried herbs that they'd walked into last night, and then through another door to the right, and then they were on the landing of the back stairs.

The door to the yarn room swung shut and they found themselves in semi-darkness. A glowing thread outlined the outer door that opened onto the herb garden, just enough light to show them each other's too-pale face.

"Maura?" Rebecca called softly. "You down there?"

No answer. "Maybe she went up." Wib looked hopefully up the flight that led to the upper floors, with their tall windows and bright sunlight. But Henry had said *celar*.

Rebecca touched his arm. "Listen." A sound came from below: a

77

footstep on wood, something that flexed with a creak. "We need to get down there," she whispered.

"Not in the dark." There was no light switch on the landing. He took a step down, brushing a hand along the stone wall. No switch here either. "Flashlights. Probably in the kitchen." But even as he said it he knew there was no time. *Hury*, Henry had begged.

He took another step. Rebecca slipped down after him. At once, strangely, the darkness was less intense. Something was glowing down below.

"Maura?" Another step and another, easier now that the light gave shape to things: rough wall on the right, a wooden railing on the left. Step and step and step and then they reached a tiny landing, turned a corner and went down half a dozen more stairs, and at last set foot on a stone floor, smooth underfoot, and cold clear through the soles of their shoes.

Still no Maura. The room was smallish and square and empty. The light came through an open doorway in the near wall.

They found Maura in the next room, sitting cross-legged on the cold floor with the white cat in her lap. She was cuddling and petting it. It looked at Wib and Rebecca, purred loudly and winked its glinting eyes. Its fur stood out in a silver-white fuzz.

Rebecca pointed and mouthed, *The cat*. All the light here came from the cat. How was that possible?

The cat-light glinted on glass jars, rows and rows of them, in shelves all around the walls. Wib stared around, diverted. "This is where they store the jams and pickles." He'd expect that of Dulcey, that she would never waste so much as a bean from the garden. But it looked like hundreds and hundreds of jars, and they'd only been here what, a year? That was a lot of preserving.

Still, they brought his courage back, all those jars filled with jam for somebody's breakfast toast, pickles for their dinner. So right and useful and ordinary.

"Maura?" Rebecca knelt beside her. "C'mon, time to go home. Your mom's here."

Rebecca, Wib thought, never lost courage. Or if she did, she had enough nerve to make up for it. Now she tugged at the hand that was petting the cat. He wouldn't have wanted to get anywhere near that animal, if it was an animal. Maura let her hand be dragged off but she didn't look away from the cat. It flattened its ears and hissed — not at Rebecca, but at Wib.

Then it leaped off Maura's lap and stalked across the room, the light moving with it. Maura scrambled up and went after it.

"Maura, wait!" Rebecca caught at her arm. Maura twisted and clawed. Rebecca yelled "Ow!" and jumped back.

Meanwhile the cat had butted a lower shelf with its head. The shelf clicked, then slowly swung out from the wall. It was a door made of jam-jar shelves.

The room beyond was pitch black. Something stirred in the blackness. There was a rustle like sliding silk, or like dry hands rubbing together. Whispers.

The cat walked in through the door, tail high, taking its light with it. Maura started to follow. Wib knew in his gut that she must not go in there. *Dont let him get her.*

"Maura, no!" Rebecca grabbed her arm again and Maura spun, hissing and spitting. Wib grabbed her other arm and between them they dragged her across the room and through the door to the room with the stairs. Behind them came another click and a clink of glass jars, and the darkness became total. Wib found the bottom of the stairs by running his elbow into the end of the wooden railing. He yelled. His grip loosened and Maura yanked away, but Rebecca hung on.

They wrestled her up step by step. The steps began to appear out of the darkness as they got near the top. They reached the ground floor landing and stood gasping, still locking a struggling Maura between them. Then a thread of sunlight from around the outside door crossed her face and she went quiet.

She stayed quiet as they marched her through the house to the kitchen. "Look who we found!" Rebecca proclaimed cheerfully, pushing Maura into the room ahead of her.

Mrs. Norton dropped a mug of tea on the kitchen table (Dulcey caught it), jumped up and flung her arms around her daughter. "Maura! Are you all right?" She held her off and looked her over. "You're so cold! And what's all this dirt on your clothes? Where have you been? I was worried sick!"

Aster, stepping into the kitchen from the garden, rolled her eyes. Dulcey watched, calm but not smiling. Maura looked around vaguely.

"She was playing with the cat, that's all," Rebecca said. "In the cellar."

"Cat!" Mrs. Norton hugged Maura close. "Maura's allergic to cats! No wonder she looks ill!"

"She does look a little peaky," Dulcey said. "Maura, try a sip of this. It's rosemary tea." She reached behind her to the stove and brought forward a steaming mug. To Mrs. Norton she said: "It will buffer her system against allergens, although I doubt the contact was sustained enough to cause a serious reaction." Maura's mom nodded anxiously, but Maura grimaced and pushed the mug away.

Wib caught her eye as she left the house, her mother's arm around her. He stood on the porch beside Rebecca and watched the car turn onto Circle Road.

"Allergies?" Rebecca leaned against a white-painted column and held out her right arm. It was scored with thin red marks, like cat scratches. "Could allergies change her like that?"

"I guess, if they were really bad allergies. Peanuts can kill you if you're allergic. Who knows what cats can do?" He turned back to the house. "What colour are Maura's eyes?"

"Oh... blue. Like a doll's."

"That's what I thought. But just now I'm pretty sure they looked sort of yellow-green. Like a cat's."

Chapter 15

"THERE YOU ARE!" Aster appeared in the doorway and waved them in. Rebecca protested, but Aster marched her back to the kitchen, where she handed her a bar of yellow soap and turned on the hot water faucet. "Scrub! Cat scratches can turn septic."

"Cat? But it was Maura, not—"

"Just do it, okay?"

"Oh, all right." Rebecca scrubbed, yelping at the sting. Then Aster handed her a clean white towel to dry her hands and arms with.

"Thanks a lot," Rebecca said. She was about to say more, but instead closed her mouth and took a step back. Aster and Dulcey were standing shoulder-to-shoulder in front of her. Dulcey smiled, but there was a no-nonsense look in her eyes.

Aster poked her chin at Wib, who had come forward to stand beside Rebecca. "So, a cat."

He looked up at her uneasily. "Uh, yeah?"

"We don't have a cat." It sounded like an accusation. *Liar!*

"We've seen it twice," he snapped back, surprising himself. "You have a cat."

"Couldn't miss it." Rebecca shaped the air with spread hands. "About so big. Fluffy and really white. Sort of glowy."

"Glowy." Dulcey nodded, smiling. "And what else have you seen and heard around the house? Wib?"

"Um." Looking up into Dulcey's warm sky-blue eyes, he felt the pull. It would have been a huge relief to spill everything. But he couldn't. Wouldn't. And yet he didn't want to lie to her. He let himself go blank.

Dulcey moved her eyes. "Rebecca?"

Rebecca tossed her head like a colt. "Not a thing!"

"Well, forewarned is forearmed, remember that. Thanks for all your help today. Here are some extras for you both." Dulcey handed each of them a warm paper bag that smelled like butter and ginger and cloves, and another, smaller bag that smelled like medicine.

Rebecca sniffed at the smaller bag. "Isn't this that rosemary tea that Maura wouldn't drink? Thanks, but I don't have allergies."

"Me neither," Wib said.

"It's not for allergies. It's protective in other ways."

"Like what?" He wasn't going to drink some mystery brew. He could tell from the way Rebecca was holding the package, by the tips of her fingers, that she wasn't going to either.

"Against things like that white cat." Dulcey's eyes sparkled with amusement. "It also promotes the healthy circulation of the blood. Share it with your families. Now, off you go. See you tomorrow!"

BEFORE THEY separated on the sidewalk, Rebecca to head north and Wib south, Rebecca stopped and gazed up into the trees. Dozens of big maples and chestnuts marched along the boulevard edging Circle Road. Two of them bracketed the street end of the Morley house driveway.

Wib had an inkling of what she was looking for. He'd wondered himself. "You won't find one."

"There's got to be a security camera." She kept turning and searching with her eyes. "How else would Dulcey know right away how I changed the sign?"

"But when we found her, she was in the garden. And not looking at any video screen."

"Right, but Aster could've...." She spun to face him, alight. "Yes! That's how they do it! Aster monitors the video and then she phones

83

Dulcey. You know, on those little tiny earphones that you can hardly see. I bet they're both wired like that."

Wib thought about it. Aster, with her trick telescope.... Maybe. But wired? "Don't think so."

"But it would explain so much!"

"Dulcey wearing a phone? Really?" He tilted his head at the trees. "I'm guessing you could search every branch in every tree around here and not find a camera."

Rebecca threw her hands in the air. "Somehow, I think you're right."

Chapter 16

THAT EVENING Wib and his mother tried to cool their hot house by opening all the windows and doors and turning the ceiling fans on high. While the evening air flooded through the rooms, they sat on the front porch steps with the bag of fresh ginger cookies between them and cold glasses in their hands. Wib was drinking milk, while his mom had a glass full of an iced tea that she had made from that rosemary junk from Dulcey. She seemed to like it.

"A good day's labour." She toasted Wib with her glass of tea. "Here's to us workers!"

She looked tired and smudgy, her hands scratched from ripping up floor tiles. But it was good tired, Wib thought: contented, not stressed out. Not the way she used to look after work at her programming job. He hoped this new job would be better, wouldn't leave her wrung out and twitching with nerves.

As they sipped and munched, they looked across the street at the houses there, a row of small wood-siding buildings like this one. Some with weedy yards and scabby paint and old sofas growing moss on the verandahs. Some weeded, mown, geranium-bordered and spruce. Scrubby or spruce, their western facades reflected the setting sun and shone like cheerful faces.

A teenage girl in jeans and T-shirt backed out of the house opposite, pulling a baby stroller after her. She levered it down the steps and along the cement walk and onto the street; looked across, beamed and waved. Wib's mom waved back. The girl lifted an arm and pointed a finger. "Your boy?" she shouted.

"Yes! This is Wib!"

"Mom, for gosh sake," Wib muttered through his teeth.

The girl waved again. "Hi, Wib! How ya doing?"

He waved back. "Fine, thanks."

She wafted off one last wave and walked away, pushing the stroller.

"That's Pippa and her daughter Nebula," his mom said. "There are some nice folks around here. Friendly. I think we'll be okay, Wib." She slipped an arm around his shoulders and hugged him: just a quick, brief squeeze, knowing how he felt about that, how he was too old for hugs now. Mostly.

"This house is a lot of work, though," he said. "Lots more to do."

"Sure is, but we can make a go of it, don't you think? It looks kind of shabby, true, but that's just the surface. The structure is solid. Plumbing, wiring, woodwork, all good. The rest: well, it'll take elbow grease, but we've got lots of that on hand, right? Or on elbow." She laughed.

Wib looked sideways at her smudged face and thought: It sounds as if she's actually looking forward to all the work. Then he knew. She *was* looking forward to it. Much more than to her new paying job, which was to start tomorrow.

"But starting tomorrow," she said, as if she'd read his mind, "I won't have as much time to work on the house, so I'll be counting on you to keep on helping out, okay?"

"You bet."

She picked another cookie out of the bag. "Oh! Guess who I met today at Canadian Tire? Rowena's dad!"

"Um... Rowena?" The name was familiar, but it took him a moment to place it. "Oh, you mean Rebecca!"

She looked puzzled. "Is that what she calls herself? Anyway, Keith, Mr. MacBeth, says you two seem to be really wrapped up in some club you joined. Run by an outfit called the Three Sisters." She bit into the cookie. "What club is this?"

Wib nearly choked. He was startled to realize that he hadn't mentioned the club to his mother. He'd started off with the search for his secret place and the thing hidden there, and of course he'd wanted to keep all that from her. And then he'd got absorbed in the mystery of Henry and the black dog, and the white cat, and....

"Well, um, you're so busy." He huddled, feeling guilty.

"I'm not busy right now. Where is this club? What do you do?"

"It's a sort of a drop-in centre, afternoons, I think just to fill in the time before school starts in fall. Crafts and stuff. Today we made paper with plant bits in it. I'll show you that tomorrow, if it turns out any good." He tried to sound upbeat, as if he was really pumped about this stuff.

She didn't buy it. "Crafts! That's doesn't sound like your sort of thing. Where is it?"

He'd been hoping she wouldn't ask. "It's, ah, actually in that house where we used to live. On Circle Road. Funny thing, right?"

She leaned back, as if to get a better look at him. "The old Morphy house!"

"That's it."

"Good grief! What a place to have a club for kids. I'd better go see."

"No, Mom, it's okay! These three women run it, Aster and Dulcey and Mrs. Doun, and they're really good at crafts and baking, and Dulcey, especially, you'd like her. She made these cookies. It's educational, too, we learn all about plants and things in the garden. And it's free!"

"So you really like it? Are you getting to know lots of other kids?"

"Yeah, it's for boys and girls from 10 to 14. There's more than a dozen of us."

She held the cool glass against her cheek and gazed at the glowing roofs across the street. "Well, if Keith is okay with it, I'm sure it's all right. It's just that..." She lowered the glass. "You know, Wib, even if we hadn't had to move away from Amstey, after your father died, I think we would have left that house quite soon."

"Cause we couldn't afford it?"

"Not that so much. I never really wanted to live there, you know. It was your dad's idea to buy it, he was tickled by the notion of owning the famous Morphy mansion. His very own haunted house! Plus it was going cheap, and there was that huge yard that would be good for kids."

"But you didn't like it?"

"Uh-uhn. Too much house, too much work. And I never felt it was ours." She shivered a little and shrugged something away. "Maybe because so much of the original furniture was still there, and I never felt it was ours to use, or get rid of. It was like the previous owners were hanging around and breathing down our necks."

Wib sat up straight. "You mean ghosts?"

"No!" She laughed, but Wib thought it sounded forced. "But if there were ghosts, they were a real pain in the neck. Things kept getting knocked over. Things changed places, and I could never remember if I'd moved them or not. Doors closed themselves. Things went missing." She looked meditative again and a little sad, and Wib knew she was thinking about *it*.

"So what's Rebecca's dad like?" he asked, to distract her. "Is he like that grandmother of hers?"

"Not a bit! He's tall and thin and quite a nice man — not that Flora isn't nice, but Keith is much more comfortable. Quiet. Quite shy, really." She laughed, a real laugh now, and shook her head. "But my gosh, for somebody in real estate, he has no notion at all of how things work in a house. I had to help him buy a drain snake to clear a blocked downspout. That's how we got introduced. He'd never heard of such a thing as a drain snake before."

"Me neither. Is it venomous?"

She gurgled and punched his shoulder.

Chapter 17

"THIS, FOR YOUR enlightenment, is a drain snake." Keith exhibited the roll of coiled steel wire. "And guess who helped me buy it? Wib's mom!"

"Yeah?" Rebecca couldn't work up any enthusiasm about the hardware. Her dad meeting Wib's mom was more interesting. "You like her?"

"She seems quite nice. And so handy! For somebody who works with computers, she knows an awful lot about tools and how to fix things. Seems it's her recreation, working with hammers and saws and mitre boxes. As far from software programming as it's possible to get, she says."

His mild, bony face was unusually animated. Rebecca thought: *Hmm.*

It was Keith's night to cook. Unusually for him, he had decided to take a risk and make something interesting and different, something out of a cookbook, called Country Captain. It was not a complete failure: Rebecca liked the chicken and its spicy sauce. But the rice was an overcooked sticky mass. She dumped out the rice and they sopped up the sauce with bread.

Even Flora had a good word for Keith's cooking, although not for anything else. She was getting ready for a meeting with the local New Democratic Party riding association the next day, and was too worked up to be trusted in the kitchen, even for clean-up.

At the dinner table, both Keith and Flora looked preoccupied, chewing and swallowing without conversation. Rebecca had a full load of questions to explore herself.

90

Like, if that had been Henry writing on that mirror, what exactly was he, and how did he do that? And how did he know Maura was in danger? And if Maura was in danger, what kind of danger? And what about that glow-in-the-dark cat? And....

She finished wiping her dish out with a slice of bread, ate the bread, and pushed her plate away. "Hey! Dad, Gran! Remember the old Morphy house?"

Gran glowered at her. "Rowena, I've far more pressing things on my mind than the old Morphy house!"

"I'm just asking a question. Did you ever heard of a boy named Henry, connected to that house?"

"Henry? Never."

Her dad just shook his head. She wondered if he was thinking about Wib's mom.

"Then how about a ghost named Henry?"

Flora clanged her fork on her plate. "Child, don't be daft!" Then she scowled, leaned over and squinted at Rebecca's right arm. "What's that you've done to yourself?"

"It's nothing. Cat scratch." She held up her arm. "It's already healing, see?"

"Never mind, cat scratches can turn ugly. Go and wash."

"Oh, Gran! I already—"

"Go! Now! And use the carbolic soap!"

Later they had Rebecca's spice cookies with tea. But not the rosemary tea, because she had somehow lost that bag over a neighbour's back fence on the way home.

REBECCA WOKE UP on Thursday morning with her head still buzzing with questions. She finished breakfast, but only because Flora stood over her. No junky sugar-coated cereal either: this morning it was egg-in-the-hole and a mandarin orange and a dish of yogurt.

Then she pulled on a pair of black bike shorts and her favourite purple tee with flying black birds on it, grabbed her embroidered bag and jogged down the hill and through downtown Amstey to Wib's house, wishing as usual that she could fly.

As she ran up the front steps Wib's mother stepped out, wearing a determined smile and a whiter-than-white blouse over crisp black jeans. "Wish me luck!" she said. "You want Wib? You can have him once he's finished his chores." She waved and was on her way, striding energetically along Churchill Avenue toward Highway 21 and the industrial park on the far side.

Wib was cleaning the living room windows with spray cleaner and paper towels. "We need to tackle the Sisters about Henry," Rebecca said. "In a subtle and sneaky way, of course. Can't you do that cleaning later?"

"No. I mean, yes, we need to find out what they know. But this gets done first." He went on spraying and wiping.

She watched for a couple of minutes, then dumped her bag on the sofa. "Okay, I'll help."

By one o'clock all the windows in the house were clean, and Rebecca's arms were tired. Wib said her windows were streaky, but he'd go over those bits later.

"You could thank me."

"Why? You only helped so I'd go with you sooner." But he gave her a glinting look. She thought maybe he did have a sense of humour after all, only it was dry as week-old toast.

They headed north, picked up a couple of egg salad sandwiches and a carton of milk from Padgetts', and ate as they walked.

The club sign was already set up near the sidewalk outside 3 Circle Road. It said THE THURSDAY CLUB*.... *INCLUDES ALL MONDAY, TUESDAY AND WEDNESDAY CLUB MEMBERS.

92

Rebecca scooped her black marker out of her bag and stood back to think, lips pursed.

"Again?" Wib said.

"You betcha. This has become a challenge."

"Not much you can do with Thursday."

"Sure there is!" She altered the sign to say: THE TURDSDAY CLUB. Then laughed, flipped the marker in the air, caught it, stowed it away, and walked on with a swagger in her step.

They found Dulcey in the garden again. She was hacking weeds from between the green beans with a hoe that was taller than she was, and had a broad, sharp blade that made Rebecca think of the scythe of Father Time. In spite of her swagger, Rebecca was rather glad Dulcey didn't mention the club's new name this time.

"We have a question," Wib said in his direct, serious way.

"Fire away!" Dulcey continued to chop and gouge.

"It's about the people who used to live here. I mean, before I lived here. Maybe a long time before."

"What about them?" Dulcey straightened up, gently brushed a stray ant off the shoulder of her cotton jumper, and pushed back a loose strand of hair with the back of her hand. She looked then like anybody's mom, only nicer than most, Rebecca thought.

"Well... was there ever a family with a boy named Henry?"

"I'm sorry, Wib. We've been in the house less than a year, you know."

"That's not really an answer, is it?" Rebecca said, in her politest voice. "Would Mrs. Doun know?"

Dulcey's sky-blue eyes glinted with laughter. "Perhaps. She's been everywhere and she remembers everything." The glint brightened. "Whether or not she would tell you is another matter."

"Mrs. Doun." Wib looked uneasy. "Where..."

"The cellar, right?" Rebecca put in.

"That's right," Dulcey said. "Be careful, both of you."

"Careful of what? The dark?" Rebecca grinned.

"The dark, and what lives in the dark. Take care." She looked at Rebecca. "You especially. Don't be too sure of yourself."

"Why do you do that? Tweak Dulcey like that?" Wib demanded as they circled the house to the front.

"Well, talk about being too sure of yourself! That's her all over. Aster, too. You'd think they're in charge of the world, sometimes."

"I wonder what Mrs. Doun is like."

"Old, weird, and wobbly. Don't worry, I'll behave."

Chapter 18

WALKING THROUGH the house to the back corner stairs, Rebecca got a good look at the downstairs rooms for the first time. She stuck her head into arched doorways as they passed. Most of the rooms opened off the central hall, which held only that squat cupboard (she looked in and saw boots and shoes), an umbrella stand, a marble-and-brass clock on a shelf, and the tall coat stand with brass hooks up the sides and a man-high mirror in its back.

"I wonder what they use these rooms for?" Rebecca pulled her head out of a satin-gilt-crystal living room, or was it sitting room, straight out of Downton Abbey. It looked excruciatingly uncomfortable to sit in.

"Not for anything at all, I'm guessing," Wib said.

Next to the sitting room, farther back near the kitchen, was what Wib called the breakfast room, although his family had never had breakfast there. It should have smelled of toast and bacon and coffee, but instead it only smelled of old wood and wax polish.

Across the hall at the front, on the right as you came in, was another possible sitting room. This one was all floral upholstery with crocheted lace doilies, braided rugs, and cute china dogs and cats in glass-fronted cabinets.

"Not a speck of dust," Wib said, bending to look into a shining-clean fireplace, its ash-free cavity filled with a basket of brilliantly coloured dried flowers.

"I have a feeling they don't use most of the house." Rebecca blinked at a glittering display of tiny cut-glass birds on the mantelpiece. "I mean, none of this looks much like Dulcey's style, does it? Or Aster's, either."

"No. It doesn't. It wasn't my mother's style when we were here, either." Wib stopped under the wide arch of the doorway leading to the room beyond the floral parlour. "Here's something different."

Rebecca followed him in. They'd run through here yesterday looking for Maura, in too much of a hurry to notice much of anything in passing. This room had dark wood panelling halfway up the walls and plaster roses all around the top edges of the ceiling. Despite the wide bow window it was dim, the sunlight slanting in through close-growing cedars.

"This used to be the dining room," Wib said. "We ate in here when we had visitors."

"Not much eating going on here now. What's that thing?"

The one piece of furniture in the room was a wooden machine about the size of a grand piano. It was not one Rebecca had ever seen before. Its frame of upright beams stood as tall as she was. The uprights were joined by crosspieces, with smaller frames nested inside, and other long pieces lined up in a row across the bottom from front to back. Several round wooden things with handles, like pirate ship's wheels, stuck out at the sides. A bench stood in front.

"Okay, now I got it," Wib said. "Remember that first night, when we got in the back door and we heard some machine going and Dulcey singing? That was in here."

"Holy Harry!" Rebecca craned to get a closer view without going too near. The thing looked clunky and old, and madly complicated, as if it could only be worked by an alien with eight arms.

"I saw one of these at Black Creek Pioneer Village," Wib said. "It's a loom."

"Loom?"

"Yeah, you know, for weaving cloth. That's what those machine sounds were."

Weaving. Well, no real surprise. It was the sort of crafty, old-fashioned thing Dulcey would do.

Except for the loom and its bench, the room was empty. At first Rebecca thought the loom was empty too. Then Wib sidled closer, cautiously, as if it might start up by itself and maim him. He leaned forward to look at the inner frames. Then leaned back, tilting his head sideways. Then backed away, shaking his head. "Wild!"

When Rebecca stepped up beside him she understood what he meant. There was a piece of fabric on the loom, but you couldn't get a good look at it. You had to squint to see it, so fine it seemed printed on the air. If you looked at it the wrong way it disappeared, only to shine out at you when you turned your head again.

She realized she was mashing Wib's wrist. There was something dangerous here. And also something very precious and private.

"It's beautiful," she murmured. "But..." She leaned forward and reached....

"Do not touch it."

Wib jumped and Rebecca gasped and they both whipped around. Dulcey stood right behind them. "This web belongs to someone else," she said.

Rebecca searched Dulcey's face. She was different. No trace of a smile, not even in the eyes. Distant, stern. It took some nerve to question her. "Why, uh, why can't we see it properly?"

"Because it is not entirely here."

That made a nonsensical kind of sense. Rebecca set it aside to chew on later. "There's something wrong with it, too."

"You have good eyes." Dulcey almost smiled.

"But can't you fix it?"

"That's not for me to decide. Perhaps not. Or perhaps it will correct itself, given time. Or perhaps the distortions will become part of the overall pattern."

"You said..." Wib looked at the fabric. "You said it belongs to somebody else."

"I did."

"Who?"

She tilted her head at the door in the back corner. "You have an errand." She turned and walked from the room, her totally uncool mom-ish cotton jumper swaying about her like a cloak of shadow. Wib stood looking after her until Rebecca pulled at his arm. "C'mon!"

On the landing of the stairs that led down to the cellar, they stopped and pulled themselves together. "So here we are without flashlights again," Wib said.

"What's this?" Rebecca bent and picked up something from the floor beside the outer door. It was a candle stuck in an iron holder shaped like a leaf, with a frosted glass chimney over the candle.

"Candle lantern. Good." Wib bent and came up with a small box of wooden matches. "Take off the glass."

She lifted it off and held the holder while Wib struck a match and lit the candle. Then she set the chimney down over the candle. Wib laid the burnt-out match carefully on the stone threshold, then put the box of matches in a pocket of his chinos and reached for the lantern. Rebecca held onto it. "I'll lead. You went first the last time."

The stairs seemed to go down a longer way than they had yesterday. (But yesterday we were in a hurry, Rebecca thought, and today we, I, am not totally sure I want to go down there at all.)

At the bottom she held the lantern high. The first room was bare and clean: no grit underfoot, no cobwebs in the corners. The floor was paved with irregularly shaped flat stones, smooth as if scoured by a river. There were two doors: one in the south wall near the base of the stairs, and another, which they hadn't noticed before, in the east wall.

Wib went over and opened that one and peered in. Rebecca held the lantern up over his head so they could see. "Goes a long way," Wib said, "but I think it's just for the furnace and laundry and stuff like that." He closed the door and looked around. "Mrs. Doun?" he called out.

Rebecca wished he'd kept his voice down. There were echoes. From some far place came a tangle of voices that murmured and babbled and then died away. Of course they were just Wib's voice multiplied, but they sounded like a reply. He hunched his shoulders and opened his mouth, then closed it again.

"Come on," Rebecca muttered. She held the lantern in front like a shield and opened the door in the south wall. Beyond was the room where they'd found Maura yesterday. It had three doors: the one they'd come in by, the one disguised as a set of shelves, and a third door, closed, in the wall opposite the first one.

Except for the doors, the walls were completely filled with rows and rows of gleaming jars. "Look: no labels." Rebecca moved the light closer. "No labels on any of these. How will they ever know what's what, and when it was packed?"

"We have a good memory," said a voice. A cold, dark voice, a deep voice, but not a man's voice. The fine hairs rose on the back of Rebecca's neck. Wib shuddered once, then went very still. They looked, and a vague figure loomed in the gap where the third door now stood open. Without another word or sound it melted back into the darkness.

Chapter 19

WIB AND REBECCA looked at each other. "Well, come, if you're coming," the voice said sharply, now sounding like anybody's cranky old gran and a lot like Flora, Rebecca thought. That made her feel braver. She held the candle lantern out in front and stepped across the threshold to the next room, with Wib close at her heels.

She stared around. She wasn't sure what she'd expected, but this wasn't it. "Mushrooms?"

The walls of this room were lined with wooden planters: beds of dirt and what looked like wood chips, arranged in tiers on racks that rose from the floor to chest height. The beds were dotted with small white globes, singly and in clusters. "It's another garden," Wib said in a wondering voice.

"A garden in the dark. A night garden." Rebecca felt cold, and not just because the cellar's earthy-smelling chill was starting to soak into her bones.

"You sell these just like Dulcey sells tomatoes and cantaloupes," Wib said, in a determinedly daylight voice. "Organic produce. Right?"

"Douse that candle," said the deep dark voice.

"But then we won't be able to—" Rebecca began, but Mrs. Doun nodded once at the lantern and it went out.

Blackness pounced. Rebecca froze, purple afterimages from the candle flaring across the dark. Small sounds crept in all around: Wib's uneven breathing and her own. Tiny scurrying footsteps that made Rebecca wish she were wearing tall boots. Distant voices too, maybe from upstairs, but they sounded as if they came from miles deep.

Then the dark was no longer total. Small pale things showed all around. As her eyes adjusted, she saw that some of the mushrooms glowed with a strange greenish light, the colour of light that cancels all red tones. It made Wib look sick, his eyes big and black. She suspected she looked the same.

She made a mental note. *Never, ever let Dad or Gran buy mushrooms from here.*

In this cold, sickly light Mrs. Doun was all black and white. The face white and ancient, the eyes pale as sea glass under heavy lids, no-coloured hair scraped back into a granite knot. She was square-built, not tall, like a slab of rock (a tombstone, Rebecca thought). In fact she was about the same size and shape as Flora, but that was the only way they resembled each other.

It was reassuring to see that the old girl was wearing ordinary, depressing old-lady clothes: some sort of long, black dress, probably polyester. With a wide black belt and a black leather sheath on one side holding what must be a really big knife. Which was not so ordinary. Rebecca took a half step back. No, wait, it was scissors, or shears, you could tell by the handles.

That wasn't all, but she wasn't sure she really saw the rest or only imagined it. A hint of shadowy robe or cloak that covered the old woman from head to toes and hung over her face. It only showed when she moved. Did Wib see it? He was staring, and his face had gone even whiter.

Mrs. Doun waited, still and silent.

Wib cleared his throat. "We, uh, Dulcey said to come down here."

"We need to find out about the people who used to live in this house," Rebecca said. "Before Wib. Maybe a long time before. Was there ever a boy named Henry who lived here?"

After a long silent moment, Mrs. Doun said: "Yes. But he is not a boy now."

"He's grown up?" Made sense, Rebecca thought.

"No."

Wib's breath hissed in. "What is he?"

Mrs. Doun didn't answer. She seemed to be listening. Wib and Rebecca listened. Again Rebecca heard distant voices, only now they were more like cries. And somebody weeping.

The mushroom glow faded. The voices grew louder. "Light your glim," said Mrs. Doun.

Wib fumbled the match box out of his pocket, nearly dropping it. Rebecca lifted the glass chimney and Wib lit the candle just as darkness closed down again. The friendly yellow flame rose; the voices faded.

Rebecca drew a shaky breath. "What just happened?"

"The dog is growing strong. He can change what you think you see." She turned and moved toward another unlit open doorway. Her dark voice came back to them: "And have a care for your third." She was gone.

"Wait!" Wib teetered on the threshold of the room beyond. "Wait! What did you mean about Henry?"

No answer came. Rebecca held up the lantern but it showed nothing past the frame of the doorway where Mrs. Doun had gone. They looked into darkness thick as tar. Out of its depths came the sound of water flowing and a smell like a riverbank in a forest.

"Out." Wib stepped back from the threshold. They headed back the way they'd come, only faster. Rebecca couldn't wait to get out of that black, buried place. In the next room she was glad to see the shelves of jars, so ordinary-looking.

One thing was different. A single bank of shelving stood open like a door. It was the hidden door that the cat had opened yesterday, the door they had wrestled Maura away from as if from a nest of rattlesnakes.

Wib, insanely, walked over to it and was looking in. "Hey, you should see this."

"You mean you can see? There's light in there?"

"Sort of."

Peering over his shoulder, she saw what he meant. The room beyond was huge: much bigger than the ballroom, so far as she could tell. To get to it you had to go down a short flight of steps. The stone floor was bare, except for a rectangle of what might have been faded carpet that covered a space in the centre almost as big as Dulcey's kitchen.

All of that was hard to make out, because the far wall and corners faded into dense shadow. But there was light, a bluish twilight glow that seemed to come from the silky, cobweb-fine and cobweb-grey hangings that stirred on the walls and swathed the ceiling. The room looked like the inside of a big tent.

Wib took a step forward. Rebecca grabbed his arm and held on. "You're not going in there!"

"I need to know what this is. Is this why Henry warned me to stay out of the cellar?"

"If he said stay out, you should listen!"

"Sh!" He held up a hand.

There was sound in the room now. The silken hangings stirred and whispered. Rebecca could almost hear words. Then from the dusky corners came a soft chanting, and a drumbeat: slow, deep, insistent. The hangings stirred again. Then they rippled. As if things behind them were elbowing their way out.

Rebecca yanked at Wib's arm and they scrambled backward together. Wib pushed the bank of shelves back into place and it closed with a click. In two seconds they were out of the room; another two and they were up the stairs. On the ground-floor landing Rebecca blew out the candle lantern and set it down and sprang out through the door that Wib held open. He slammed it behind them.

They stood on the grass beside the herb garden. The sun beat down. Rebecca lifted her face to it, to the wonderful hot, healing sunlight. The breeze teased her nose with scents of thyme and sage. Wib stood rubbing his goosebumped arms. He was trembling. She discovered that she was too.

"I wish I knew exactly what happened in there." Wib looked at the closed door.

"You're not going back!"

He grimaced. "No, not right now. But I don't think I'm finished with that place. Especially not that big room with the blue light."

"There is no way I'm going back in there!"

Wib looked at her coolly. "I didn't say you, I said me."

She jabbed him with a look. "I don't weasel out on my friends!"

"But you just said—"

"I know. If you go back there I'd have to go with you, and I'd hate it. So you better not!"

"Know what? Your dad's right, you're getting like your gran."

They started back around the house, heading for the front door. "Well," Rebecca said, "we found Mrs. Doun. She wasn't much help, was she? I've got more questions now than before."

"Yeah. Like, what did she mean, Henry is not a boy now? And the dog getting stronger, what did that mean?"

"And who's the third we should take care of? Third what?"

"Not take care of." Wib picked a young green bean as they skirted the vegetable rows and crunched it in his teeth. "She said 'Have a care for.'"

"So what does that mean, they're dangerous? Or they need help?"

"Maybe both."

104

"Two meanings. Typical of this bunch," Rebecca said bitterly. "And did you hear? Sounds like they've got an underground stream in that back room, or maybe a broken water pipe. Was it like that when you lived here?"

"I don't think so. But I never went down in the cellar, so I don't know. Henry always said that was *the* place I should stay away from." Wib finished the last bite of bean and threw away the stem.

Chapter 20

WIB WAS STARTLED to hear voices upstairs and the lobby clock chiming half-past two when they came in the front door. They must have spent more than an hour in the cellar. How could that be? It hadn't felt anything like that long.

Kids were already gathering in the ballroom, where their dried handmade papers were laid out on the long tables. The girls were milling about making comparisons, laughing, exclaiming, sniping, admiring. Maura wasn't there.

Some of the papers did look okay, he had to admit. Rebecca's, with its border of green basil leaf bits, looked like a clearing in a forest. Not much room left for writing, though. Wib's paper should have had yellow petals and tiny pods from the birdsfoot trefoil arranged in a frame around the edges, but somehow they had drifted into clusters and...

He looked, frowned, looked again, then glanced around to make sure nobody else was watching. The bits spelled out WIB across the top. Then down the right-hand edge he could clearly read: FIND ME, then a space, then WE NEED TO TA. That was all. The bottom edge had cut off part of the last word. He could guess what it meant to say, though.

"Hey, cool," Aster said over his shoulder. "You spelled your name in weeds." She cracked her cold smile and didn't mention the rest of what was spelled out there, although she must have seen it.

Before she would whirl and walk away he said, "Where's Maura?"

"Home."

"Is she okay?"

She looked straight at him. "What do you think?"

They spent the next hour and a half flattening their papers under stacks of heavy books, then discussing whether to trim the edges straight or leave the deckle (the wavy bits) on, then breaking up into groups to explore ideas for how to use the papers. You could fold them into origami cranes or cut them to cover picture frames or roll them up and tie pretty ribbons around the rolls... and on and on.

Then they had to get busy and actually make things. Wib carefully folded a sheet of his paper into a fan, for his mother, and glued one end. He had to keep refolding and regluing it because he was too busy thinking about important things to be bothered with what his hands were doing. Ingrid ignored him, Venice giggled at him, and Zira offered advice which he half-heard and didn't take.

When a green-speckled paper airplane bounced off his head and fell to the floor beside him, he remembered Rebecca. He looked around and spotted her across the room grinning at him. He signalled with his head to meet over by the piano. Once they were away from the others, he showed her his paper with the embedded message.

"Talk, yes!" she hissed. "But how?"

"I need to get into my secret space. That's where I always used to find him."

At four o'clock Dulcey brought a tray of warm, densely chocolaty brownies and a jug of cold milk, as well as a pitcher of homemade ginger ale for those who were lactose intolerant.

While they were snacking, she called for their attention. Silence fell instantly and completely, something Wib had never seen happen in any classroom or camp or club he'd been in before. She sent her golden smile around and announced: "I hope you'll all be here tomorrow, because we have a wonderful treat in store! Maura Norton is having a birthday and she will be eleven!" She paused. (Polite clapping.) "So, during our regular club time, we will have a party here. There will be a scavenger hunt with clues and prizes and, of course, delicious party food!" (Enthusiastic applause.)

"Okay!" Aster snapped, looking around with narrowed eyes. "That's tomorrow. Here's today. To get you in the groove, we'll have a game of hide and seek. Last one out frees the bunch and wins a prize. You can hide anywhere in the house and grounds, except the cellar. Got that? Not the cellar. This spot," she stabbed down at the floor, where she stood on the inlaid star under the chandelier, "is Home. I'm It. Now scatter!"

She closed her eyes and started counting down rapidly from one hundred. The girls scattered. Wib and Rebecca ran with the rest. Most headed down the stairs; a few went up. Wib raced up the stairs with Rebecca at his heels.

On the third floor girls were barging in and out of rooms, Emily and Cecily among them. "Nowhere to hide!" Emily chirped, passing Rebecca at a run.

"Nothing in there!" Cecily snipped. "Stay here and you're toast!" The two ran laughing down the front stairs. Wib and Rebecca were suddenly alone. The house fell quiet.

"Nowhere to hide? In all these rooms?" White-painted doors opened onto the corridor on either side of the main stairwell. Rebecca walked along sticking her head in, pulling it out, shaking it. "That's funny. No beds, no furniture, no— Wait, here's something. Looks like a playroom. There's a rocking chair, a dollhouse, a—"

"I know what's in there. Not what we're looking for." Wib trotted on toward the back of the hall.

Rebecca closed the playroom door. "But it's really weird. No beds! Where do they sleep?"

"Maybe they don't." Wib knelt at the walled-in side of the back stairs.

108

Rebecca knelt beside him. "So where is it, this secret space of yours?"

"It's...." He moved his fingertips over the wallpaper, feeling for the crack between two panels. "Here!" He got out his pocket knife, opened it and ran the tip of the blade delicately down the wall. "This is the way in. The left side of this panel has hinges. It opens on this side." He pushed hard at the right-hand edge of the panel, then hit it with the heel of his hand. "Only it doesn't!"

Rebecca looked over her shoulder. "Someone's coming." A quick, sharp sound came from the direction of the front stairs. The clickety-click of clawed feet. "Some *thing*." She stood up. Wib whammed the edge of the panel with the side of his fist. Still solid.

Boom. Boom. Boom. All the doors in the corridor swung closed, one after the other. Rebecca ran back and tried the nearest, the play-room door. Locked.

The corridor darkened. The clicking sound grew louder. A smoky cloud poured up out of the front stairwell and swirled around the banister.

"Wib! We gotta get out of here!"

"Two seconds, that's all I need." He pounded the side of the panel with all his strength. "I know it's here!"

The smoky cloud rolled toward them. As it neared it darkened and grew denser, and shapes pushed out of it. Feet that didn't quite touch the floor yet still went clickety-click. A heavy head, two shining red glints where the eyes should be.

Rebecca hauled at Wib's arm. "Come on! Down the back stairs! We can make it if we go now!"

"No, look!" Something, some invisible spike or nail was scratching lines in the wallpaper right in front of his eyes. Curled paper shreds littered the floor. The scratches wrote: TOP LEFT HIT HARD. Rebecca hit the top left corner with her fist. Nothing happened.

Too near, something growled: a growl with teeth in it. Wib thumped the spot, harder. The panel popped an inch open, inward, tearing the paper. He pushed it wide. The two of them lunged at it and slithered in side by side. They stuck. Rebecca wrenched free and squirmed in first. Wib yelled. He yanked his feet in and Rebecca grabbed the panel and banged it shut.

There were two wing nuts on the free edge. Wib twisted them and they nested into two grooves cut into a wood strut inside the wall. They looked like no protection at all. But whatever was outside didn't try to batter its way in.

They lay there breathing hard. "It got one of my sneakers!" Wib said, when he had his breath back. Growling sounds came from outside. He put his ear to the panel. "I think it's eating it."

"Could be worse," Rebecca said. "Could've been your foot."

Chapter 21

"HOW LONG DO you think it'll wait out there?" Rebecca asked.

"I guess we'll find out." Wib rolled away from the flimsy panel and burrowed into the depths of his secret space. Rebecca burrowed after him. The space was longer and wider than she'd expected, although if she'd thought about it she might have guessed that Wib's secret space would have the same footprint as the flight of stairs above.

But it wasn't very high. The ceiling slanted from zero inches to five feet over a distance of roughly seven feet, from the inner end to the outer wall. At first they had to squirm, then they crawled. In five seconds Rebecca's bicycle shorts and her black and purple tee and her arms and legs were grey with dust.

The surfaces were bare wood, splintery in places, yet the space gave Rebecca a feeling of safety and softness, of being cuddled. Maybe it was the air in here, warm and smelling of dry old wood. Maybe it was the light and the colours. The wooden walls and ceiling had aged to the deep gold of buckwheat honey; and the sun, now halfway down the western sky, shone in through a small round window at the outer end and painted stripes of bright green, blue and yellow on the walls.

When they were far enough along to sit up without banging their heads, Rebecca sat up and looked around. "This is fantastic! I wish I'd had a secret place like this when I was six. Or even now!"

"I liked it," Wib said, offhand but obviously pleased.

"I specially like the window." She scooted closer to get a good look. It was made of stained glass and showed a brown owl with golden eyes perched on a tree branch among green leaves. The other parts of the window were made of dimpled glass, some pieces amber, some sky-blue.

"Yeah. Funny thing, though. The way I remember, it was a robin on that branch, not an owl. And the door," he tilted his head backward, "had hinges on the left, not the right."

"You could've got that mixed up. It was six years ago."

"No. Some things stick with you. That window had a robin."

"So, how..."

"Henry."

"I get it — I think. If Henry could scratch up the wallpaper to send us a message, and crack the back of the piano, what else has he changed?"

"That's what I'm thinking."

"Anyway, we found the place, hurrah! See anything else different?"

They looked around. There wasn't a lot to see. Wib's younger self had scavenged an old, torn patchwork quilt and folded it and laid it along one wall, for a place to sit or lie. Under the window sat a flat, square metal box printed with a red plaid pattern and the words Walker's Scottish Shortbread. Wib picked it up and wrenched it open. He tipped it to show what was inside: a drift of hard flakes that looked like yellowed plaster, a silver spoon black with tarnish, and a steel butter knife.

He wrinkled his nose in a kind of smile. "That was my food cupboard. Those crumbs are from Ritz crackers. I used to smuggle tubes of squeezy cheese up here and spread the stuff on the crackers." He picked some flakes up and let them fall back into the tin. They made a sound like sand.

Then he gave her a strange, almost embarrassed look. "I had another box. I'm scared to see if it's still here."

"Your treasure box?"

"I guess that's what it was. Treasure when I was six. Now it'll be junk. Most of it."

Most, not all, Rebecca thought. *Here it comes: the special thing he's looking for. The reason he joined the Tombstone Club.*

He drew a deep breath, held it, let it out. Then pulled back the end of the quilt closest to the window and uncovered another box. He set it on the floor in front of his crossed knees. It was about a foot square and six inches high, the top and sides decorated with scenes of a snowy village at Christmas time.

"Looks like a cookie box," Rebecca said.

"That's what it used to be. Chocolate-covered biscuits. I begged it off my mother when the cookies were finished and I put all the things in it that I thought were cool, or precious. I had Henry's things here, too."

"Henry's things?" She sat up straight. "What things?"

"Things of his I found when I discovered this space. I was really young then, about four. So of course when I found his things, that meant Henry was alive and real." Wib shook his head at his four-year-old self. "I figured it out later: he left those things behind when he really was alive. Check the dates."

"Dates?"

"You'll see." He gripped the lid of the box, as if bracing himself. Then pried it up: it was tight and slightly rusted. Rebecca leaned in to see over his arm. Looked like a lot of paper in there. He lifted out a comic book — a Classics Illustrated *Ivanhoe*, which he tossed over to her. "That's for you, Rowena!" She caught it and laughed.

"That was Henry's. So was this, and these things." A yellowed, brittle copy of the *Amstey Gazette*, the local weekly newspaper, dated Friday, August 14, 1970. A tangle of bent nails that Wib had figured out was a puzzle. A small black-covered notebook with a stub of yellow pencil tied to the spine by a string. (Somebody had been writing in it, Rebecca noticed.) A small flashlight, its corroded batteries stuck in the tube, no use at all.

"And my stuff is still all here. I think." Wib went tense. He sat for a moment just breathing. Then dug in again and lifted out half a dozen Spiderman comics. He froze. Then held the box upside down and let the rest fall: a plastic mesh bag of scuffed and nicked marbles, a small yellow toy pickup truck that clattered over the floorboards, a chunk of rock glittering with mica, a chestnut in a wrinkled shell. "It's not here!" He dropped the box with a clang and pawed through the strewn treasures.

Rebecca crawled over to look at them. "You're sure?"

"Yes!" He picked up the metal truck and hurled it. It hit the window, cracking one of the owl's golden eyes. He picked up the bag of marbles and fired it savagely at the wall.

Rebecca stared in shock. She'd never have guessed so much rage and violence could be brewing under Wib's quiet surface.

"It was in a little blue velvet bag with a gold string." His voice sounded strangled. "It's gone!" He thumped his fists on the floorboards. "I was right! Somebody got in here and took it!" He bent over, knees up, arms clasped around himself, rocking back and forth. Rebecca reached out and laid a light hand on his shoulder. He jerked away.

They sat like that, Wib curled into himself, Rebecca watching him out of the corner of one eye, for what seemed to her a long time. Long enough for the splashes of coloured light to move along the wall. She watched for when he stopped rocking, and when his shoulders started to uncurl. Then she said: "We have to find out who took it."

"Oh yeah, how?" He didn't turn around.

"We could try asking Henry. Maybe he saw."

114

Wib straightened up, turned around, and looked at her with no expression.

"Can't hurt to try," she said.

He lifted one shoulder. "Go ahead."

"Okay." She tilted up her face. "Henry!" she called, but softly. No good if all they did was let everybody in the house know where Wib's secret space was.

"Henry!" Wib called, a little louder. "Are you there?"

"Henry?"

Rebecca was about to call again when Wib touched her wrist. "Listen."

At first all she heard was the hiss of wind. Wib pointed at the window. Air was hissing through the crack in the owl's eye. Then the wind took on tone and pitch. It sounded like a flute: a flute that talked, or sang.

It sang: "So you found our place again. I'm glad. I wish you wouldn't break things, though."

Chapter 22

REBECCA SWALLOWED a gulp of panic. Until that moment, Henry the protective ghost had only been half real to her, in spite of the evidence, the messages he'd already sent. In this place he seemed to be right there with them. If she closed her eyes she could picture him sitting cross-legged in the corner near the window, hands on knees, looking at Wib and smiling.

So this was what it was like to be in the presence of a ghost. Cold and sick-making.

Wib had been sitting with his eyes tight shut. He whispered something Rebecca couldn't catch. Then opened his eyes and glared. "What's with that owl? Didn't it used to be a robin?" A weird first question, Rebecca thought. Wib must have really liked that old window.

"Yess," the wind hissed. "And before that, long before your time, it was a cardinal."

"How did it change?"

"I got tired of the cardinal," Henry fluted. "And I like robins. The owl happened by itself. I'm not sure why. Sometimes when I change or grow or learn something new, that makes other things change."

"What other things? The house seems different. But maybe that's just because I was younger then, and I didn't notice things so much."

"No, you're right. I think." The voice wavered. "I fell asleep after you left, Wib. I only started waking up again when the Sisters came. I haven't been really awake very long. So I'm still confused. But I feel it too, something in the house has changed. I think there's something I need to do."

Rebecca's stomach was settling. The fluty voice sounded so normal, so unghostly, you couldn't be scared of it. She took a breath. "Henry. This is Rebecca."

"Yes, I know. I can see." There was a smile in the voice.

"Oh. Okay, I want to get this straight. You can actually change things in the house just by thinking? Like, scratch paint and crack wood and stuff?"

"Well, yes, but it's not just thinking. It's not that simple. And anything like that, I fix it after. Always clean up your own mess, that's what I was taught."

"So you could change the owl in that window to, um, a raccoon? Right now?"

"I could, but not right now. Lead and glass are not hard to change: I could fix this crack in a minute. But it would take time, days at least, to form something new." The flute made a disgusted whistling sound. "Besides, I don't like raccoons. They poop in the attic and it's hard to get rid of them."

"Henry, what happened to Wib's... um... " She looked at Wib, eyes wide in question.

Wib looked into the corner by the window. "Henry, d'you remember my father's medal? Remember when I showed it to you?"

"Medal? Let me think. Umm..." The flute ran up and down a skein of notes. Then: "Oh! Yes, now I remember. It's your special treasure."

"Was." Wib's voice tightened up. "I can't find it. Did you move it?"

"Me! No, I wouldn't. Anyway, I couldn't."

"Couldn't?" Rebecca asked. "Why not?"

"Because it's not part of the house. It's part of Wib. I couldn't move it so long as I'm stuck in the house."

The voice broke off and the soft melody floated up and down

117

again. Rebecca had an idea that meant Henry was thinking. She was just going to ask, when he said, in a new harder, sharper tone: "The only one who could've taken it is the black dog."

"The black dog?" Wib flinched. "Why would that thing want it?"

"I don't know," Henry fluted. "Normally he'd just wreck it, to hurt somebody, if it wasn't any use to him. So he must have found a use for it. And a place to hide it."

"But how could anybody *use* the medal?" Wib shook his head, frustrated and angry. "It's not a tool."

"Wait," Rebecca said. "What is this black dog, anyway? Some kind of demon? And what about that white cat?"

"The black dog is a ghost. The cat is a ghost too, it's one of his slaves. He's strong: he can do that. He could do it in life, too: force people to be his slaves, to do what he wanted."

"So you knew it... uh, him... when he was alive?"

"Yes." The flute shaded darker, mournful. "He was human once, but he let himself change. When he died, he changed more."

"Well, if he's only a ghost," Wib began.

The flute piped up: "He's not only a ghost. I mean, he's not like other ghosts. They're just weak, wispy things, mostly. He's strong. He can actually do things. He can hurt people. Just like in life."

"So, did you..." Rebecca wondered how best to put this. "Did you, um, like, die at the same time?"

The flute let out an indignant whoop. "Die? I never died! I'm not a ghost!"

Wib tried to say something, but Rebecca wasn't going to let this go. She needed to know. "Then what the heck are you?"

"I'm a boy, like Wib. In fact, I think we're the same age now. Twelve, right?"

"That's right," Wib said. "But—"

"So, we're the same. Only, I'm stuck in the house and I don't

118

know how to get out."

There was a baffled silence. Finally Wib said: "I don't understand. Where are you hiding? Why can't you leave? How can you talk to us like this, invisible, if you're just a regular kid?"

"Because I am *in* the house," the flute sang. "I am *in* the walls. In the foundation stones and roof timbers. In the glass and wood and plaster. In the copper pipes. In the fireplaces. In the dust."

There was a breathy silence. More mildly, Henry said: "I'm even in the garden, a bit, close to the house. In some of the trees. I like being in the trees." Another long silence. "I guess that's all," he added in a meditative tone. "I guess I'm in everything except the wiring. Electricity scares me. Oh, and the water."

In the house. Rebecca stared into the corner by the window. In. The house. She was getting the strangest feeling about this. Wib was staring too, his eyes unfocused, as if he was remembering.

"But how did you get *in* the house?" she asked.

"I'm not even sure myself," said the flute. "I know when it happened, and why, but not how. And I'm still not all the way awake, so—" The flute stopped with a squeak. "It's them! I have to go!"

There was a gasp, as if the airstream had sucked itself back through the crack in the owl's eye. Then a sense of emptiness, someone suddenly not there.

A voice spoke in the corridor, near the secret panel. "I give up!"

Wib mouthed, *Aster*. Rebecca nodded.

"Come out, come out wherever you are!" Silence. "Okay, suit yourselves! But if you don't show up in five minutes, you don't get your prizes!" Silence. And more silence.

Rebecca picked up the newspaper and notebook Henry had left behind. "You keeping these?"

"Phooey, no. Take what you want. It's all junk."

She folded and stuffed the papers, with the *Ivanhoe* comic, into

119

her bag, which had travelled with her all this way, and wound the strap of the bag around her arm. They shuffled and then crawled and finally wormed their way, as the ceiling slanted down, back to the entrance. After a breathless moment listening, Wib untwisted the wing nuts and pulled open the panel and put his head out. "Clear." He slithered out, with Rebecca close behind. Then he eased the panel back into place with the blade of his pocket knife.

The scratches in the wallpaper were gone as if they had never been. There were no shreds on the floor. But Wib's left sneaker lay nearby, the toe case ripped, the rubber sole punctured. He put it on.

They ran downstairs and found that everyone else was packing up and going home. Dulcey and Aster met Wib and Rebecca in the lobby. Aster stood on one foot with her arms clasped behind her neck and needled them with her pale, black-bordered eyes. Dulcey said, "Well done!" and handed them each a quart-sized mason jar. "Your prizes for being the last ones free." She laughingly shooed them out.

Standing in the doorway she called after them: "Be sure to come back tomorrow! Don't forget Maura's party!"

"Yeah. The game's afoot!" Aster said, and slammed the door.

Chapter 23

HALFWAY ALONG the driveway Rebecca stopped under one of the silver maples and looked at her prize. "Hey, look, they gave us preserves from the cellar."

"Oh wow," Wib muttered.

"It's marinated mushrooms." She looked at his jar. "Yours, too. I hope they're not those glow-in-the-dark ones."

He hadn't even looked at his jar. He was frowning back at the house. "What did that last crack mean? 'The game's afoot.'"

"The scavenger hunt? It would be just like Aster to make it sound sinister. She does it on purpose."

"I'm not so sure." He walked on up the driveway, shoulders hunched, eyes on the ground.

Rebecca trailed him, face lifted, gazing up into the tall, gangly silver maples. *He loves being in the trees.* "Wib! If he's not a ghost, if he's really alive.... d'you think he's happy like that?"

"Huh?" He didn't turn around, didn't stop walking.

"D'you think Henry's happy being stuck in the house? Or d'you think he wants out?"

"I can't talk now. I'm thinking."

There was a wall around him. Rebecca wanted to run after him, poke at him and knock holes in the wall. She hated being shut out. But a shred of sense held her back. That wall was solid and would only get solider if she tried poking it. "You coming back tomorrow?" she yelled after him. No answer. She stood and watched him go.

A warm stillness settled around her like a big glass jar. It was quieter here, she thought, than anywhere else in town. Maybe it was the stone walls on three sides, and the big trees, and all the green, growing stuff. Maybe they sopped up noise. Couldn't even hear a car whiz past, or a door slam, or a dog bark. Nothing but the wind whuffling through the long grass and stirring the leaves of the trees.

Trees. Henry liked the trees. Rebecca laid a hand on the trunk nearest her. Its rough surface, wrinkled and fissured like an elephant's hide, felt warm and alive. "Henry?" The tree murmured again. "Henry, can you talk?" She looked up, and listened. The leaves went *hush... hush....* Tree talk, she thought. Not very useful.

What had he said? That he was *in* the garden a little, close to the house. Rebecca walked back and stopped under the maple next to the house, the biggest tree, with branch tips swaying only a metre from the third-floor windows and leaves dipping to brush the roof of the porch.

She hid from the house behind the massive tree, put the jar of mushrooms down at her feet, set her back against the trunk and tilted her head to look up. The green leaves on the blue sky were so bright they hurt her eyes. *Tree, you're gorgeous. I love you.* The branches creaked in the wind. The leaves surged back and forth. They sang *Yess... yesss...*

"Henry, are you there?"

Yessss....

He was there. In the tree. She turned around and stretched her arms around the trunk as far as they would go. "Henry. Are you happy?"

The tree fell still a moment, as if thinking, then stirred. *Ssometimesss...*

"Don't you want to get unstuck? I mean, to get out and live like a normal boy?"

Wishhh....

"You wish you could? I thought so! But then why don't you?"

Hhhhelp....

She stepped away from the tree so she could look up into its branches. "You need help?"

Yessss.... The branches waved, the leaves hissed and sang. *Pleassse....*

Rebecca felt eyes on her face. She glanced at the house and caught sight of someone ducking back from one of the tall ballroom windows. It was a furtive movement: not like Aster or Dulcey, she thought, or even Mrs. Doun. But it was a person, not a dog or a cat.

"Henry! I have to go now but I'll be back! I'll help, I promise! And Wib too! We'll get you out!"

The leaves danced and made a sound like breathy laughter. Then the tree fell still and silent.

Rebecca picked up the jar of mushrooms, walked back to the driveway, sent the house a bright grin and a wave, then strode confidently away. But with every step up the drive to the street, she felt those eyes on her back.

"I'M THINKING," he'd said, but Wib wasn't thinking as he walked up the driveway to Circle Road. He'd only said that to keep Rebecca off. She seemed to understand that thinking needed quiet and space. She didn't seem to understand that feelings needed the same. His feelings did, anyway.

He was packed full of them, too full to think. A startled joy at having found Henry again. At the same time, all mixed up with the joy: frustration, bitter disappointment, anger, and a kind of pain in the chest that he didn't understand until he remembered his dad and knew the pain was grief.

He'd lost so much. He'd lost his dad and he'd lost his dad's medal, years ago. And now he'd lost the medal again. He felt guilt, too. Guilt was like a queasy stomach that took all the satisfaction out

123

of life.

If only I hadn't stolen it in the first place! Things would be so different now.

The feelings seeped away, little by little, as he walked. That was the great thing about walking, it almost always helped. He began to feel sorry he'd groused at Rebecca. As he crossed the Hay Street bridge he started getting his brain in gear. He stopped to lean on the stone parapet, the jar of mushrooms balanced beside his elbow, and watched the water flowing past from under the bridge. He felt himself loosen up, felt his thoughts start to flow like the water.

Henry and the black dog. Everything centred on them. The black dog was a ghost, Henry said, but not like other ghosts. It was strong, able to do things, able to hurt people. Maybe it (he?) had taken the medal. But why?

Meanwhile Henry was only just awake, still confused, his memories hazy. He knew there was something he needed to do but couldn't remember what.

And Henry was *in* the house. Whatever that meant. Not a ghost, but not exactly alive and normal, either. Maybe if he could get out of the house into the here and now, his thinking and memory would sharpen up. He seemed to know all about the dog. Maybe he knew what would beat it.

We'd be two against one, Wib thought. We could do it. Then he thought of Rebecca and grinned in spite of himself. Three against one. Just try leaving her out!

Three against one. Was that what Mrs. Doun meant when she said that thing about a third? *Have a care for your third.* Maybe it was important that they should work together, the three of them.

Work together, fine. But first, they had to break Henry free of whatever held him in the house. To start doing that, they needed to talk to him again. Which meant getting time with him alone, out of the reach and hearing of the Three Sisters. Which, Wib suspected, would be a clever trick if they could manage it.

A clock struck somewhere, southward. That clock on the Town Hall. Six bongs. Wib grabbed the jar, left the bridge and put on a burst of speed. He was home by six-fifteen. He just had time to wash off the dust of the secret space and change his clothes before his mother got home, exhausted and tense as an overtuned guitar string.

"Had supper?" She forced a smile and fluffed his hair.

"No. I'll make it. You go shower or whatever."

Wib made spaghetti and meatballs, with a dish of sliced tomatoes and mayonnaise on the side. He gnawed his lip as he studied the jar of marinated mushrooms. Then opened it and picked one out, the smallest he could see, and gingerly bit into it. He was ready to spit it out, but he didn't. It was surprisingly good, pickley and a bit garlicky. He spooned some into a small bowl and set that on the table beside the tomatoes.

His mother came down, fresh and damp and looking more like herself in an old T-shirt and shorts. By the time the meal was over and they were doing the dishes together, she seemed her best self again.

"And those mushrooms: mm, really good. So you won that as a prize? What for?"

"Hide and seek. Rebecca and me. She got a jar too. Because we didn't get caught."

"Oh, yes. I remember." Her eyes looked inward a moment, then they crinkled at Wib. "So you haven't forgotten how to go invisible."

He laughed and was on the brink of telling her about his secret space, but then, catching her eye, he guessed that she already knew. She had always known.

Chapter 24

AS SOON AS SHE got home, Rebecca climbed to her third-floor bedroom, washed, and changed into a white tee and capris. She stowed the jar of marinated mushrooms on the shelf at the back of her closet, then wadded up today's dusty clothes and stuffed them in around the jar to hide it.

Then she upended her embroidered bag on the bed and slid out the things she'd salvaged from Wib's secret space. An old copy of the *Amstey Gazette*, an even older comic book, and a cheap little black-bound notebook with a stub of pencil tied on. She made a gagging noise at the *Ivanhoe* comic and threw it under the bed. She flipped through the newspaper, flipped back to stare at one particular page, then dropped it on the pillow for later.

The notebook was sure to be the most interesting, the most personal. She sat cross-legged on the bed and opened it carefully. Then dropped it in disgust. "Shoot!" Most of the pages were torn out.

Still, there might be something useful here, no matter how small. She picked it up again. On the inside of the front cover was written "Property of Henry Vance". The words were enclosed in a carefully drawn box. The handwriting was small, rounded and very neat, almost like the print in a book.

Vance. Until then she hadn't known his full name, and she suspected Wib hadn't either.

The first page after the cover was black with writing from edge to edge, as if in an effort to save precious space. It began: "I stole this book from Tailer becase I need something to write on but I have no money so cant buy one and anyways even if I had money I cant pass

126

the gate becase Jared woud know right away if I did."

Rebecca blinked and reread the sentence. Then she read on. "I cant let him know what I am thinking. Its hard enough to keep my thouts secret but if he finds this I will not have a second chance. Jared he says to call him that always even in my thouts so as not to call him by his real name by misteak. I cant call him what he really is that doesnt feel right it never did but specally not after what he said about Mom. But even so what I have to do will be hard. I still dont know if I can do it."

There was no date on it, so it wasn't a diary. The spelling was really bad in places, a contrast to the perfect handwriting.

What I have to do will be hard. What did Henry have to do? And this Jared: why didn't he want Henry using his real name? Who was he? And what was this about Henry's mom?

"Rowena!" came Flora's penetrating voice from two floors down. "Dinner! Get your skates on!"

Flora had cooked today, some kind of Hungarian-style veal stew with dumplings and sour cream. And it was delicious — nine stars out of ten, Rebecca judged after the first few bites. Gran was exuberant because the meeting with the NDP riding association had gone so well. "I'm almost certain I'll be their candidate," she said, and forked up a chunk of tender veal.

"Super!" Rebecca said. Then a thought struck her. She set down her fork. "But if you run in the next election, and you win, then you'll have to go and live in Ottawa. Right?"

"That's right, kidlet. Part of the time, at any rate."

"So you won't be here to manage everything I do."

Keith paused, fork in air, and watched his daughter warily.

"Your father will pick up the slack." Flora gave Keith a pointed look.

"Oh, sure." Rebecca waved that away. Her dad had never paid

her much critical attention, leaving that to Flora, so she didn't think he would get in the habit of it any time soon. "But it means I'll be free to eat what I want for breakfast, and get my ears pierced and decide what to wear and what colour to dye my hair and all that, right?"

"You're not eighteen yet," Keith said. For a moment he looked and sounded unnervingly like Flora.

Rebecca decided to drop the subject for the time being. She dug into her veal stew again. "So, Gran, the game's afoot, eh?"

"What game?" Flora ladled sour cream on her dumplings.

"That's just something I heard. It means exciting things are happening, right?"

"It's from Sherlock Holmes, lass. He said it when he was off to pursue some miscreant." Flora grinned. "And it's true, there are some of those in Parliament. But we'll soon roust 'em out!"

"Yes, but Mother, before that it came from Shakespeare," Keith put in. He sat up straight in his chair and made dramatic gestures with his knife and fork. "The game's afoot! Um, something something, and upon this charge cry God for Harry, England, and Saint George!" He lowered his cutlery and smiled at Rebecca. "That's from *Henry Fifth.*"

She stared. "Henry? Fifth?"

Keith sighed. "It's a play, Rowena. Henry was an English king. That speech came just before the Battle of Harfleur, which you haven't heard of either."

"Battle! Did he win? Henry, I mean."

"Yes, but he lost a lot of men."

"Bummer."

ONCE THE DISHES were cleared and washed, Rebecca was free. On her way through the living room to the stairs she spotted a copy of the latest issue of the *Amstey Gazette*. It lay on the floor beside

Gran's favourite armchair, folded open at the editorial page. She picked it up. "May I have this?" She showed it to Flora, who was setting up her laptop on the dining table.

"You may let the pigs have it!" Flora flapped a hand. "That man hasn't the sense he was born with."

"What man?"

"Brendan Ryder. Just look at that editorial! I don't think there's been a single decision of council that he's wholeheartedly agreed with, not once in all these years."

Keith looked out from the kitchen, dish towel in hand. "It's not his job to agree with council, Mother. It's his job to keep them on their toes."

"But need he do it with such relish? Bah!"

Except for Flora, Rebecca had never, ever heard anyone say "Bah!"

She carried the newspaper up to her room and opened it again to the editorial page. The editorial was headed "Demolition rarely the best choice." She didn't bother reading that because she was only interested in the section at the bottom of the page where they named the people who worked on the paper and showed a tiny photo of each, along with an email address. Brendan Ryder was the editor-in-chief.

She spread out the issue, then opened the copy of the *Gazette* from August 14, 1970, that they'd found in the secret space. The copy that Henry had originally put there, Wib thought. A copy that Henry had considered important enough to hide and save.

She checked through the 1970 issue. The editor then was different, but there was an article by Brendan Ryder, staff reporter, that started on the front page and continued on page three. There was also a small photo of him on the editorial page. He looked younger then, of course, and his hair was a lot longer and not grey and there was more of it on top, but the thin face with the cocksure grin and heavy black-framed glasses looked much the same.

The article was headed: "Commune will aid orphans, Morphy claims." Rebecca settled against the headboard of her bed with the old issue spread over her knees. "The Circle Road commune," she murmured in wonder. That house where the Three Sisters now lived really did have a strange history.

Much of the piece was based on an interview with Taylor Morphy, "the last living member of one of Amstey's oldest and most prominent families," and the only member of the commune who had agreed to speak to the press. (Taylor, Rebecca thought. Tailer?) Front and centre was a photo of Morphy, bearded and long-haired, hammering at strips of leather on a bench in the sunshine with the old house in the background behind him.

"People don't understand what we're all about. We're not communists or potheads," he was quoted as saying. "The money we raise through the sale of our vegetables and handwork goes to the foundation we've set up to aid African orphans."

As for their leader, Jared Skye, "When I met him I knew at once that I was in the presence of a truly good man. A saint. But please understand: we have no leader in the conventional sense. We are all equal. Jared insists he is a seeker like the rest of us. We are all walking the same path toward enlightenment."

(Jared, Rebecca thought. Jared Skye. Not his real name, and Henry knew it.)

Asked what his forebears would think of their house being turned into a back-to-the-land commune, Morphy said: "My forebears were money-grubbing capitalists who exploited their workers, so I really don't care what they would think."

The rest of the article was a short history of Number 3 Circle Road. "Built in 1890 by merchant Philemon Morphy, it is a showplace in the height of Queen Anne style. Features include a turret

130

with a telescope and revolving dome, the only full-sized ballroom in the county, and a sunken room below the level of the cellar where Philemon Morphy installed a swimming pool and gymnasium. Later the pool was covered and the room fell into disuse."

The article ended: "It is noteworthy that in this town of spiralling streets, the Morphy mansion is one of a very few houses of which the four sides are precisely aligned to the four cardinal points of the compass."

Rebecca folded the paper and shook her head at it. "Swimming pool and gymnasium! Can you imagine?" She thought of the big room in the cellar with the steps going down, and the voices, and the strangely moving draperies, and shivered.

She picked up the little black notebook again and turned to where she'd left off. After the first page, almost all the rest were torn out, leaving only some shreds close to the stapled centre and then four more pages at the end. The next piece of writing began on the first of the four pages. She frowned at it and held it close to her eyes.

"Dear Mr. Ryder," it began, or she guessed it did, but the words had been scribbled over with pencil and it was hard to make them out. She squinted. Yes, it did say "Dear Mr. Ryder."

Her breath caught and she let it out slowly. So Henry had written a letter to Brendan Ryder. When? Sometime in 1970? It must have been about the commune. And here, in the notebook, was where he'd tried to work out what he wanted to say. He probably copied it out nice and neat for the finished letter. She wondered if the letter actually got sent.

He must have had a ton of trouble deciding how to word things. The first page was almost unreadable, thickly smudged with erasings and rewritings and black with crossings-out. She could make out only a word here and there: *Owen*, and *steel* (steal?) and *serprise*, and.... No, that was it for page one.

She turned the page. The reverse was worse, the paper torn where the eraser had worn through. The next two pages were just as bad. The last page had only a handful of lines, and they were blacked out.

Henry must have been worried about leaving evidence of what he'd told the newspaperman. In case somebody (Jared?) should find it and know what he'd done.

No, he was more than worried. He was afraid.

Rebecca knew he was afraid because he had leaned so hard on the pencil at the end, it had left a colourless imprint on the inside of the back cover. She could read the words if she held the notebook so that the light from the window slanted along the surface. The letter had ended: "He may suspec me so dont tell anyone about this letter. If he suspecs me someone could die."

Chapter 25

NEXT MORNING there was no time to lose. Luckily Flora was already out and about, and Keith was reading the back of a Shredded Wheat box with a faraway look on his face. Rebecca pulled on the first clothes that came to hand — yesterday evening's plain white tee and capris off the end of the bed, and her favourite shiny white sandals — wolfed down a cheese sandwich and a glass of milk, grabbed Henry's notebook and the important pages from the two issues of the *Amstey Gazette*, stuffed them into her embroidered bag, and raced from the house.

She arrived at Wib's place in time to see his mom walking, with a determined stride, east along Churchill Avenue on her way to work.

She found Wib washing the breakfast dishes. Rebecca found a towel and dried, and as she worked she talked, describing what she'd found in the *Gazette* and the little black notebook. She'd laid out these pieces of evidence on the kitchen table.

"So you can see our next step," she said, energetically polishing a plate until Wib took it from her and put it away in a cupboard.

"Which is what?" He drained the sink, sprayed it with tea tree oil cleanser and rinsed it. Rebecca was impressed. He was pickier about cleanliness than she was, by a long shot. Almost as picky as Flora. But he wasn't perking up the way she'd expected, after she'd brought all this exciting news. He plodded around as if he was still groggy from sleep. Not a morning person, maybe.

"Which is, we go talk to this Brendan Ryder and find out what he knows about Henry. He must know everything about what happened back in 1970. He may even have that letter from Henry and that may explain everything!"

Wib looked grim. He got two bottles of orange juice out of the fridge, handed one to Rebecca, and walked out to the front porch, where he sat on the steps in the sun. It was going to be another hot day, they could tell that from the soft air that would be muggy later on, but right now it was still fresh and fine. Rebecca sat down, opened her juice and gulped some down. She bopped on the spot a little to vent some of her overflowing gladness. It seemed to her that the Henry mystery was as good as solved.

"You've changed," Wib said. He'd been looking at her sideways.

"What? How? Since when?"

"Since that time I met you, Tuesday. Up in that tree sulking, mad as a wet hen because you had to join this stupid club. And for a while you stayed like that, moping around. Not happy with anything or anybody. And now look at you."

"What about me?"

"Bobbing around, cheer-up cheer-up. Isn't there an old song about that? The red, red robin." He bent up one side of his mouth, not quite smiling. "I guess you're not a sparrow after all."

"Sparrow? Robin? Hen? It's like you're talking in code, some-times." She laughed. "Life has got interesting since you came to town, Wib. Scary sometimes, but not boring." She elbowed him on the arm. "Oh! Remember that thing Aster said to us yesterday? The game's afoot? I found out what it means."

She told him what Flora and her father had said last night at din-ner. "I think Aster was trying to encourage us," she finished.

"Yeah, like how?"

"Like, King Henry in the play won that battle, right?"

"Or it could mean nothing at all and Aster was just being a jerk as usual."

Rebecca made an exasperated noise. "What is your problem?"

He rolled the juice bottle between his palms and gloomed at the bright eastern sky. Finally he said: "I didn't sleep much last night. I was trying to figure out ways to help Henry get free of whatever has him trapped. But I couldn't think of a darn thing."

"But Brendan Ryder—"

"Wait. See, there's a problem here. I'm pretty sure we have to talk with Henry if we want to help him get out of wherever he is. But so long as he's in there, wherever, I'm guessing he's not going to be able to think very straight. So talking won't get us very far."

"That's where Mr. Ryder could help."

"I dunno. It was what, 44, 45 years ago? Not likely he'll remember much, or care what happened back then. And even if he does, he can't help me find the medal, can he? That had nothing to do with 1970."

"Lordy!" Rebecca banged her juice bottle down on the wooden step. "You're such a wet blanket sometimes!"

"Take it or leave it." He went on glooming at the sky.

"O—kay." *Never be a quitter.* She took another gulp of juice. "Okay, think of it like this. Henry suspects the black dog took the medal and he has some idea about why and what for. He seems to know what kind of thing this black dog is. Okay?" She held up one finger.

"Mm."

"Next. Henry said he remembers when he got stuck in the house and why, but not how. Now, the last real fact we know about Henry is he was around in 1970, and not stuck in the house, because he saved that newspaper. So whatever it was that got him stuck in the house, the how, that probably happened then. Maybe after he wrote his letter." She held up a second finger. "Okay?"

"Maybe." Wib drained his juice. "So..."

"So if we can find out what happened then, if we can nail the how, we could tell Henry and maybe he could undo it. And get out!" She spread her hands triumphantly wide. "And then he can help you get that medal back, because he knows about the black dog."

Wib rubbed his eyes, growled under his breath, then gave himself a shake. "I've been a pain in the butt."

"You sure have!" She laughed and elbowed him gently.

"And you've been better at this stuff, working out the way we should go. Even though there's nothing at stake for you."

"Nothing at stake?"

"Right. Why are you so go-go about this? It's not like the medal means anything to you."

That thought had never crossed her mind. When she caught it in passing now and looked hard at it, she saw it wasn't true. *Because you mean something to me and so does Henry.* Now she set it aside, sensing that Wib was finally ready to really open up and she wasn't going to miss this chance. "And what's it mean to you? Are you ever going to tell me that?"

He made a grim mouth, then dipped his head. "Right. I owe you that." He stood up. "Let's walk."

Rebecca ran back into the house to get her bag and the notebook and papers, and Wib dropped the bottles in the recycling bin. He locked the front and side doors. Then they headed west to the board-walk, and walked north with Lake Huron's incoming waves swelling and gently breaking on their left and the gulls swooping and crying.

Then softly, so that at times she had to lean close to hear, he told her about the really, really bad thing he'd done.

"MY FATHER," Wib said, "was a newspaper reporter, a good one, and everybody knew him. Griffin Willett. My mother was very proud of him. I think she must have been afraid for him, too, because he made a lot of bad people hate him.

136

"But mostly she was proud. She collected all his articles and printed them out and kept them in a binder. I wanted her to read them to me but she never would, because they were about awful things. Murder, gangs, drugs, people-smuggling. I found that out when I was old enough to read them for myself.

"The year I turned six, he won a National Newspaper Award for a series of articles on gangs in Toronto. He won $1,000 for it, and a certificate. My mom thought he should have a medal too, not just a piece of paper. So, I think half for a joke, half serious, she had a medal made for him. It was a silver disk about so big," (he shaped a two-inch circle with his fingers) "with silver rays sticking out from it all around, and it hung from a bright red satin ribbon attached to a pin, so he could wear it pinned to his shirt. And the disk had a crown on it, and the words DAUNTLESS - BRILLIANT - UNSTOPPABLE in a circle around the crown.

"I thought it was absolutely beautiful. Remember, I was only about five. Maybe if I saw it today I'd think it was sort of cheesy. And maybe that's what my dad thought, because he took one look and he just laughed and laughed. And my mom laughed and laughed. Then he got her to pin it on, and then they laughed some more and hugged each other, and they hugged me.

"A while after that, he went away for the last time. He went to Asia and didn't come back. I remember the funeral, but that wasn't the same as him coming back."

Rebecca muttered something and lifted her hand. He talked on, fast, and walked faster, so she wouldn't have a chance to hug him.

"So we didn't have my dad, but we still had the medal. Mom kept it pinned to a velvet-covered card beside his photo on the mantelpiece in the living room. Right, that room in the Morphy house with the fireplace and the flowered furniture. Every time I saw that medal, it made me think of the moment when my dad first saw it. I wanted to go back in time and find that moment and stay there, my dad home with us, my mom happy, all of us laughing and hugging.

"Every time I saw the medal I reached up and touched it. Sometimes I took the card down and held it. It was like if I kept hold of the medal, that could keep my dad with us. I missed him and I wanted the medal more and more. And finally....

"Well, it was during the move. Mom got a job out west. So everything got packed up. Mom put the medal in a little blue velvet bag with a gold drawstring and put it in a box, and put that into one of the big cartons. I was there and I saw.

"And when she wasn't there I..."

He clamped his mouth shut and walked on, watching the gulls and the lake and the slope of Sentinel Hill coming nearer, and carefully not looking at Rebecca's face. After a while he picked up the pathetic little story.

"I took it out of the carton. I hid it in my treasure box in my secret space. I meant to pack it in my suitcase just before we moved. I never meant to leave it behind.

"What happened was, I got sick. A couple of weeks before the move. Appendicitis. I had to go to hospital. There was never a chance for me to get to my secret space. When I got out of hospital somebody else was moving into our house.

"Mom only found out the medal was gone when we got to our new house out west and unpacked. She thought the movers took it, or they were careless and let it get lost. She phoned the moving company and shouted at somebody. But of course she never got it back.

"And of course, after I saw how angry and upset she was, I couldn't tell her. I'd never heard my mom shout before. I kept it secret. I felt sick to my stomach with guilt, but I still couldn't tell her. I couldn't let her know what a bad thing I'd done. What a bad person I was.

"My mother never mentioned the medal again, not once. But she was often sad, and I worried that it was my fault. I had made her sad.

"Over the years I tried to shove the whole mess to the back of my mind and bury it. But I never really forgot it. As soon as I learned we were going to move back to Amstey, it was like the sun came up. I started thinking of how I could get into the house and find my way to the secret space and get the medal back.

"I pictured it: me putting the medal into her hand, and the amazed look on her face. And she would ask where I'd found it. And then I would tell her the truth, all of it. I would tell her what I'd done. And because I'd got the medal back for her, she would be happy and forgive me and everything would be fine.

"So you see, this chance to get into the Morphy house was a gift. It was going to make everything all right for my mom and me. And now I've lost the medal again. The End."

Chapter 26

THE OFFICES of the *Amstey Gazette* occupied a beaten-up-looking two-storey building on Albert Circle, a couple of streets away from the Town Hall. "I'm sorry, kids," said the harried-looking woman behind the reception desk. "This is a busy morning — the issue comes from the printer and we have to get on with distribution. But I'll ask." She turned and yelled "Bren!" into the interior. "Got a moment?"

"Not even half of one," somebody yelled back. Rebecca and Wib exchanged disappointed looks. Then a little old man trotted up behind the desk. He was talking into a cell phone. "Gotcha," he said to the phone, then peered over the desk at Wib and Rebecca. "What's this?"

They gave their names but Rebecca could tell he was only half listening: he kept muttering into the phone.

"We're in the kids' club at the Morphy house," Wib said loudly. "We're interested in the history of the house."

That caught his attention. He thumbed off the phone and pocketed it. "Aha! So you've met the Three Sisters?"

"Yes," Rebecca said, "but what we want to know—"

"You can tell me all about them." He darted out from behind the desk and held out a hand to shake. "Brendan Ryder, editor-in-chief." He grinned a wide, bright grin. His eyes gleamed through heavy black-framed glasses. He wasn't much taller than Rebecca and looked about a hundred years old, she thought, with that crow's nest of grey hair, and those old-man clothes: checked shirt tucked into belted pants — but he moved like an over-excited teenager. "And you are?"

"I'm Rebecca and this is Wib." She tapped Wib's shoulder. "He actually lived in the Morphy house when he was little. So of course he's interested."

"He... Wait." Ryder's eyes narrowed. He stuck a knobby finger at Wib. "What's your last name?"

Wib looked for a moment as if he was going to turn and walk away. Then he squared his shoulders. "Willett."

Ryder reared back. "Don't tell me you're Griff Willett's son!"

"Yes, I am," Wib said defiantly.

"But this is wonderful! Everybody!" He turned and waved an arm at the unseen rest of the building. "Guess who's here? Griff Willett's boy!"

There was a small uproar as people jumped up from desks and poked their heads around doorframes and called down from the stairs above. It settled down within minutes, through. A good thing this was their busy morning, Rebecca thought, watching Wib's tight face slowly relax. He still wore a guarded look, though, as Ryder, who seemed to have forgotten he had no time, went on and on about Griffin — "Superlative newspaperman, dedicated, absolutely fearless — yet not too big to do a little work for the hometown paper when he was in Amstey." He beamed at Wib. "You have the look of him, anyone tell you that? So, you're following in your dad's footsteps, eh? Doing some investigative reporting?"

"No, we—"

"Actually, yes, we are," Rebecca put in quickly. "We're writing a report about the old Morphy house, including who the Sisters are and where they come from. Interested?" She tilted her head and looked as cute and endearing as she knew how.

"Now, look," Wib said, and she could tell he was going to blow it. She elbowed him. He elbowed her back. "That's not true," he said. "We just want to know what happened in 1970. Did you ever hear

141

about a boy named Henry who lived in the Morphy house about that time?"

Ryder stared. "Henry? 1970?" A flicker in his eyes told Rebecca he was what Flora would call *dumfoond*. "You mean the time of the Circle Road commune. No, there was no boy there." He stepped back, holding up his hands, smiling. "Sorry, kids. I've got a gazillion things to do. Maybe another time."

"There was a boy," Wib said doggedly, "named Henry."

Ryder backed up some more. "No, if you read the police reports or my own articles — I wrote a series of four, be happy to get you copies when I've a moment — you'll find no boy was ever mentioned."

"But he wrote you a letter," Rebecca said. She took a step after him.

"Letter? No! Sorry." He took another step back. In half a second he'd be off.

"Look." She'd been holding Henry's black-bound notebook in one hand and now held it out to him, open. "See that? And check the inside of the back cover."

He took the notebook and stared at the first page, where Henry had written his name. Then flipped to the back, squinted, and held it up to catch the light. He whistled softly. Flipped back to the front again and gazed at the name. He murmured something that sounded like "Son-of-a-gun." Then closed the notebook and pressed it between his palms and looked at Rebecca. He'd gone strangely quiet. "Where did you find this?"

"In the house, hidden," Rebecca said. "Along with this." She showed him the front-page article from the old issue of the *Gazette*. "Well?"

Ryder gave Rebecca a long, considering look that moved to Wib, then back again. "Wait a minute, haven't I seen you someplace before? What's your name again?"

"Rebecca. MacBeth."

"Uh-oh." His eyes widened behind the thick lenses. "Flora's granddaughter? The tomato-thrower?"

"That's me." Rebecca giggled.

Ryder grinned. "Well, you got me, the pair of you. I'll talk." He handed back the notebook. "On one condition."

Wib looked wary. "What's that?"

"You get me into the Morphy house and introduce me to the Sisters."

"Why them?"

Ryder laughed. "Are you kidding? They are *the* story. In my entire career they are my only failure. Just can't get at them. Who and what are they? What's their background? Where do they come from? And how did they convince the Building and Properties Committee, which is run by that pitbull Flora MacBeth, to let them ignore two, maybe three bylaws? And why did everybody come out of that meeting smiling? Don't tell me there's not a story there." He switched his bright grin from face to face. "So, will you do it?"

"Don't know if we can," Wib said.

"Sure we can!" Rebecca said.

"I'll hold you to that." He wagged a finger at her. "Okay, give me an hour. After that I'll have all the time in the world."

Chapter 27

AN HOUR WAS more than enough time for them to walk to Padgetts' Coffee Shop, buy cinnamon buns, and walk slowly back, munching.

"You didn't like that one bit, did you?" Rebecca said, between bites. "All that fuss over you. Me, I wouldn't mind a little fuss."

"It isn't just the fuss. It's the way they talk about my dad, and compare me to him. They say I look like him, but I don't think I do, so much. They talk about how wonderful and brave he was, and how I must want to be exactly like him and follow in his footsteps."

"Hm." Rebecca eyed him sideways. Wib's voice and eyes were dead flat, like lids clamped down. "I can see how that could be tough."

"Tough!" A lid flew up, something flared. "I'm not wonderful! I'm nothing like him. I'm afraid of all kinds of things! I lie awake worrying about my mom and, and everything. And I don't know what I want to be, but probably not a journalist — I'm not very good at writing stuff. I wish people would stop saying I must want to be just like my dad. Because I don't want to be. Even though I'm proud of him and I miss him. I don't want to be a copy of him."

Coming from Wib, that was an hurricane of words. "I know exactly how you feel!" Rebecca stopped him with a sticky hand on the wrist so they could talk face to face. "My dad wants me to be something I'm not. Something I'll never be."

"And what's that, Rowena?" He was still fierce.

"Exactly."

Wib blinked and then bit back a smile, which was okay. She'd been aiming for a smile. From Wib, even a squashed one was good news.

THEY STOOD on the street outside the *Gazette* office, finished their cinnamon buns and watched people come and take away bundles of newspapers. Brendan Ryder came out to meet them fifteen minutes late. He waved them over to a scraped and dented white Mercury Cougar at least ten years old that was parked by the curb. "We'll ride," he said. "It's uphill, where we're going. I can talk and I can climb, but I can't do both at the same time."

Wib was going to ask if he had any wet wipes for their hands, so they wouldn't get the upholstery sticky, but after a look inside the car he shrugged and slid into the back seat, pushing aside an old pizza carton, still with bits of dried-up pizza sliding around inside. Rebecca picked a stack of newspapers and magazines off the seat and put them on the floor under her feet.

"Guess you're not married, Mr. Ryder?" Wib couldn't see his mom tolerating this mess for a minute. The floor mats weren't even visible.

"Was," Ryder said cheerfully, pulling away from the curb with a screech. "Three times! Never lasted. I was already married to my work. And please, call me Brendan. Or Bren. If we're to be associates we should be on a first-name basis."

He talked as he drove, often turning halfway around to look at their faces or make a point. He hardly ever had two hands on the wheel: one was always waving or drawing shapes. Sometimes both were in the air.

"So, this story that I'm telling you comes from several sources," he said. "Something to remember, Wib: the more sources the better. Some of it came from my interviews with Taylor Morphy and other commune members after the event—"

145

"What event?" Rebecca asked.

"Wait for it! Some came from what the police dug up. And some came from an anonymous letter."

"Henry's—" Wib began, then shut up and concentrated on holding tight to the back of the front seat as the Cougar swirled clockwise around Albert Circle and took the corner onto Ambrose Street on two wheels.

"Yes, it was Henry's letter, though I didn't know about Henry then. Talk about a story! That Jared Skye, now, he was quite the character. Almost certainly a sociopath. But he had genuine charisma. Seems he could make people believe almost anything."

"So he — wasn't a — saint after all?" Rebecca said between gasps.

"Saint!" Brendan laughed aloud. "He was a con man. Wanted by police all over North America. He'd been caught a couple of times and held, though not for long. He'd never faced a judge, never been convicted or served time. Always seemed to find his way out of the system and vanish again before any of that could happen."

The Cougar shot over the Church Street bridge and sailed up the hill to Summit Road, then swooped around onto Park Circle. It squealed to a stop in front of a church with a tall steeple — St. Michael's — two feet out from the curb. Brendan turned off the engine and got out.

"What are we doing here?" Rebecca looked alarmed.

"I often come up here. I like to sit there and enjoy the view." Brendan pointed at the little park that formed the core of Park Circle, crowning the hill. A circle of grass, with a drinking fountain and sandbox and some swings and slides under the trees. A few small children played there, with adults watching from wooden benches. "Here's my seat," Brendan said, settling onto a bench that stood on the southmost edge of the green and faced out over the town.

"Wow, relief!" Rebecca muttered in Wib's ear. "For a minute there I thought he was going to go in and talk to my dad or gran about me. I think they're both out, though." She tipped her head south-west, across the street. "That's my house there, the one like a duck."

Wib looked. It was no mansion, not compared to the Morphy house, but he liked the look of it. A wide, tall house with wooden siding painted yellow, with a deep porch sticking out the front (like a duck's bill) and big old wide-spreading trees all around.

They sat down, Rebecca on Brendan's left, Wib on his right. Brendan pulled a tiny pair of binoculars out of his pants pocket, unfolded and aimed them. "The Morphy house," he said, lowering the glasses and grinning from one face to the other. "I hardly ever see anything, though, with all those trees. Just sometimes, somebody at a window or in the garden. But somebody sure spends a lot of time in that turret. Any idea who?"

"Aster," Wib said. "She likes to look at the stars."

Rebecca poked Brendan's arm. "What were you going to tell us about 1970?"

"Okay, here goes. A capsule history." He raised the binoculars to his eyes again, and went on talking.

Chapter 28

"FOR US," said Brendan Ryder, "the story starts when Jared Skye came to Atmstey in 1969 and met Taylor Morphy in a bar. Taylor was an orphan, but not a poor orphan. He'd been left in charge of a big house and a fortune at the age of twenty and had no idea what to do with either of them. He was exactly the sort of not-very-bright, aimless kid who could be dominated by somebody like Jared. He was an emptiness waiting to be filled. And he had a circle of young friends with too much money and not enough brains.

"It must have been too easy. Jared nudged them into creating a commune dedicated to social justice and spiritual enlightenment, and establishing a foundation to aid African orphans. He made them think it was all their idea and he was just helping out. In fact it was a scheme to suck their wealth into Jared's secret offshore bank account. If he'd made it, he'd have gotten away with more than a million dollars.

"But it wasn't the theft or even the betrayal of trust that left Taylor broken, and haunted most of the others for years afterward. It was what Jared did to them mentally and emotionally. The money was just income. What he really loved was controlling minds. Playing God.

"They held their so-called spiritual exercises in the ballroom, which they called their 'ashram'. Jared pieced together prayers, meditations and mantras from Buddhism, Taoism, and faux-Celtic paganism. When he led the exercises, that charisma of his came into play. None of them could explain it later, but it seems he was able to make himself appear holy, even godlike. They felt the air shiver, they heard faint music, and sometimes, usually at moments of 'enlighten-ment,' they saw a fuzzy gold light around Jared. He seemed to be unaware this was happening, and when his disciples told him about these effects and haloes and whatever, he was awed and humbled. Apparently.

"There was also a room in the cellar, very private and solemn, where Jared led special sessions with so-called advanced souls. Puri-fying their spirits. Testing if they were worthy to go on up that path to enlightenment. I think, personally, he did it for fun. Taylor would never talk much about these sessions. He mentioned monsters coming out of the walls. And yet he couldn't break free, because Jared had made him believe that *he* was at fault, he was a failure, and the mon-sters came from his own heart.

"How Jared did all that we'll never know. The house was later searched from top to bottom, and no hidden wires or electronics were found.

"I was just twenty-two then, fresh out of Ryerson, interning at the *Amstey Gazette*. Never meant to stay: just meant to score a solid in-vestigative piece that would get me a job on a big-city daily. That year, 1970, the Circle Road commune was the big local story waiting to be cracked. There were so many unanswered questions, so much secrecy. I knew there had to be dirt there, only I couldn't get at it. After that first interview with Taylor, they all clammed up. Wouldn't even let me in the gate. I got a lucky zoom photo of Jared, but never got any closer.

"Then in October, the break. Some kid phones the *Gazette* office and asks for me. He says he's calling from the commune at 3 Circle Road. He said, and I think this is accurate, 'There's a big silver maple that reaches over the wall on the west side. There's a crack in the branch that lies on the wall. Go there when it's dark so nobody can see you and get the letter that will be in the crack. It'll be wrapped in black so the people here won't see it.' And No, he says, this is not a joke, and he can't give his name. 'You can't ever know who I am,' he says. 'Someone will die if anyone knows.' *Bang*, he hangs up.

"The call appealed to me. If it was a hoax it was a good one: the voice sounded dead serious. Just a kid, I guessed, young enough that his voice hadn't broken. But it was the first I'd ever heard there were kids in the commune.

"So that night, after dark, I borrowed a stepladder from the office, drove up to the Morphy house, snuck around to the west side, located the overhanging tree and used the stepladder to reach the top of the wall and find the crack in the branch. And there, hard to see in the dark, was a small packet wrapped in black plastic. I took it back to the office."

"And it was Henry's letter?" Rebecca prompted.

"Yes, and it was a bombshell. A detailed account of what the commune was really for and how the members were being rooked. The writer gave Jared Skye's real name and a lot of his history. He described where to find a notebook with bank account information, names and addresses of prospective victims, and a list of Jared's false names, in a camouflaged alcove behind one of the fireplaces. All the evidence needed to make an arrest.

"I still have that letter in a file and I've looked at it since, so I remember it well. It ended much like this: 'I don't know how you can get in. I can't help you in case I get caught. If you go to the police, make sure it is in secret and if they come in it must be a surprise or else he will take his papers and get away. You need to do this soon, because he is getting ready to leave. Better not put any of this in the newspaper until after. He may suspect me so don't tell anyone about this letter. If he suspects me someone could die.'"

"I wonder who he meant," Wib muttered. "Who could die?"

"Never found that out," Brendan said. "The letter wasn't signed and there was no clue to the writer's identity. As a newsman I had a natural suspicion of anonymous messages, but this one hooked me. It was badly misspelled but clearly written and well-organized, and it was convincing. I thought about it overnight, then decided to honour the request for secrecy. I copied out the important details and took them to the police, along with the photo I'd taken of Jared Skye. Within a day or so they confirmed that this fellow Skye was a con man and thief who was wanted across North America. His real name was Owen Vance."

Rebecca let out a squeak. Wib said: "Vance?" But he wasn't really surprised. He'd had a feeling that was coming.

"That's right, Vance. Owen was Henry's father — not that I made that connection until later. Anyway, a few days after I got the letter, the police moved in and Jared a.k.a. Owen was arrested. His followers protested, but when they found out the facts, they all turned against him.

"Now, here's where things get really weird. That night Owen was held in the county jail, which was then in the basement of the Town Hall. Somewhere around midnight, he got out. Nobody knows how, least of all the officers who had, for some reason they couldn't explain, unlocked his cell and then forgotten all about him. Bribery? Hypnosis? Who knows?

"And then, instead of skipping town as you'd expect, he walked back to 3 Circle Road. Why? My guess: to look for the whistle-blower. Taylor and some of his friends were there but something about the look of their former holy man scared them so badly that they scrammed. They called the police after they got their wits back, about an hour later.

"When the police arrived they found Owen's body—"

"Body!" Rebecca said. "He was dead?"

"As a doornail. He was flat out on the driveway near the front

151

steps, his head bashed in. Beside him was a brick that they later found had fallen from a chimney. They also found a gas can and matches on the ground nearby. They concluded he had meant to burn the place down.

"Of course I looked for the person who had sent the letter. Taylor and some of the others vaguely recalled some kid hanging around but they were never clear who he was. He seemed to fade into the woodwork, Taylor said.

"But then, when the police looked deeper into Owen's background, they traced him back to the little town in Alberta where he was born, raised and married. His wife divorced him soon after their son, Henry, was born. Owen came back when the boy was eight and kidnapped him, I'm not sure why. Maybe to get even.

"So when the police found out about the kidnapping, they got in touch with Henry's mother, who came here looking for him. But he'd disappeared. Not a trace of him in or around Amstey. It was assumed he ran away. He was never seen or heard of again."

Chapter 29

"THAT IS SO horribly sad," Rebecca said. "His poor mom!" She jumped up from the bench and stretched her arms out sideways, airplane style, as if the only way to vent her feelings was out through her fingertips.

Brendan leaned over to pull a well-stuffed wallet out of his back pocket. He fingered through its contents and brought out a small black-and-white photo. It showed a boy with a thatch of dark hair, big dark eyes and a gap-toothed grin, leaning over a cake with candles and a big icing "8" on it. On the back was written "Henry 1966 / 8 years old."

Wib took the photo and was glad his fingers didn't quiver the way his insides were doing. The face in the picture looked younger than the one he'd seen looking at him out of mirrors, but they belonged to the same person.

Rebecca veered in to grab the photo from Wib. She stared at it for a long moment, front and back, with a look of horror. Then handed it back and turned away, counting on her fingers.

Brendan carefully eased the photo back into his wallet. "Henry's mother gave me that. I used it with an article in the *Gazette*. Ever since then, I've kept it to remind me that the story isn't finished. It won't be finished until we know what happened to Henry."

"We should tell his mom," Wib said huskily.

Brendan looked surprised. "About what, that notebook? It's a nice thought, but too late. I kept in touch with Mrs. Vance in case she ever got news about Henry. She never stopped searching. But there was never any real news, just a few false leads. She died three years ago. She was in her seventies."

Wib couldn't speak. His chest hurt. He was thinking of a mother who had spent more than half a lifetime searching for her son. And all that time he'd been trapped in a place that kept him forever twelve years old.

"Can you see why I was so gobsmacked when I saw that notebook?" Brendan twiddled the binoculars between his fingers, but he'd stopped trying to spy on the Sisters a long while back. "I always wondered if the whistleblower might be Henry. I was never certain. But that notebook, with his name and the bits from the letter in it, and his handwriting — yes, I recognized his writing. All that proves it. Henry turned his father in to the police. I can't blame him, can you?" Brendan gazed out at the lake, not seeing it. "But you can see how Owen would look at it. To him it would be the worst kind of disloyalty. His own son ratting him out! That's why he went back to the Morphy house, I'm sure of it. He went back to punish Henry."

Rebecca thumped down on the bench. "You think he murdered Henry? But... um." She looked as startled and puzzled as Wib felt. If Henry had been murdered, then he was a ghost after all.

"No. In fact, he couldn't have. Between escaping from jail and getting mashed by that brick, there might have been time to murder somebody, but not enough time to hide the body. And no body was ever found. My guess is, Henry made himself scarce before the police came in. I think it was because he feared, or knew, exactly what did happen: that his father would slip free the way he'd so often done before, and then he'd come looking for him."

Brendan got up stiffly from the bench, pressed his hands to the small of his back and stretched. He folded the binoculars and stuck them back in a pocket. "Well, my friends, there you have it. The sum and total of what I know about Henry Vance and the events of 1970. And what do you plan to do with all that?"

154

"We'll think about it," Wib said.

"And not tell me what this is really all about, right?" Brendan flashed his bright grin. "Okay, now it's your turn. Hop in the car, we're off to pay a visit to the mysterious ladies of the aptly named Number 3 Circle Road."

He circled the car to the driver's side and jackknifed himself in. As they walked to the passengers' side, Rebecca hissed in Wib's ear: "I realized something when I was looking at that photo. Henry's really fifty-five years old!"

"Yes, and?"

"If we help him get free, will he suddenly turn old? Like him?" She tilted her head at the car, where Brendan was keying the ignition.

"I don't know. But if I was Henry, I'd rather be old and free than young and trapped."

Chapter 30

THE DISTANCE from Park Circle, where Brendan Ryder had parked, in a direct line to the curb outside the old Morphy house was barely two flaps of a crow's wings. In Brendan's Mercury Cougar it involved a right turn onto Summit Road, a nearly full circle around the hilltop, then a left onto Circle Road.

All the same, Rebecca didn't think a crow would have gotten there much sooner than Brendan did. The car screamed to a juddering stop at the curb at Rebecca's request, so she could see if the A-frame sign was out.

It was there. Brendan got out with her and watched, eyebrows up, as Rebecca pulled out her black marker and altered THE FRIDAY CLUB to read THE FRIGHTDAY CLUB.

"Why?"

She explained about being forced, and joining under protest, and that this was her daily statement of opposition.

"But you're not opposed any more," Wib said impatiently.

"No, but it's about pride now. I can't back down."

Brendan grinned. "That's exactly what I'd do, in your shoes. But if they charge you with vandalism, I don't know you!"

They got back in the car and Brendan swung it around slowly and sailed up the driveway to a quiet stop in front of the house. "Best behaviour," he explained, seeing Wib and Rebecca's looks of surprise.

They found Dulcey in the garden, as always. She was standing with her back to them, picking big clusters of glossy purplish-black berries from a bush by the rear stone wall. "Elderberries!" she called out over her shoulder, as they came within earshot. "Lovely and ripe!"

"Making elderberry jam?" Brendan called back cheerfully. "My mother used to do that."

"Jam, and wine, and syrup for colds, and of course the berries make a nice blue dye for our yarn." She set a double handful in an already heaped basket at her feet, and held out a slightly purple-stained hand. "Dulcey Blythe," she said warmly.

"Brendan Ryder." He flashed his brashest, brightest grin. "Heard about this club you're running for young people. Wonderful idea! My two friends here are enthusiastic members and I thought, 'Hey, I wonder if Ms Blythe and Ms Morgenstern would like more kids to know about this great venture. I bet they would!'"

Piling it on with a shovel, Rebecca thought. But Dulcey took it in stride. "How nice of you to visit! Why haven't we seen you here before?"

"Ah. I've tried, but..."

"Well, better late than never. You must let me show you around the grounds and the house, and meet my sisters. But first, why not come to the kitchen for a nice cup of tea and fresh-baked cookies? Let me guess, you're a molasses cookie man. Am I right?" She was moving toward the kitchen door as she spoke, the basket over her arm.

"Fresh-baked molasses cookies?" Brendan's voice softened, but his eyes still gleamed sceptically. "Sounds wonderful! Tell me, are you really sisters by blood?"

"In a sense, yes. Not the genetic sense."

"Mm. So: Aster Morgenstern, Dulcey Blythe and Mrs. Doun: are those your real names?"

She laughed. "Ah, there's a story behind that."

"I'm sure there is. What's Mrs. Doun's first name?"

"You'll have to ask her." Dulcey twinkled at him, then paused at

157

the kitchen door. "Wib and Rebecca, do you still want to make yourselves useful?"

"Sure," Wib said.

"You betcha," said Rebecca.

"Good. Then would you go up to the crafts room and look in on Maura, please?"

"Maura?" Rebecca felt a qualm. "She's here?"

"Yes, she came early to work on her knitting project, even though I think she's still not quite herself. I think she'd be the better for your company." She sent them a grave smile and a nod, and then waved Brendan into the kitchen.

Rebecca giggled as they tramped around the house to the front door. "Any bets he won't get a thing out of her that she doesn't want him to know?"

"No kidding! About Maura, though: I'm pretty sure Dulcey's worried about her."

"You think? If she's hard at work knitting, she's probably back to normal." She pushed open the front door and they stepped into the cool dimness of the hall. "I think we should get to the secret space and find Henry. Ask him about that stuff we learned from Mr. Ryder."

Wib shrugged. "I do too, but I still don't see how all that history will help. It told us a lot about Henry, but didn't explain how he got trapped in the house."

"But if we remind him of what happened, about his father, and how he blew the whistle, and how the police raided the place, maybe that would jog his memory!"

Wib looked doubtful. "Maybe. But we should check on Maura first."

They headed up the front stairs, Wib first. Rebecca glanced up at the stained glass picture with the mirror in the old man's robe that was set into the back wall of the landing. She stopped to take a better look. "Hey! Wib?" But he'd gone on up. She shook her head at where he'd disappeared, then studied the picture.

It had changed, and not in a small way. The old man's face had become a young boy's face. The white hair had darkened, the beard warped into a white collar. The robe made of pieces of mirror was the same. The figure still held up a lantern, but he no longer gazed into the darkness as if searching. Instead he was looking outward and down. Looking right at Rebecca.

"Henry?" she whispered. Nothing happened. She leaned in and breathed on the mirror. It fogged a little, a patch the size of her hand, then cleared. She knocked on the glass with a knuckle. Still nothing. "Anybody home?"

A wave of cold air washed over her. She took a step back and stared. The mirror, all of it, was fogging over.

"Um. Henry?"

yes me the invisible fingertip wrote. *Im starting to remmber*

"Great! Like, how you got stuck?"

no but I member when owen kidnaped me he did it to hurt my mom but then he fund out I coud help with his work The mirror filled with a neat, swift printing, clearing as fast as it filled.

"His work? His scams, you mean. Brendan Ryder told us all about that."

mr ryder you met him thats grate but he dint know all owen coud do — he had talnts I had talnts too and he traned me

"Henry! You sound as if you admired him!"

no I did some bad stuff like my gif for not been notised I used it to help owen steal stuff — my mom will be so upset

Rebecca thought: I don't think he realizes it's been forty-five years since he's been out in the world. He talks as if he's only been away a few weeks or months, and all the people he knew are still

159

there.

wait the thing I need to tell wib — I have a idea why the dog

The writing stopped. Rebecca thought the stained glass face looked alarmed, although the features hadn't changed.

"Henry?"

o no wibs in danger go hury

"Danger? What—"

HURY!

Rebecca sprinted up the stairs.

Chapter 31

WIB FOUND MAURA all by herself in the middle of the ballroom. She was sitting on one of the insect-thin gilt chairs on the central piece of the inlaid star, under the chandelier. It struck Wib as a dangerous place to park yourself. Like sitting at the centre of a giant target.

She was knitting, her needles flying. Every minute or so she pulled more yarn from the quilted bag beside her chair.

"Oh, hi, Maura." He looked around, hands in pockets, as if he'd just happened to wander in and wondered who else was here.

She released a small, cold smile without looking up.

"Are you, uh, okay now? I mean, um, your cat allergy worn off?"

"Oh, Mom thinks I have all kinds of allergies. She likes to fuss." This sounded like a different Maura, cool and older and amused: not the soft, nervous mommy's girl he met on Tuesday. In theory the new Maura should be better company, but she made him uncomfortable.

As he strolled across the floor, he noticed she'd made progress on her project. The beautifully smooth and perfect blue-violet piece was now twice as long and wide as it had been the last time he'd seen it, and she'd done something to shape it into a tube. It looked almost big enough to climb into. He pointed his chin at it. "What're you making, anyway?"

She darted a grin up at him. Her mouth was small and childlike, but he hadn't noticed before how pointy some of her teeth looked. "It was going to be a shawl for my mom, but I've changed my mind. I'm making something for you, Wib!"

"For me?" He felt alarmed. "You shouldn't do that."

"Oh, why not?"

"Your mom will be disappointed."

"Uh-uhn. She only cares if I make my quota. Discipline, Wib!"

He tried to find another argument that would head her off from making anything for him that he might have to wear in public, but she gave him no time. "Why don't you go get your project and we'll work together? I could help you with it."

He hesitated, thinking of Henry, then thought: *There's definitely something not right about Maura. And Dulcey did say she'd be better off with company. Where's Rebecca got to?*

He went and got his ugly pink bundle and a sturdy wooden chair and carried them over to sit beside Maura. When he unrolled his work, the holes in the knitting looked as if they were mouthing words.

"Here, let me." Maura took the piece, pulled out the needle and unravelled it to below where the holes started, then slid the inch of knitting that remained back on the needle. "You don't want your knitting making faces at you!" She showed him again how to hold both needles and place the tips and move the yarn around so as to avoid making holes. "There, you're doing better. That's great!"

She kept on talking softly as she worked, he was no longer sure about what. Listening to the purr of her voice, Wib relaxed. This knitting wasn't so bad after all. And maybe she'd relaxed too, maybe she'd only been acting strange because her mother was always on her back, poor kid.

Cloud-soft wool stroked his arms. He hadn't thought his yarn was that soft. This was so soothing, you could almost fall asleep. You could knit yourself to sleep, what an idea! He smiled. Warm, lulled, he sank into a soft blue-violet cloud... so tired... no wonder, didn't sleep well last night...

A blast of cool air hit him in the face. He stirred and opened an eye. Then he opened the other, but that didn't help. He peered out past a web of something that caught on his lashes and cut his view into tiny bars and dots of dark and light.

He caught a glimpse of Maura's face turned away. Beyond her across the ballroom floor he saw the white cat primly walking toward him, waving its plumy tail. The black dog paced behind. A speck of red and a glint of silver showed in the dark fur of its chest.

The medal. It's wearing Dad's medal!

Outrage blazed through his mind. He tried to get up from the chair and found he couldn't move his arms and legs. He rocked the chair back and forth. The cat miauled. The dog growled. It expanded as it came, legs growing longer and more muscular, head growing heavy, teeth showing yellow and strong and sharp.

REBECCA LEAPED and scrambled up the stairs and halted in the ballroom doorway. Maura was there in the middle of the floor, kneeling up on a gold chair. Something weird swayed in the wooden chair beside her. A long, fuzzy blue-purple shape that looked like a giant cocoon. Or a mummy. Maura was busily knitting at the top of it with four long double-pointed steel needles that could have been used to roast corn with. The cocoon rocked back and forth, struggling and bending, and making muffled noises. Maura swayed with it, her needles flashing, yarn whipping up out of her quilted bag.

Rebecca at first could make no sense of what she saw. She stood there goggling. Then saw a torn sneaker poking out at the bottom of the cocoon. "Wib!" She leaped forward, then again skidded to a halt. Pacing across the floor from the west came the black dog. Taking its time, comfortably sure that its victim, if that's what Wib was meant to be, would still be waiting when it arrived.

Rebecca dashed across the room, grabbed Maura around the waist, dragged her off the gold chair and dumped her on the floor.

Maura squalled angrily. Rebecca ignored her and tore at the stuff that was wrapped around Wib, pinning his arms and legs, covering his face.

But it wasn't wrapped: it was knitted. It was a huge piece of knitting, a giant whole-body tube sock. So, how... right! Unravel!

She pulled the needles out of the top end, tossed them over her shoulder (Maura squalled again), found the free end of the yarn and pulled it out hand over hand. The dog's hard nails clicked on the polished wood, not far enough away. Wib kept lurching, which didn't help.

A knocking sound made her glance up. Something moved in the nearest of the mirror wall panels. It was a boy. A familiar-looking boy. A boy on the other side of the glass, on the *inside*, looking out. He was rapping his knuckles on the glass and mouthing words at her. *Hurry up!* She didn't need the reminder. A glance over her shoulder: the dog was mastiff size now and no more than two dozen paces away. Slow paces, but steady and relentless.

She ripped and ripped at the knitting around Wib's head, pulling off handfuls of yarn. His eyes blinked free, then his nose showed, then his mouth. He sneezed. Then gasped, "Scissors!"

"Scissors! Yes! Where?"

"Maura's bag!"

She swivelled, teetered and caught her balance, arms whirling. She looked down. Her feet were tied together with layers of soft blue yarn that had snaked out of Maura's bag. Maura, who had settled back onto the gilt chair like a spectator, smiled up at her with a cat's eyes.

Rebecca grabbed another glance at the black dog. It was closer, its jaws starting to grin. The quilted bag stood at Maura's feet. Rebecca threw herself at it. Maura moved it farther away with her foot. Rebecca squirmed like a snake and grabbed the bag. She upended it.

Balls of yarn, spare needles, crochet hooks, little coloured plastic rings, a dozen other bits and pieces clattered and bounced over the floor.

A small pair of scissors with thin sharp blades tried to skitter out of reach, striding on its pointy tips toward the dog. Rebecca rolled, grabbed the scissors, yelled "Ow!" when they nipped her fingers, cut the yarn around her feet, leaped up and ran the blades up the length of Wib's cocoon from bottom to top.

Wib was off the chair as she sliced, lengths of yarn clinging and waving. "Out! Quick! And Maura too!"

"Out, how?" The dog was between them and the arched doorway now. It was the size of a pony.

The mirror behind them banged. Rebecca glanced back. The boy in the mirror scooped his hands, beckoning them toward him. *Here!* he mouthed. They backed up against the glass. "Trapped," Wib said.

Rebecca had no breath to answer. *Now would be the perfect time for a secret panel to open behind us.* Something touched her shoulder. She turned her head and saw the boy's hands flattened on the inside of the glass as if it was a window. Her reflection slid over and through his image in a stomach-churning way. He jerked his head backward. *Come on!*

She gaped, then gasped. "Wib! I think he means—"

"Get ready," Wib muttered through his teeth. "Soon as I move, you run for the door. And keep going no matter what!" He took a step away from the mirror and she knew he meant to tackle the dog.

"No!" She grabbed his arm, pulled his hand back to the glass. The boy's hand darted to cover it. Wib's mouth opened wide and suddenly he was only half there, half in the mirror and half out, sliding into his reflection until just one waving arm still stuck out. Then all of him was gone.

A shadow fell over Rebecca. She turned around and looked up

into the eyes of the black dog. Its massive head dipped toward her, its jaws grinned, scarlet tongue lolling over teeth as long as her hand. But those eyes were all she could see: hard black eyes with a flicker of red light deep inside.

Chapter 32

SHE BARELY FELT the touch of hands on her shoulders, or herself sliding backward through something cold and fragile as a crust of frost.

Then a hard landing on polished wood. She sat up rubbing her bruised elbows and looked fearfully into the mirror an inch from her nose. She was looking at Maura standing bewildered several paces away on the other side of the glass, a tangle of ravelled blue-violet yarn in her hands. Rebecca's embroidered bag, fat with all the folded paper inside it, lay on the floor out there where she'd dropped it, but she couldn't see the black dog, or the white cat. Or her own reflection.

She looked back over her shoulder. This was still the ballroom, or seemed to be. At first glance everything looked the same. Except Maura wasn't here, she was out there. And Wib wasn't out there, he was in here. He was standing elbow to elbow with another boy, a thin boy with dark eyes and a ragged too-long thatch of dark hair.

Wib was white and pinched about the mouth and looked as if he felt like being sick to his stomach. Which was much the way Rebecca felt.

The dark-haired boy was beaming. He stretched his arms wide and laughed. "Hey, Rebecca! Welcome to my world!"

She picked herself up off the floor and rubbed her bruised left hip. Then she walked over to the boy and walked all around him. She took a good close look at him from every angle. Henry the imaginary playmate, Henry the ghost, Henry who lived in glass and stone and wood and took the wind for a voice. And who was this?

167

She stopped in front of him and gazed into his face. He was just her height. "So you're Henry."

"That's right."

"For real?"

"Absolutely." He sounded and looked completely normal. Not ordinary, because with the life he'd led, he couldn't be. But normal.

She understood now why she hadn't instantly known him, even though he'd looked familiar. She'd only seen an old photo of him. It looked like him, but that was very different, she now discovered, from seeing the same face lit by thoughts and feelings, changing, full of life.

"All right!" She threw her arms around him and hugged him. He let out a little gasp, and after a moment hugged her back. He felt as real as Wib. He even had that slightly sweaty forgot-to-shower-this-morning smell that some people had, mostly boys.

His clothes didn't look especially strange either, just sort of dorky. She guessed Wib would never wear pants with flared bottoms like that, or that brown sweater vest over a grey plaid shirt with a collar and buttoned cuffs. Or black leather shoes with laces, except for weddings and funerals.

Wib had been looking at him too. Not face-on: just glancing, as if he was afraid of not seeing what he hoped to see. Suddenly he reached over and grabbed Henry's hand, gripped it a moment, then dropped it. "It's really you," he said wonderingly.

Henry clapped his hands to his face, turned away and burst into tears. "I'm sorry! I'm sorry!" he hiccupped between sobs. "It's just that n-nobody's t-touched me for so long. Or really talked to me. N-nobody's been near enough."

While Henry sniffled himself quiet and wiped his face on his sleeves, Rebecca and Wib looked around. "So here we are inside the mirror," Rebecca said. "Like *Alice in Wonderland*!"

"Wonderland?"Wib's voice was tight. "What's so wonderful? We're *in* the house. Like Henry."

Henry cleared his throat. "That's right. But it's okay, you're safe in here. The black dog can't get at you."

"Hm," Wib said. Rebecca caught his eye and guessed he was wondering what she was wondering. Were they stuck in here, like Henry? Would they ever get out?

"I know what you're thinking," Henry said. "I'd be worried too, if I were in your shoes. But you don't need to be, really." He turned away from the mirror. "Okay, let's get you out." Rebecca thought his mouth looked sad.

"You too!" Wib said. "Have you remembered yet how you got sucked into the house in the first place?"

"If you can remember, maybe we could reverse it," Rebecca put in.

Henry shook his head. "There's a lot that's still hazy. And other things seem more real, and they get in the way. Things like last night's stars and the smell of Dulcey's cooking and the news the winds and the birds bring me, and—"

"News?" And here she'd been worried he'd be way out of date, and confused. "Like, about airplane crashes? And wars? And the Stanley Cup finals? And Chris Hadfield? The birds tell you about all that?"

"No, I mean real news." He waved a hand at the ceiling. "Things like the air getting thin way up there, and the bees getting sick, and the Earth getting angry. Important things."

"Oh, right." But nothing about mothers being alive or dead.

"Hey, shouldn't we be going that way?" Wib pointed back over his shoulder. "Back the way we came?"

"I don't think that way's safe. Anyway, the ballroom's a funny place. Owen used it for chants and stuff, and I think some of that

169

stuck, but it must've been a funny place even before we came here."

"Funny how?" Wib asked.

"Well, I've seen..."

Rebecca was only half listening. She was looking around at the room, with its beautifully patterned inlaid wood floor and gorgeous crystal chandelier, and the satin- and mirror-panelled walls, and wondering why it looked exactly like the one outside the mirror, yet not the same at all. The air felt a degree or two cooler, and the sunshine lighting the trees outside the windows wasn't so bright.

But it wasn't just that. The trouble was... Of course! "The door's in the wrong place! It should be that way!" She pointed south. "It's all backwards!"

"Well, yeah," Wib said, just barely not rolling his eyes.

"Does that mean everything in here is backwards? Am I backwards?" She looked down at her white T-shirt. There was no writing or graphic on it. She looked at Wib. He wore a plain, clean tee over jeans. She looked at Henry. "Henry! What's that on your wrist? A watch?"

A steel band showed under his right sleeve. Or was it his left? He pushed back the cuff. "It's one that Owen stole but it was scratched, so he gave it to me. It works, but not in here." It was one of the old kind with hands and a round dial. The numbers around the edge were backward, sure enough. Printed in the middle was the word XEMIT, with the E wrong way around.

"But that's nothing," Wib said. He had stopped in front of one of the mirror panels and was squinting at his own reflection. "Look at this, if you want a puzzle. See? It's me in a mirror in the mirror. And in that mirror there's me again."

Rebecca leaned in beside him and saw the two of them reflected back and back. She wondered: Would all the backward things turn the right way around again in the next mirror? And would a mirror inside a mirror feel hard and glassy? Or would it be soft, so you could get through?

She reached out, touched, and felt the glass give faintly, like hard rubber. Back and back and back and...

Henry reached across and slapped her hand down. "Never do that!"

"Ow! Why not?"

"Cause it's dangerous. I got into a mirror in here once, and then another by mistake, and it was like those fun houses at the fair, only much worse. And not fun at all! It got colder and colder and darker and darker and I thought I'd never get back to the outer layer."

"But we'd be careful—"

"No! Don't even look in there." He had them each by an arm and was pulling them around as he spoke, away from the glass and toward the door. "You get in there, you could get lost forever."

Chapter 33

HENRY HAD THEM out in the corridor and was herding them toward the main staircase, when Rebecca spotted the archway opposite the ballroom. "Isn't that the library?" She'd looked in there before, in the real world, but never had a chance to explore.

"I don't think we want to go in that room," Henry said.

"Sure we do!" She walked in and spun to see all around. "A library, books, *Through the Looking Glass* — maybe 'Jabberwocky' would make sense here, what d'you think?"

"I doubt it." He followed her into the room. Wib leaned against the doorframe and put a hand on his stomach. He seemed to have lost all spirit of adventure, if he ever had any.

Rebecca wandered around, peering sideways at titles, poking into corners. She wished she'd explored this room before, in the real world outside the mirror. It was more interesting than the ballroom and as nice as the kitchen, in a different way.

There were bookshelves all over, floor to ceiling, and little stepladders with wheels to reach the top shelves. There was a fireplace with a big mirror over top (she didn't look in), a soft dark-green leather sofa facing it, easy chairs here and there under lamps that bent brass necks to light your book, cabinets and desks and cupboards with glass fronts and dozens of little drawers with crystal knobs or gilded rings to pull on, and one tall bureau packed with layers of wide, long, shallow drawers that held — "Hey, look at this!"— big maps laid flat. Maps of weirdly shaped places with alien-looking names, like Ocixem and Lizarb and Natshkazak.

"We should get out." Henry was glancing about nervously. "You can't read the books anyway."

"Yeah, I guess." She couldn't resist taking one down and opening it: a tall, thick book with a picture of flocking gold and red butterflies on the cover, and a title that she could just make out, reading backward. *Winged Insects of the New World.* She flipped through until she found a page showing those lovely blue ones with wings like pieces of sky. She was still puzzling out their name, Mor-something, when one of them stirred, unfolded its wings and lifted off the page.

They all watched it, a miraculously beautiful thing, a floating jewel. "Oh," Rebecca breathed. Wib's eyes were big, and even Henry stared, mouth open. It lilted about the room and finally came to rest on the front of a cabinet with glass doors. Inside was a collection of little boxes, some with figurines on top.

"That was amazing!" Rebecca looked down at the open book in her hands. There was a light, alive, stirring feel to it, as if all the butterflies wanted to get free. And why not? She looked at Henry, smiling, eyebrows up.

"Winged insects," he said. "That includes wasps and hornets, right?"

"Uh." The book wasn't just stirring now; it was buzzing. She slammed it shut, shoved it back on the shelf, and backed away.

"That butterfly will just die in here," Wib said.

"Huh." He was right. "Then we'll have to catch it and put it out a window. Henry, can we get one of those windows open?"

"I don't know. I've never tried. Somehow it never seemed like a safe thing to do." They looked at the nearest window, which was set between two banks of shelves. Nothing to see out there but sunlit leaves. Yet from this side of the house they should be able to see down the hill to the lake.

"Never mind," Wib said. "Look!" He had walked over to the glass-fronted cabinet where the butterfly had landed. It was clinging to the end of a brass key that stuck out of the black wooden door-frame. He touched the butterfly before Rebecca could stop him. It didn't move. He touched it again. "It's turned to metal. It's part of the key."

Rebecca felt like she'd been kicked. It was as if something in this place had killed the beautiful little creature just to be mean, because she'd loved it. She looked at Henry. "You're sure the black dog can't get in through the mirror?"

"Positive. But there are other things in here. And this place has its own rules. Ready to go?"

"I am," Wib said.

"Me too," Rebecca muttered.

She was nearly out the door when a tinkling sound made her stop and look back. It came from the cabinet where the butterfly had turned to brass. One of the boxes inside had started up, its globe revolving, music playing. Strange music, half familiar yet all wrong, because it was backward.

Ice ran up her spine. She backed out of the room. They started down the steps, while the sinister tinkling faded behind them.

Chapter 34

THE STAIRCASE curved like the one outside the mirror, only in the wrong direction. The wrongness made Rebecca feel queasy.

Wib swayed and grabbed the banister and slid down onto a step. "Whoa, dizzy."

"Take a rest," Henry said. "This mirror place affects different people different ways, I guess." He sat down beside Wib.

Rebecca leaned on the banister and wondered if it would make her sick to slide down it. "It doesn't seem to bother you."

"It does. Gives me the willies. You never know what you might come across in here. Like that butterfly. That's why I never stay long."

"So, what makes this house the way it is? I mean, in most houses you can't get into the mirrors, and there isn't a stream in the basement."

"Oh, you found that?" Henry looked up, eyes bright. "It's a spring, not a stream. It comes out of the hill under the house and then it goes underground again. But why the house is like this, I don't know. Maybe the Sisters could tell you."

Rebecca wanted to ask him what he knew or guessed about the Sisters, but then Wib pulled himself up and started on down the stairs. They stopped on the landing to look up at the glass picture. It had changed again. Instead of a man, young or old, in a long mirrored robe holding up a lantern toward the left, it now showed a woman with a flashlight, wearing a long red metallic coat and gold cowboy boots, striding toward the right.

Rebecca pointed at it. "Henry? Did you do that?"

"No way." Henry blinked up at it. "I have a feeling we've stirred something up."

"The black dog?" Wib looked nervously back up the stairs.

"No, I told you, he can't get in here. But wait, that reminds me. I was going to tell you something. An idea I had about the dog. Now that I've had time to think, I'm pretty sure I know why he took the medal. He wants to lure you into danger."

Wib stopped with a foot on the next step down. "Me? Why?"

"Because you're my friend, why else? He can't get at me, so he'll get at you instead. He's mean that way."

"But he's a ghost. Why should I be afraid of him?" Wib went on down the stairs. "I mean, what can he do to me?"

"Look what he did to Maura," Henry said, following behind. "He's in her head. He's got her doing what he wants."

"So that's what's wrong with her? But why would he pick on Maura?"

"Don't know. Maybe to get her away from you. Maybe she's a friend you're going to need."

Rebecca thought about Maura. Quiet, soft, pathetic Maura, scared — when she was in her right mind, anyway — to stick a foot out of line. "What use could she be?"

"Well, maybe he did it just to be mean, then. It's exactly what he used to do to people when he was alive. He liked to control what they saw and did and thought. He liked to hurt them."

"Wait!" Rebecca grabbed Henry's shoulder. "You're talking about Owen, aren't you? Your father. Your father is the black dog?"

He looked back up at her, mouth flattened, eyes dark. "That's not my father, not any more. But yes, he used to be."

Wib stepped off at the bottom of the stairs. "So that's why you wrote that letter to Brendan Ryder? You had to stop all the bad stuff he was doing to people. Right?"

"That too. But especially I had to stop what he was doing to himself."

They stood in a knot in the middle of the front hall, which looked the same as the real one, only dimmer, and backward. The coat stand stood on the right as you faced the door, instead of the left, and the clock's second hand was travelling in the wrong direction.

"I knew he was not a good man, but I never knew he was actually a bad man," Henry said. "Not until we came here, and he had all those people looking up to him, and calling him Father, and telling each other how holy he was. And he pretended to be so humble and like he didn't want all that, but really he loved it. He just drank it up. Only it was poison."

Henry's eyes were black with memory. Pain and dread came off him in waves. "How did you know?" Rebecca asked softly.

"We had the ashram in the ballroom. The ashram, that was what he called the gathering, sort of like church. They made a circle and they chanted and prayed and read things.

"I always stood at one side, against the wall, and I watched. That was my job. Mostly they didn't know I was there. I had this talent, I could fade into the background until I was almost invisible. Owen told me to watch their faces, then later report who really believed and who was faking. They all believed, I could see that.

"But I watched him, too. I saw that glow he made around himself, to make them think he was really close to God. I knew the others saw it and they thought he was really holy then. But they didn't see the other thing, the thing that I saw." Henry closed his eyes and took two deep breaths. He opened his eyes. "When it reversed."

"When what?" Wib asked.

"When that glow went black. When it made a halo of darkness all around him. I knew what it meant. And I knew I had to stop him, to save him. Even if it meant getting him thrown in jail."

He stared at his shoes. Rebecca touched his hand; it was cold and trembling. He looked at Wib. "See, Wib, that shows you what he can do. I know what he did to Taylor Morphy, too. He hurt him real bad, in his mind. You can't let him get anywhere near you." He added, "Best thing would be if you go away and stay away."

"Not a chance," Wib said quietly.

They crossed to the coat stand, with its full-length mirror. It was weird, looking in there and not seeing their reflections. Henry stepped onto the low ledge at the bottom, put his face close to the glass and peered both ways. "Coast is clear. Take my hands. I'll ease you out: Wib first, then you, Rebecca. It shouldn't feel as bad as coming in." They grabbed hands. "Okay, both of you, ready?"

"Ready!" Rebecca said, and gripped tight. Then relaxed her grip. "What do we do now?"

"Don't know. Never did this before. Maybe if you both just push through ahead of me, and then let go when you feel me stick." He stepped back.

Wib, frowning, moved his free hand close to the mirror's surface. Then pulled it back. "Wait! Why can't it work both ways?"

"Um?"

"Yes!" Rebecca whooped. "Wib, you're right! If Henry could pull us in, why can't we pull him out?"

"But...." Henry shrank back. "I've tried. It never worked."

"But you never had us to pull you." She swung his hand. "A human chain with you in the middle. We can do this!"

"The mirror's not wide enough," Wib said. "Not for all three of us to go through at once."

"It will be if we scrunch together. C'mon, everybody up close to the mirror." Rebecca squeezed against Henry. "Wib, scrunch!"

"Oof. Ugh. Okay," Wib growled. "This better work."

"Henry, you ready?"

"I... well..." He looked at her, then at Wib. "W-worth a try."

"And after you're out," Wib said, "we'll get you away from this house. To a place where you'll be safe and the dog can't get at you."

"I..." Henry was shaking. "I don't know if I can..."

"Wib, jump!" Rebecca shouted. "Now!"

She lunged with head ducked, eyes shut, face screwed up, expecting to feel glass shatter on her forehead. Nothing broke, but a veil of cold slid across her body and at the same moment Henry's hand slipped from hers. She grabbed but it was gone.

She landed sprawling. Wib picked himself up and threw himself at the mirror. "Henry!"

Henry was still inside, his hands flattened on the glass. He was shouting, but they couldn't hear him. Their reflections cut through him. Rebecca put a hand on one of his and felt warmth through the glass. She pulled at him, or tried to. Wib had his hands on the glass too. "Come on, Henry!" he yelled. "Come on, push!"

Henry mouthed: *I'm trying — but — I — can't — I can't —*

He clenched his fists and pounded the mirror. It broke in a glittering spray.

"Henry!" Rebecca leaped forward, hands out, ready to catch him. But only the glass burst out. The marble floor glittered with shards and splinters. In all the bigger pieces there were broken bits of him: a clenched hand, an ear, a mouth wide open, silently shouting.

Chapter 35

"WELL! AND WHAT'S all the fuss?"

Rebecca was crouching on her heels, trying to pick up pieces of Henry without kneeling on them or getting cut. She had the notion that if she could piece the mirrored bits of him together they might have the whole of him, and he would be out and free.

She looked up now into Dulcey's smiling face. Wib stood frozen and speechless. Rebecca got to her feet and opened her hands down at the wreckage. "It's Henry. We have to..." But the mirror bits now reflected only the ceiling.

She looked around. Half a dozen girls stood in tiers on the stairs, making "ooh" sounds. Two heads poked in through the partly open doorway: Emily and Cecily. Emily made a mock-shocked "Are you ever in deep doo-doo!" face. Cecily smirked.

"Nothing you can do here!" Dulcey made a shooing motion at the girls on the stairs. "Back to the crafts room, please!" The stairs emptied. She looked at the two in the doorway, who instantly blanked their faces. "Emily and Cecily, will you go around by the back door, please, and up the back stairs?" They vanished. The door closed.

Wib looked around haggardly. "I'm sorry. It was an accident. We — I'll pay for the mirror."

"We both will," Rebecca said. She hoped it wouldn't cost so much that she'd need to ask her dad or gran for the money. She dreaded hearing what Flora would say.

"Never mind that now. Give yourselves a shake."

Wib flicked his head back and forth. Splinters of glass flew. Rebecca stared. "Whoa!" She gave herself a vigorous whole-body

180

shake, and so did Wib, and Dulcey brushed sparkling fragments from their hair. It was astonishing that nobody got so much as a nick, Rebecca thought.

She nudged the glittering debris with the toe of one sandal. "Where's a broom? We'll sweep that up."

"No, dear. Not your job. We'll talk about this later, if it's still an issue. Off you go now!"

"Go?" Wib looked puzzled.

"Club." Dulcey laughed. "Remember? You have fifteen minutes before Maura's party gets under way. Oh, and Wib? Thanks so much for bringing Mr. Ryder for a visit. We had a lovely chat." She sent a smile around and was off back to the kitchen. Savoury odours drifted from that direction, butter and bacon and something mapley.

"What a kick in the butt that was." Rebecca crunched across the littered floor to the stairs. Wib was ahead of her, two steps up. She looked back, stopped, and reached to pull at his T-shirt. "Look!"

The air near the coat stand was twinkling. Tiny bits of glass drifted up into the empty frame. After watching, fascinated, for a couple of minutes, Wib laughed quietly. "He did say he always cleans up his own messes."

"She knew that would happen, didn't she?"

"Well, they live in the house. They must've noticed things."

WIB SHOOK his head at the weirdness of everything, then wished he hadn't. His brain was bumping around like a soccer ball inside his skull. "You okay?" Rebecca put a hand on his shoulder. "You look shaky."

He sat down on the step above the landing and cradled his head in his hands. "Got a headache from that mirror place. Nothing major."

"We really blew that, didn't we?" She dropped onto the step be-

181

side him. "I mean, he saved us. We didn't save him."

"I've thought about that a bit. Maybe it's just as well that Henry is trapped."

"What!" She slapped her knees.

"Yes." He straightened up and winced. "Think. What does the black dog really want? Not to get me, that's second-best. He, Owen, Henry's dad, wants to punish Henry for turning him in. For not being loyal. But so long as Henry stays stuck in the house, he's safe."

"I figured that out by myself," Rebecca said. "The real reason Owen would go after you, and maybe me too, would be to force Henry out where the dog can get him. Because Henry will always try to protect you. And if you're in real bad danger, that might be enough to bust him out."

"And that is why I've got to find the medal by myself and get away from here. And Henry has to stay away from me. You too."

"No way! Are you crazy?"

"Makes sense to me." He pushed himself to his feet, holding tight to the banister. The headache was getting better, but he still felt slightly dizzy, as if the Earth was turning the wrong way.

"No!" Rebecca was up and flaring, ever inch alight. "We're friends! Friends don't dump each other! And what about that black dog?"

"It'll be okay. I'll handle it." He started up the stairs.

"Like you handled it back there in the ballroom?" She darted up in front of him and blocked the staircase. "Like when you got yarn-bombed and I had to cut you out? Like when you were going to tackle the dog on your own? That was brave, by the way, but really, really stupid."

"It was the only thing I could do. C'mon, get out of my way."

She stayed planted on the step above him. "Face it, we need help."

He blinked up at her wearily. "I know who you mean but that's hopeless."

"Never hurts to try. Okay? Me for the kitchen, you for... wherever." She grinned, pranced down the stairs past him, and couldn't resist a poke on the arm in passing. He made up his mind they would need to have a talk about the poking very soon.

Chapter 36

HAND-MADE PIZZA with the works, buttery cheese scones, dollar-sized potato latkes all golden and crunchy, with thick sour cream, sausages wrapped in puff pastry, heaps of fresh fruit and veggies, and a dozen different kinds of cookies. It was all ready to be carried up to the crafts room, which was the party room today. Rebecca could tell by sight and smell, and even sound — the delicate faint crickling of the puff pasty as it came out of one of the Aga's ovens, the sizzling of the pizza as it came out of another — that this would be a feast to remember.

"I don't understand how you can do all this for free," she said, as she piled the scones into a pyramid.

"Oh, it's all paid for in the end." Dulcey carried two jugs of raspberry fizz to the table. "One way or another."

A typically teasing remark, Rebecca thought. She said: "You help people, don't you? The Three Sisters, I mean. That's what you're all about. Am I right?"

"Only in a very limited way."

"But you could help Henry, if you wanted, couldn't you?"

Dulcey stopped stacking glasses and gave her a blank look. "Who's Henry?"

This was what Flora would call stonewalling, Rebecca decided. "At least, you could help me and Wib help Henry. Because we really need help." She leaned on the table and aimed her most beseeching look at Dulcey's face.

Dulcey's eyes sparkled with laughter. Rebecca saw nothing to laugh at. *Try a different angle, shake things up.* "Henry says the water in the cellar is a secret spring that comes from higher up the hill. D'you think maybe that's what makes this house so weird?"

"What an idea!" But Dulcey's hands stilled. She gave Rebecca a long look that might have meant approval or surprise. "It is a natural spring, but it's hardly secret. The first owner of this house even diverted part of it to fill his swimming pool. And you've probably seen where it comes out finally, through a culvert under Circle Road South."

"Oh, yeah." There was a little stream that came out there and flowed into Lake Huron a few yards farther down. "But it goes under this house, right? Maybe it, um, sets up an electric current. Or, um, vibrations." She broke off, because Dulcey was laughing out loud. Rebecca stepped away, cheeks flaring.

"Oh my goodness!" Dulcey wiped her eyes with the hem of her apron and flicked a strand of gold-brown hair off her nose. "Dear girl, I'm not making fun of you. Listen, I'll tell you what I think. I think it was a mistake to build a house over a spring-fed stream, and not for the obvious reasons, wet cellars and mildew and so forth."

"Why, then?"

"Because water is powerful stuff. Pure, flowing water especially. It's the stuff of life, just as much as blood is. And so it, well, it enlivens." She looked serious now, but at the same time she smiled. "Evil things hate it, or so the old stories say. Quite apart from that, it may even, sometimes, have a magical effect. That may in part be why this is such a *lively* house. But only in part. The people who came here brought their histories and their hopes and troubles. And the house remembers."

She picked up the platter of pizza and pointed Rebecca at the sausage rolls and scones. "We'll have to make several trips, so we'd better get on with it. What a wonderful helper you are!"

TEN MINUTES till the club starts, Wib thought. Might be enough. Instead of going on into the crafts room, where there was already a headache-making hubbub, he walked to the back of the house and climbed the narrow stairs all the way to the top.

Aster was there, bare feet firmly planted, arms crossed, gazing out through the opening in the cupola, which was oriented northwest at the moment. That reminded Wib of something that had been knocking at his attention for a couple of days.

"A while back, when you let me look through the telescope, the first time." He tipped his head at the set of nested brass tubes on its curly-legged tripod. "I saw Georgian Bay."

"Congratulations." She didn't look at him.

"Georgian Bay is a hundred miles from here. I shouldn't be able to see it. The horizon isn't that far."

"Well, gosh."

"You made me see that — that impossible thing. You wanted me to know you could."

"Took you long enough to notice," She went on gazing at the sky.

"So, if you can do things like that, you can protect Henry while we search for my dad's medal."

She turned around finally and flared her eyebrows at him. "Who's Henry?"

"You *know*."

She gazed, and he thought maybe she smiled, but it was hard to tell. "It's not our job to interfere with yours," she said in a different, older voice. "Your path is your own to choose. So is Rebecca's. So is Henry's, whoever he is."

"Okay, so if I decide to keep looking for the medal?"

She shrugged minimally. "Then that's your quest."

"Uh, quest?"

186

"Didn't I just say that?"

"Y-yeah." She was making him stammer again. Dulcey never made him stammer. Maybe it was because she was young, and those brilliant, black-fringed eyes...

"Focus!" she snapped. "Will you turn aside from your quest?"

"No way!" He squared his shoulders.

She smiled coldly. "But you realize, if you stay on this path you're going into deadly danger."

"I... I think I knew that."

"Good, because we won't be able to help."

"Okay!" Suddenly he was fed up. "I don't need help! For Henry, yes, but not for me. I never asked for any help."

"You did," Aster said silkily. "You asked Rebecca."

"Well yeah, but only because she..." He caught her eye. It would have flash-frozen a mammoth. "Okay, yeah, I did."

She grinned, which was no more reassuring than her scowl. Maybe less. "Take a look, Magellan." She waved a hand at the telescope.

Gingerly, Wib positioned himself at the small end of the telescope and aimed an eye. At first he couldn't make out what he was looking at. Wherever it was, it was dark, with light from somewhere else stencilled across the darkness in a pattern of diamonds. A curved brown thing might be the toe cap of a leather shoe or boot. Next to it lay a shapeless, soft-looking thing. It took a minute or so for him to puzzle it out. It was a leather glove coloured the yellow-brown of dried mustard, a man's glove with thick fingers and a wide palm.

One of the diamond shapes of light struck a gleam off something metallic that lay across the wrist edge of the glove, half fallen out. It was a brass key with a strangely shaped bow, the part you held while turning. As he watched, the edge of the glove lapped out like a tongue and slid the key back in.

187

I've seen that key before, or something like it.

"Time's up!" Aster said.

He was still thinking about the oddly shaped key as she herded him down to the ballroom, a thin hand hard on his shoulder.

Just short of the ballroom doorway her fingers dug in and she pulled him to a halt. "Hey. Something to remember. Three is a strong number. Three legs to a stool, three leaflets to a shamrock, three heads better than two. Go." She shoved him through the door.

It looked like the birthday party was about to start. Dulcey was arranging platters of food and pitchers of drink on one of the long wooden tables. Rebecca was at her elbow, tidying up a pyramid of scones.

She stepped back, licking crumbs off her fingers and admiring her pyramid. "Well?" Wib muttered in her ear, and she jumped.

"Well, what?"

Wib watched Dulcey move to the other end of the banquet table. "Did she say she'd help?"

"Nope," Rebecca muttered back. "Did Aster?"

"She said no, flat out. She also says I've got a quest, and we all have our own paths to follow. What use are they anyway, except for making creepy remarks?"

"Party time!" Dulcey called out. "Where's the birthday girl? Come over here, Maura, and help me cut the cake."

Chapter 37

DULCEY HAD BAKED a birthday cake. A big chocolate cake, frosted in pink and decorated with real fresh-picked pink and white rosebuds and tiny silver candy balls, which Rebecca whispered was embarrassingly girly, but which Maura should really like.

She didn't like it, though, Wib could see that. The flames of the eleven candles reflected like a bonfire in her eyes. She backed off, her soft hair bristling.

Everybody else liked the cake; even better when they found a tiny paper-wrapped silver charm in each piece. Each charm had a meaning, which you were supposed to guess. Some were obvious. Emily got a miniscule piano, which meant she was good at music. She walked around flaunting it.

Some were not so obvious. Rebecca got a dime, with the schooner *Bluenose* on it. She waggled it in the air ("I'll be rich!") but Dulcey said No, it meant she would make a journey by water.

Wib's charm was shaped like a dog: a mastiff. He buried it in the remains of his piece of cake and looked around. Nobody paid him any attention, except Maura. He got up and walked over to where she sat, at a table by herself near the project storage shelves. She watched him come, her eyes half-lidded. He noticed that his pink monstrosity lay on the shelf, neatly rolled, next to Rebecca's embroidered bag, but Maura's blue-violet knitting with the diamond patterns was missing. He decided not to mention that.

"Nice cake," he said.

She shrugged. The piece lay untouched at her elbow.

"Don't you want to know what surprise you got?"

189

She shrugged again. He wondered if she'd forgotten how to talk, except in cat language.

Rebecca sauntered up, bouncing the shiny dime on her palm. "Come on, Maura, let's see!"

Dainty and deliberate, Maura picked up her fork and dug into the slice of cake. The little paper-wrapped piece popped up and Rebecca grabbed and unwrapped it. "Huh." She looked at Wib and dropped the charm onto the table. It was a tiny silver medal, just like the one Wib had described, silver rays and ribbon and all. Maura stretched and yawned, showing sharp little white teeth, and turned her back on them.

"I got the dog," Wib said quietly. "Somebody's messing with us."

"Scavenger hunt!" Aster snapped. She stood at the centre of the inlaid star under the chandelier and rapped a steel ruler on her clipboard. "Form teams! Three people each. You, you and you. Come on, let's go!" She pointed them into triads and got five teams lined up in seconds flat. "And you and you and you. Yes, you!"

Wib and Rebecca gaped at her, then at each other, then at Maura. "You've got to be kidding!" Rebecca said.

"Here's the first clue." Aster dealt out squares of cardboard all around. "Rule one and only: No sharing or collaborating between teams. Okay go!"

Wib frowned down at the card. Printed on it in black marker was: CHARMS.

"What the heck does that mean?" Wib tossed the card in the air. "This is stupid! Us three a team? I'm fed up and I'm going to tell Aster—" He glared around the room, but Aster wasn't there. The last of the others crowded out the door and then they were alone in the ballroom, the three of them. Wib scanned the mirrors, but there was no sign of Henry, either. He hoped Henry hadn't been hurt when that mirror broke.

Rebecca kicked the card across the floor. "We don't have to do this. Whatever game this is, and whoever set it up, we don't have to play."

"Oh, come on, let's!" Maura had her voice back. They stared at her. She picked up the card as she spoke, and set it on a table. That would be like her, Wib thought. Tidy. Her eyes still looked strange, not quite blue, not quite round, but she sounded more like herself. Maybe she was all right now.

She sent her eyes from Wib to Rebecca. "Oh, come on! I love puzzles, don't you?"

Rebecca looked at Wib. "It may not be a total loss. We just might find out something useful. Better than sitting on our hands doing nothing."

"Maybe," he said grimly. "Okay, charms. Those things from the cake." He went and got the dog figure from his partly demolished slice and set it on the table next to Maura's medal. Rebecca set her dime beside them.

"See what I got?" Maura chirped. "A medal! It means I'll be really good at something. Wait till I show my mom!"

Rebecca said: "Dog, medal, dime. DMD. Doesn't make a word." She moved them around. "No matter how you scramble it."

Wib found he was getting sucked into this game despite the fear and worry and anger that churned inside him. "Try the names. Owen, Bluenose, Griffin."

"OBG," Rebecca said. "GOB. BOG. Bog?" She laughed. "That's what my gran sometimes calls the washroom. The bog."

Wib flipped the dime over. "How about this? Elizabeth Regina. ER. Put it with Griffin and Owen and you get ERGO."

"Omigosh!" Maura bounced. "That's from math. It's Latin for 'therefore.' It must mean something!"

"Can't imagine what," Rebecca said. "What else is there?"

"GERO," Wib said. "ROGE."

"REGO," Rebecca said. "GREO. EGOR."

"OGRE," Maura said. "Ogrrrrr." She put her hands to her mouth, giggling, although Wib saw nothing funny about it.

Ogre sounded less silly than bog, and made a sinister kind of sense. But it wasn't much help. At least bog pointed them in a direction.

"Bring these with us." Rebecca handed Maura the tiny silver medal, pocketed the dime and held out the dog image to Wib. He didn't really want the ugly thing, but took it anyway and stuck it in a back pocket of his jeans.

There were two washrooms on this storey, both at the west end, near the turret stairs. One was dark, and the light didn't work. They closed the door and tried the next. Rebecca walked in, stopped dead and breathed "Whoa!"

"Oh my goodness gracious!" said Maura, and clapped her hands.

It was a big room, about six times the size of the little bathroom in Wib's new home, walled and floored with gleaming ceramic tiles, some with designs of shells and fish and mermaids on them in green, blue and gold.

Along one wall stood a row of four wash basins with brass faucets, and above each hung an oval mirror in a gilded frame. Along the opposite wall was a row of cubicles with polished wooden doors.

Wib stared around. "I remember now. This wasn't the family's washroom. This was for the guests at the ball."

"Then this was for the ladies," Rebecca said. "I bet the men's room isn't half as nice."

"It isn't."

Another mirror, large enough to reflect an entire tall person with billowy skirts, hung in a wooden rack on rods so you could tip it back and forward. Next to it stood a sofa upholstered in pink-and-green satin.

"If this is the right place," Wib said, "there should be some object we need to collect, and another clue."

Maura looked behind the tall mirror. Wib went and looked inside the cubicles. Rebecca got down on hands and knees and peered under the sofa. Up again and turned around, she said: "Where's Maura?"

"We had our backs turned for ten seconds," Wib said.

"So where is she?"

He stepped out the door and called. No answer. No Maura. He stepped back in. "She must've run off scared." He bent and picked something silver off the floor: the charm shaped like a medal. "She dropped this. I guess —"

Rebecca grabbed his arm and pointed. The tall mirror had fogged over. An invisible fingertip was writing in the fog. HANDS AND FEET, it printed.

Wib felt his chest expand as a weight of worry lifted. "Henry?"

NO

They stared at it. "Aster, you think?" Rebecca asked.

"Has to be." But he wasn't even close to sure.

The fog cleared. Rebecca rubbed her goosebumped arms. "Any bets the other kids have way less creepy clues than ours? And easier ones. Hands and feet, huh?"

There was nothing to scavenge here, so far as Wib could see. Unless it was Maura's charm. He slipped it into his jeans pocket with the dog charm. He mulled over the fog message on the way to the ballroom, where they looked in. No Maura there, either.

"Gone to Dulcey, I bet," Wib said.

"Think so?"

"Yeah, she'd feel safe there. So we're not a legal team any more. Fine with me."

"But wait a minute." She caught at his T-shirt sleeve. "What if we're supposed to be? A team, I mean. Remember what Mrs. Doun said about our third? 'Have a care for your third,' she said."

"And three is a strong number, according to Aster." Wib shrugged that away. "Henry's our third, that's obvious. He's the one we need to find, not Maura."

"Okay, only..." Rebecca rocked back and forth on her feet, shuffling her thoughts into order. Then she stopped rocking and looked at Wib. "I'm not so sure Maura's back to normal. I mean, all that chirpy oh-my-goodness stuff, that was just a bit much, don't you think? Like she was acting. Pretending to be herself."

Wib rubbed his forehead, which still ached slightly. He didn't want this Maura problem, on top of everything else. But now that he put his mind to it, Rebecca was right. "So she's in danger."

"Remember what Henry said, when we were in the mirror? He said the black dog's in her head. Wib, we've got to find her!"

Chapter 38

THEY RAN DOWNSTAIRS and burst into the kitchen. Rebecca knew without thinking about it that there, if anywhere in this house, was help and heart and strength. They found Dulcey at the long table singing a song in some nonsense language and twisting snakes of dough into a football-sized braid.

Rebecca skidded to a halt at the table and Wib piled up beside her. "Maura's gone!" they shouted over each other.

"Then you must find her." Dulcey smiled but her hands never stopped their work.

"But we can't!" Rebecca pleaded. "We need help!"

Dulcey shook her head and went on placidly braiding and pinching dough, and singing softly. No help here. They slumped back to the deserted front hall.

"Aster?" Rebecca said hopefully.

"Aster already told me she won't help."

"Then Mrs. Doun—"

"Mrs. Doun, who talks in riddles?" Wib laughed bitterly. "Totally useless, the three of them. We'll have to do this ourselves."

They searched the house, upstairs and down, everywhere but the cellar. Maura would never go there on her own, Wib said.

Only, Rebecca thought uneasily, maybe Maura wasn't on her own.

OUT OF BREATH, they sprawled on the stairs between the first and second floors. "Maybe she just went home," Rebecca said. "What now?"

"We should follow up the last clue. I'm sure this scavenger hunt is all about Henry and the black dog, no matter what it means to the other teams. Look at the charms we got."

"Except for mine. A dime? Journey by water?"

He flapped a hand. "Not everything has to fit. Anyway, I think I know where we're supposed to go next." He told her about his visit to the cupola before the party and what he'd seen in the telescope.

"A glove and maybe a boot. Hands and feet." Rebecca slapped the step beside her and jumped up. "Hey! I know the place you mean."

The boot cupboard stood in the entrance hall, to the left of the front door as you came in, facing the coat stand with its mirror (which was once again all there, and not even scratched). The cupboard was a squat boxy thing built of dark wood with two doors, each door inset with a grille made of criss-crossed strips of brass.

"When I looked in the telescope," Wib said, "I saw a dark place with light spotted through it in diamond shapes, like the spaces between those brass strips. The glove is the important thing."

They knelt side by side and Rebecca opened the doors. Inside were two shelves filled with boots and shoes neatly paired, everything clean and polished and looking ready to put on your feet. Some of them were really old-style, like those ladies' boots buttoned all down one side. Where did they come from, and why would the Sisters want them?

Rebecca added that to the list of questions in her mind that would probably never get answered, and started pulling out boots and shoes. In a corner she felt something unpleasantly soft and moist, like a sweaty, pudgy live hand. She sat back with a cry of disgust.

Wib reached in and pulled the thing out. It was a man's leather glove the colour of dried mustard. "This must be it." He stood up dangling the ugly thing from his hand.

"And we need this why?" Rebecca got up off her knees and took it from his hand. It squirmed like a caterpillar in her grip and she yelled and the glove dropped to the floor with a splat. A large brass key jolted out and spun away across the polished marble floor. They both dove after it and landed hard, bruising knees and elbows and cracking heads.

"Ow!" Wib was up first. "I'll get it!"

THE KEY SKIDDED through the arched doorway of the floral parlour and fetched up under the edge of a braided rug. While Rebecca was still picking herself up off the floor Wib was in there after it. He snatched it up, bobbled it, grabbed for it and knocked it high in the air. He grabbed again and it bounced off his fingertips, cracked against the stone mantelpiece, rebounded across the room and vanished under a glass-fronted cabinet full of china dogs and cats.

Muttering, he lay down flat and squinted into the half-inch gap under the cabinet. Too dark to see anything in there. He pushed his hand in but it stuck at the third row of knuckles and nothing metallic met his groping fingertips.

"Rebecca?" He rolled over and scrambled up. "It's here but I can't get at it." He tried shoving the cabinet away from the wall but it stood so solid it might have been set in cement. "Hey! I could use some help here!"

She didn't answer, so he looked around for something to fish the key out with. Something long and thin, a ruler or knife or... *Okay, good.* He crossed to the hearth and pulled an iron poker out of a rack of fireplace tools. "Perfect!" He waved it like a sword. Then knelt down beside the cabinet and slid the poker into the gap. A couple of swipes and the key came spinning out into his hand.

It quivered like a tiny live thing in his grip. It made him think of the blue butterfly. At that he nearly opened his hand, then clenched it instead and the quivering stopped, as if he'd crushed it. He fought down a queasy feeling of guilt. Then he rolled away from the cabinet, climbed to his feet, picked up the poker and dropped it back into its rack.

"Rebecca? Look at this." He was examining the key as he walked, so it wasn't until he came into the hall that he realized she still wasn't there.

The mustard-coloured glove lay on the floor like a boneless hand. He picked it up in his fingertips and flung it back into the boot cupboard, then closed the doors. As he straightened he saw something silver gleaming on the floor. He picked it up. Rebecca's dime.

"Rebecca? Rebecca!" He knew at once there was no use calling, but he yelled anyway. No answer. The house was so quiet, you'd think it was deserted except for him. Distant voices came through the windows from the meadow and gardens. The girls were playing at being hunters and scavengers. Rebecca wouldn't be out there. She would never just run off, not at a time like this.

His right hand clenched the key and the dime together until his fingers hurt. His heart felt like it was going to jump out of his chest.

Calm down. Calm down. Can't help Rebecca if you panic. Think!

He breathed, and breathed some more. Then opened his hand and studied the key. Brass, but polished almost as bright as gold. Just two inches long, the business end intricate as lace, the bow end cast in the shape of a settling butterfly, its wings folded together.

Obvious what this belonged to. He slipped the dime into his jeans pocket with the other charms. Then closed his hand on the key and climbed the stairs to the second floor.

As he stood in the arched doorway to the library, looking around cautiously for anything weird or out of place, it struck him that Maura had disappeared when they'd solved the first clue in the scavenger hunt. And Rebecca had gone after they'd solved the next clue.

198

And this was clue number three, and he was the only one left.

He froze in the doorway. He knew, clear as two and two, that the next step would decide. This was his last chance to back away. To give up this idiotic quest, go home, be with things he understood. To be safe.

One step back into the hallway, turn on his heel, down the stairs, out the front door and gone. Or one step forward into the room, into... what? *If you stay on this path you're going into deadly danger.* There were no other choices. Wib felt, for a moment, as if he was wriggling between two pin points.

Then a face, bright in his mind: his dad, Griffin, with that "Look out, world!" gleam in his eye. And a voice, Rebecca's: "We're friends! Friends don't dump each other!" Rebecca, flaring up like a bonfire. She wouldn't hesitate a second, she'd jump in there with both feet.

Wib took a breath, felt the pin points pull away from his skin, and stepped into the library.

Chapter 39

REBECCA SNEERED at herself for dropping that glove, it was such a wimpy thing to do. The squishy, squirmy feeling of it had taken her by surprise, and she'd just reacted. And then the key went flying, and she missed her chance to nab it — but Wib hadn't wasted a split second, he got right on it, good for him!

They'd really banged their heads hard. There were actual spots floating in front of her eyes. It took a few seconds to blink them away. Wib was making a lot of noise in the floral parlour, grunting and thumping and scrambling about. Sounded like he was fighting with the thing.

"Wib! Hang on, I'm coming!"

A sound from behind caught her in mid-step and spun her around to look. A small figure was just slipping out of sight up around the curve of the stairs.

"Maura?"

The sound came again, and now she knew it for a stifled sob.

"Maura!" She sprinted for the stairs and went up them by twos. Up ahead of her ran light footsteps, swift and panicked-sounding.

Rebecca saved her breath for speed, tripped twice and bruised her knees, scrambled up painfully and climbed on: up the spiral of the stairs to the third floor. There was nobody in the hallway, but in the silence the sound of breathing was loud: somebody gasping and sobbing, down at the back end of the hall near Wib's secret cubby.

"Hey, Maura." Rebecca walked softly in that direction. This felt like trying to get close to a wild bird without spooking it. "Maura, it's just me, Rebecca. Where'd you go, we were worried—"

"Oh help!" A gasp, a clatter of sandals, the thud of feet on stairs.

Rebecca sprinted along the hall and flung herself down the back stairs. Down and down, clutching the railing, fetching up with a stagger on the landing above the cellar. She stopped to catch her breath and listen. The darkness down the stairs breathed a damp cold and, after a moment, a muffled sob.

"Maura!" She felt her way down, holding tight to the wooden railing. "Maura? You down here?"

It was thick black in the bare little room at the bottom of the stairs. Rebecca recalled how enormously glad she'd been to get out of there the last time. And then she'd had Wib for company, and a candle lantern to push back the dark. It was three times as bad being down here alone, and with no light. You felt there was nothing *but* the dark. That you were breathing it into your lungs. That you would never get out. You would be alone, buried, lost forever....

She felt backward for the stair railing.

No, wait. Her eyes were adjusting and now she could see a vague squared shape: an open doorway. That made all the difference in the world. Courage poured back and she started forward. "Maura!"

The room beyond was walled all around with glassy gleams: the shelves of jars. No Maura here.

But she did go down here! "Maura!"

Wait, suppose she went into that room, the one with the moving curtains and the creepy noises? Suppose she was lured, like before, by the white cat?

That bank of shelves on the left, that was where the cat opened the hidden door. Just poked it with its head like so, and there was a click, and.... Rebecca pushed at the shelves. No click. She pulled. They didn't move. She kicked the shelf. Not a quiver.

"Maura! Are you in there?"

Silence.

201

Maybe there's another way in.

The faint light in this room came from the doorway into the next room, the one with the glowing mushrooms. Rebecca walked on through. All around were the tiers of flats full of dirt and compost and mushrooms, some of them glowing greenish. And that damp, earthy mushroom smell. She found what she thought was the right wall and pushed and pulled at the flats there, but only managed to upset two of them on the floor, scattering dirt and mushrooms. No new door appeared.

"Um, Mrs. Doun?" Rebecca shivered. Not just because she was feeling alone and lost again. That too, but also because it was actually getting cold.

Cool air breathed from the inner room, the one where she'd never been. The doorway to that room was outlined in a sharper silver light. A sound of flowing water came from there, and a green, leafy smell.

Rebecca stood in the doorway and looked up into a sky full of stars.

Chapter 40

THE BUTTERFLY KEY went sweetly into the lock of the glass-fronted cabinet in the library. The lock turned easy as butter. Wib opened the two doors, then stood there looking in. He had no idea what he was looking for, or why.

The shelves were crowded with fancy little boxes. Music boxes, most of them, he guessed. Some had objects fixed to the tops: ballerina figurines, china roses, little leaping horses.

Maybe the thing he had to collect, the thing with the next clue, was in one of these boxes. Or maybe the medal was hidden in here. Some boxes had lids that lifted up, some had bases with little drawers in them.

One had a snow globe on top, which on second look had no snow in it, just a swirling bluish mist that settled when you stopped shaking the thing. A fog globe, maybe. Aside from the blue mist, there was nothing to see in that globe. It looked like the inside of a tent. The base didn't open. He set it down at the edge of the shelf.

He took out all the boxes, one by one, and opened the ones that would open. Scraps of tunes tinkled out, all of them creepily half-familiar, because they were backward. There was nothing inside any of them. He put them all back. *Why am I here?* He stuck a hand in and felt along the backs of the shelves behind the boxes. Nothing there. *This is useless!*

He pulled his hand out and knocked one of the boxes — the one with the fog globe — off the shelf. He lunged and caught it just in time to keep it from shattering on the floor. The jolt must have popped something loose, because the globe began to revolve on its base.

He expected some tinkling tune, but there wasn't one. He held it up at eye level. The light from the window, the straw-gold light of August, shone through the globe and changed. A cool, blue radiance bathed his hand and arm. The globe filled with swirling mist; then the mist became silky draperies fluttering and flowing.

Who would want to collect a pointless thing like this?

He was just lowering his hand to put the globe back and get out of there when something new took shape inside.

Three little figures. He held the globe close to his eyes and squinted. Three tiny people, could be a boy and two girls, one girl smaller than the other. The taller one wore white and had short hair. She looked like...

"Rebecca?"

The three stood back-to-back in a clumsy triangle. They were swinging sticks or poles — hard to tell at that scale — and batting away tiny wriggly specks of things that were mobbing them. And all around them the silky curtains rippled and more wrigglers swarmed out.

"Rebecca!"

She didn't hear him, or was too busy to listen. Then the image was gone. The globe still revolved, but now it only showed a misty tent-like room. He shoved it back into the cabinet, slammed the doors and dashed out of the library.

REBECCA HELD tight to the doorframe and gazed. This was crazy, this couldn't be real. What had Mrs. Doun said? *He can change what you think you see.*

But she held that thought only long enough to toss it aside. She felt in her bones that this illusion, if it was one, had nothing to do with the black dog. There was something clean and shining here, something brilliant even in this place of night, something that had no place with that shadowy monster.

She let go of the doorframe and stepped forward. The ground under her feet was yielding and sent up a smell of earth and growing things, not paving stones. The forest smell and the silky rustle of young leaves was all around. The air was damp and cool and new, the kind of air you get on a night of, say, mid-May. If this was an illusion, it was a good one. Almost better than real.

She looked up. Jagged shapes of leaves stirred across a starry sky: a sky such as she'd never seen before. The stars lay in drifts like jewels and jewel dust thrown down, jewels coloured rose, sapphire, pale gold, burning white. Rebecca gazed and gazed, and tears ran down her face and dripped on her hands. She didn't know why she was crying.

Wib has got to see this!

She walked on, and as she walked the trees opened up and she found herself on a steep bank looking down at an ink-dark river. A wide river, she guessed, because she couldn't see the far shore, not even the string of lights that would trace a shore. A strong river, because it didn't chatter like a shallow stream. Its song was full and rich, and drowning-deep.

And the bright stars danced on the black water. Stars above and stars below.

Rebecca gazed and gazed, and it took her a long time to remember why she'd come down here. Maura. Maybe Maura hadn't come down to the cellar at all. Maybe she should turn around and...

"Can you swim?"

The voice came from behind her. She whipped around. Maura stood there just beyond arm's reach. The white cat sat at her feet, its tailed curled over its toes.

"Maura! For heaven's sake, where the heck—" She bit that off and took a second look. Girl and cat smiled the same smug smile and stared at her with the same iridescent green eyes.

"Can you swim?" Maura said again, still smiling.

"I, um..." *Careful, now.* "I wouldn't swim in that. It looks dangerous, don't you think?"

"Maybe. Maybe not if you can swim really well. Can you?"

Why does she want to know?

Rebecca wanted to back away — from Maura, of all people! — but there was nowhere to go from here, except into the river. Her sandal heels sank into the crumbling lip of the bank. She took a half-step forward and planted her feet. "I can swim. A bit. You?"

"I have my Bronze Star." Maura smoothed back her soft brown hair. "I could train for the Bronze Medallion, my mom wants me to, but they're silly about minimum age."

The cat got up and padded past Rebecca. She tried to keep track of it while not taking her eyes off Maura. "Your mom really pushes you, right? That ever get up your nose?"

"I love my mother." Maura's eyes gleamed greener and her teeth showed.

"But she never lets you fail at anything, right? Like, you have to be perfect all the time. You must hate— Hey!"

Maura darted forward and straight-armed Rebecca in the chest. Rebecca yelled, teetered, then took a step back, or tried to. Something furry and unexpectedly solid caught her heels. Her arms windmilled and she caught at the first thing that came to hand: Maura's arm. She held on tight and Maura pulled back, but it didn't help. Rebecca toppled backward. Maura let out a yowl like an outraged cat.

They fell together and hit the water in a flailing tangle.

Chapter 41

A BIG ROOM with silky hangings and a blue light. There was only one place in the house like that. Wib bounded down the back stairs, taking the steps by twos and whirling around the turns, one hand on the railing. On the ground floor landing he stopped to look for the candle lantern. Not there. A distant sound of girls' laughter from beyond the back door tugged at him, made him think of the outdoors, the smell of grass, sunshine. He shook that off and went on down the cellar stairs, not so fast now, not willing to risk a fall.

He shuffled, half blind, through to the room with the shelves full of jars. The glow from the mushroom beds in the farther room, radiating through the doorway, gave light enough for his darkened eyes. The hidden door...

And there it was, not hidden at all. It stood an inch open. Rebecca must have gone in and left the door like that. He pulled it wide and burst out onto the landing above the short flight of stairs that led down to the floor of the sunken room.

"Rebecca?"

The room was even bigger and higher than he remembered, with vague ceiling and corners, as if darkness was a fog that gathered there. The silken hangings radiated a blue twilight, just they did in that creepy globe in the library.

But Rebecca wasn't here. Neither was the third, smaller person, who must have been Maura. No swarming wrigglers, either. The draperies hung still. The only sounds were the scuff of his sneaker soles and the quick in-out of his ragged breathing.

He stood still to catch his breath and think. That vision in the globe upstairs — the three of them together, back to back — there was no way to tell if it was something that was about to happen, or would happen sometime, or might never happen. But it looked bad. They were fighting for their lives.

He padded down the stairs and walked slowly across to the centre of the floor, the part covered by a carpet. *Crazy to leave a rug on a cellar floor.* The fabric was so grey with dust you couldn't see the pattern, if there was one. And — he wrinkled his nose — it stank of mildew.

His shoes made a different sound here. A softer, muffled sound. Also a more hollow sound.

Something twigged his memory, something Rebecca had shown him. Something printed... *Right!* That old newspaper, Brendan Ryder's article on the Circle Road commune. A little fact tucked in at the end, about how the original owner had a swimming pool dug in his cellar, but it was covered over later.

Might be a good idea to find out what was under there now.

Wib walked back off the carpet, knelt down and gingerly pulled back a corner. Underneath he found the ends of wooden boards. They were nailed to a wooden framework that rested on the stone floor and ran parallel to the edges of the carpet.

So, what's under those boards? He looked around and saw nothing to help him pry up the nailed-down planks. He got his fingers under the nearest, the one on the corner, a piece six inches wide and an inch thick, most of its length hidden under the carpet. He wrenched at it, and fell back on his rear end as it popped free with a screech of rusty nails. Too easy. The wood might have been dense and strong once, but now it was spongy with damp.

He tossed the board aside with a dull thump, knelt again, put his face in the gap and yelled: "Rebecca! Are you in there? Rebecca!" Nothing. "Maura!"

Nothing answered but the sound of flowing water.

COLD AND BLACKNESS shocked Rebecca motionless. She floated below the surface and looked up at the stars. The water pulled and pushed at her. She sensed she was moving fast, sailing along in the river's embrace, its drowning-deep song filling her ears. It was like flying. It was wonderful.

Something Dulcey had said slipped through her mind. *Pure, flowing water is powerful stuff. It's the stuff of life... It may even, sometimes, have a magical effect.*

Magical....

Instinct slapped her in the face. A kick and she broke the surface. Black water and diamonds above and all around. "Maura!"

"Behind you!" Rebecca swirled around. Maura was treading water and looking around in panic. "How did we get here?"

"Never mind! Let's just — work on — getting out!" She doubled up to pull off her sandals, one after the other, and let them go. "Shoes!" she barked at Maura.

Maura gasped, ducked, resurfaced with a splash. "But the shore — where—"

The shore was invisible. This might have been an ocean instead of a river: a world of glittering black water, and the two of them lost in it.

"There!" Maura looked past Rebecca and pointed with her chin.

Rebecca swirled again. Maura had picked out the only gleam of light in all this dazzle that was not starlight. It was yellow and shone steadily, not sparkling or dancing. It looked miles away.

"Good for you." Rebecca squinted at Maura. Hard to tell, but her eyes seemed to be back to normal. "Cats hate getting wet, right?"

"Um?" Maura shook her head, spraying water.

"Come on!" Rebecca pointed herself at the distant yellow beacon and saved her breath for swimming. She'd lied about that: swimming was one of the things she was really good at.

Maura matched her, stroke for stroke. The light slowly drew nearer. Rebecca paced herself, measuring out her strength bit by bit. Nearer, nearer, and the water grew colder, the dance of stars more dazzling and confusing.

By now Rebecca knew she would make it — barely. If her will held. Somewhere along the way she knew that Maura (who hadn't lied) could have easily left her behind. But they stayed together.

The yellow light grew and now it was only yards ahead. Next moment the stars blanked out, and the river boomed around them in a close, echoing way.

They were in a tunnel. There was a square grate in the roof above their heads. The grate let in a wavering yellow glow that looked like candlelight.

"So that..." Maura gaped up at it. "But we couldn't have seen.... We swam for miles!"

"Right." The ache in Rebecca's arms and legs told her, as if she needed telling, that they had swum a long, long way. That square of yellow light could not possibly have been visible across that distance. But it had been.

Here, it shed just enough light to show curved steel walls and roof. They were treading water in a culvert maybe six feet across, a yard or so short of a place where a smaller tunnel opened to the left.

Can't drown here, I hope. Rebecca let herself give way. She grabbed at the rough edge of a steel panel on the side wall. Faint sounds drifted from the left-hand tunnel. She strained to make them out.

Maura bobbed beside her. She nodded at the larger right-hand tunnel. "I think that must be the one that comes out near the lake. We should go that way."

"You're not going to try and drown me again, are you?"

Maura gaped. "What? I never—"

"Yes you did, but you don't remember because you were a cat then."

"Cat?" Maura moved away from her in the water. "Are you all right?"

"I am now. Don't you remember the white cat?"

"No!" Maura rubbed her eyes and looked around again, frowning. "I've worked out how we got here. We must've been looking for that spring they say comes into the cellar of the house. I can't remember, but we must've fallen in. Maybe I hit my head. But if you think I'd ever do anything as awful as—"

"All right, all right!" Rebecca held up both hands, and found that she could touch bottom with her toes. The bottom was gritty and pebbly, with some soft bits she didn't want to think about. "I believe you. I'm pretty sure the idea was to get rid of me so Wib would be alone, and it would've worked if we hadn't had that light to guide us."

"Um, Rebecca. You're not making sense."

"Never mind, it wasn't really your fault. And you stuck with me back there," Rebecca tilted her head back toward the river, "when you didn't have to."

"Of course I had to! I'm not a rat!"

"I never thought you were. Anyway, thanks."

"Or a cat!" Maura slid to the right, stroking sideways, keeping a wary eye on Rebecca. "I'm getting out now."

"Fine, you go that way. I'm going this way." Rebecca pointed to the left.

"But that pipe can't be more than two feet wide! You'll never—"

"Listen!"

They listened. There was nothing, for a moment, beyond the

211

ever-present watery sounds. Then a wooden clattering and banging. Then a voice, muffled and faint, but recognizable. It was Wib, and he was yelling: "Rebecca!"

Chapter 42

FLOWING WATER. Now, that was funny. There was water under there, but it didn't sound like a swimming pool, or any kind of pool Wib had ever seen. It sounded like water that was going somewhere in a hurry. A stream or a river.

"Rebecca!" he yelled again. Still no answer. He dug his fingers in around the second plank and was getting set to yank when a voice shouted: "Wib! Behind you!" He slewed around, still crouched; then shot to his feet.

A thing came snaking out from under the silken hangings on the left-hand wall. He had no name for it. It was dead white as if it lived in a deep cave, and it was snake-like, long and thin; but it had legs, too many legs, and the legs carried it across the floor at a terrifying speed. Its too many feet made a clickety sound on the stone floor and its jaws shimmered with needle teeth. That was all he had time to hear and see before it was almost on him, jaws opening wide.

Swift with terror, Wib scooped up the loose plank and swung it like a baseball bat as the thing leaped at him. There was a smack and a hiss and the thing sailed high and fell somewhere in the far shadowy end of the room. He listened for scrambling sounds and looked around for what else might come snaking out from under the stirring draperies.

"Good arm!" the voice said. "But this is no place for you. You'd better get out now and stay out!"

"Henry?" Wib looked around and spotted somebody on the far side of the carpet, a figure just turning away into the hazy darkness. But the voice wasn't Henry's: it belonged to a grown man. And there was something about him.... "Who are you?"

The man glanced back, then turned away again. Each step seemed to carry him metres, so that he swiftly dwindled into a distance beyond the cellar walls. "Wait!" Wib ran after him, across the squeaking carpet-covered boards, over the stone floor beyond. He caught at the man's elbow. And touched cold air, nothing else.

He backed off, breathless. The man stopped too and stood with head bent, as if making up his mind to something, or gathering his courage. Then he turned around.

Wib could see through him. Fold lines of the draperies on the wall beyond ran down through his body. What he wore was vague, except for the medal pinned on his jacket. The medal was crisp in all its details: shining silver, with silver rays sticking out all around. It hung on a ribbon of scarlet so bright that it showed blood-red even in this blue-shadowed place.

It took Wib several tries to get the word out. "D-dad."

"Wib." It was Griffin's voice, all right. And now that Wib had a chance to look, it was Griffin's face. Almost. The glasses, the floppy hair, the long nose. But so strange, so alien-looking in this cold blue light.

"I didn't want you to know this, Wib."

"To know..." Wib gulped and stopped.

"That I hadn't passed on. I thought it would make you unhappy. Even frighten you. I was right."

"Why..."

"Why did I speak up just then? I saw the danger you were in. You think I'd just stand by?"

"No, I mean..."

A wooden banging noise and muffled shouting came from somewhere near. Wib heard them without being really aware of them. Too much else was going on inside him.

He was a war zone of emotions. Joy at seeing his father and hearing his voice; grief all over again, because he hadn't got him back, not all of him, not alive. Sadness and horror, to see his father such a wrong thing: a ghost. He stared, brain-numbed by the wrongness of it, and what his father said slid through his mind only half heard, along with the voices calling and the thumping sounds.

"...the medal," Griffin said.

That woke Wib up. It was another part of the wrongness. "I thought the black dog had it. I saw it on him."

Griffin smiled, a pale copy of his real live smile. "And you believed what you saw? You should know better, Wib. Tricks and lies, that's all you'll get from that monster. No, I've always had the medal. That's the trouble, I think. It's why I'm here."

"I, I don't understand."

"It holds me. All the love your mom put into it, all the grief that made you take it and hide it, all of that has made it a thing of power." Griffin raised a hand to his chest and curled it around the medal. Its corners poked through his misty fingers. "It's so heavy with power, it's like an anchor. And until you take it from me, I'll never pass on. I'll be stuck here."

"Like Henry."

A strange look passed over Griffin's shadowy face, and for a moment it looked less like a face and more like the skull beneath the skin. Wib went cold inside. Then Griffin smiled and looked like himself again. Almost. "Not exactly like Henry," he said. "The important difference is, only Henry can free Henry. But only you can free me."

Behind Wib, on the other side of the rectangle of carpet, there was more muffled bumping. Then a squeal of rusty nails. Someone was forcing up another of the planks from below: from inside the swimming pool. "Wib!" Rebecca shouted, still muffled.

"How can I free you?" Henry raised his voice, not wanting Griffin to think of Rebecca, and too confused to know why. "You're a ghost. How can I do anything to help you?"

"Just one thing." Griffin held out his misty hands. "You have to take this medal from me, and then I can go. I can't do it myself."

"I... I..." Wib swayed, wanting to run straight to his dad, wanting to run away.

"Wib!" Griffin still held out his hands. "Don't be afraid of me. Please!" He was begging. It twisted Wib's heart, it hurt him inside.

Still he swayed, torn two ways. Most of all, he was wrestling with the strangeness of it all. If he'd had time to put his thoughts into words, and if he'd had the words he needed, he'd have said that his father had always been a sunlit man. A man firmly of this world, a man of hugs and jokes, of snow-caked mittens and hot breakfasts; of foot races in the park, where he let Wib win despite his short six-year-old legs.

This half-life, a shade among shadows, was a universe away from the father he'd known. How could his dad ever be a ghost? He'd be here, alive, or he'd be there, wherever *there* was. He wouldn't be an in-between thing like a ghost.

Wib backed away. "This is wrong."

"Wib!" Griffin reached out again, and his voice pleaded. But there was a razor edge in the pleading, and a claw-like crook to the reaching fingers.

"No! You're not my father!"

Griffin made a hissing sound, showed yellow teeth, and laughed. It sounded more like a dog's bark. Wib backed off again, edging along the hem of the carpet that covered the planks, aiming for the way out. Behind him came a slam. He looked back. The door at the top of the stairs was shut.

When he looked back again, Griffin was changing.

216

Chapter 43

HIS FACE FLOWED like hot wax, the long nose shortening, the glasses melting away, the dark hair lightening. When the change settled he was a middle-sized man, more compact than Griffin, with a tanned young-looking face under a shock of curling bronze-gold hair. A handsome man except for the teeth, that showed too large and long when he smiled, and the eyes, that looked like grey glass over red embers. He still wore the medal.

"You—" Wib caught a breath. "You're Owen."

"Also known as Henry's dad." Owen smiled, showing the dog-like teeth. "That's why I'm here, of course. Henry. All of this is his fault." He sauntered toward Wib.

Wib backed off. Where to? The door was closed and for sure it would be locked. And there was Rebecca, who had somehow turned up in the swimming pool under the carpet. He couldn't leave her. If only she would shut up, go away, escape, instead of making all that noise. More boards near the far corner of the pool were cracking.

"How could this be Henry's fault?" Slow him down, hold his attention. Keep him away from Rebecca.

Owen spread his arms wide and reared back, miming astonishment. "A son who rats on his own dad? Who gets his dad arrested? And then murders him?"

"He never murdered you!"

"Oh yes he did! Dropped a brick on me. I just wanted to talk with him, that's all, and he bashed my head in." Owen kept on coming, no hurry, his walk a casual swagger. "You think that doesn't deserve a talking-to?"

217

"I heard you were set to burn the house down with him in it."

Owen grinned. Those canine teeth were really long and pointy. "Only after he went and hid. A boy can't treat his dad like that, no sir! I figured to smoke him out. No harm intended."

Wib took another step back. "Is that what's going on now? Why you tricked me down here? You're trying to smoke him out?"

"Smart kid! Yes, Henry's safe so long as he stays where he is, but he'll come out for you, just you wait and see. Right, Henry?" He lifted his face like a dog about to howl. "Henry! You won't leave your pal in the lurch, eh?"

Wib had reached the nearest corner of the carpet now. If he pivoted and kept backing he'd come level with the corner near the door, where he'd pried off the first board. More sounds of boards cracking came from that direction. Out of the corner of his eye he glimpsed hands in the gap, gripping the tiled edge of the pool. Owen couldn't have missed that noise. Maybe he thought it was Henry busting free.

Wib raised his voice. "It won't work! Henry's too smart to fall for that. Besides, I don't need his help."

"No? Why's that?" Owen cocked his head.

"Because you're just a ghost. You're nothing. You're only a, a wisp of fog."

Owen tipped back his head and laughed. "An undigested bit of beef?" He subsided into chuckles. "No, I can rustle up a bit more fight than that, friend Wib. Lo and behold!" He spread his arms again and made a whirling motion with his hands.

On both the long walls, north and south, the silken draperies billowed. Things slithered and squirmed out from behind and swarmed across the floor. Towards Wib, towards the pool. Towards Rebecca, who would be caught down there, treading water, unable to fight back.

Wib whirled and dashed back along the side of the pool cover.

218

"Rebecca!" he yelled. "Out! Now!"

He skidded to the corner, fell to his knees and pulled at the nearest plank. It came up in long splinters and Rebecca elbowed herself up after it, water streaming off her, wood bits thick in her hair. Maura climbed after her, which made Wib stare for a half-second, but after that there were no more half-seconds to spare.

The dim blue place was crawling with little monsters, all scrambling and roiling in their direction. Maura looked around, let out a scream, then snatched up one of the broken planks and shrank up against Rebecca. Wib grabbed another plank and Rebecca another and they formed a triad with their backs to each other.

"The door!" Rebecca shouted.

Wib looked. "No!" That end of the room was so thick with critters, he couldn't see the floor.

"Other corner!" Maura shrieked. "There's another door!"

The triad moved. Wib, who still faced the door he'd come in by, found himself stumbling backward, struggling to keep his balance and stay close to the others. As they moved the critters surrounded them, charged in and out, claws scraping, jaws snapping, little button eyes shining red.

Rebecca yelled and Maura shrieked. Wib battled on, grim and silent. He swung his plank and kicked his feet, and behind him came smacks and squeals as critters sailed away left and right. "Yes!" Rebecca shouted. "C'mon! There's the other door!"

Wib grabbed a swift look over his shoulder. The other door was in the south wall near the front corner, at the top of a short flight of stairs. It was nearer than he'd expected. Still in a tight cluster, they made a rush for the stairs.

Only to pull up short when Owen appeared midway up the flight. He grinned down at them with massive jaws. More than ever he looked like a dog disguised as a man. The creatures flattened to the ground, as if they feared him too.

"This is his place," Rebecca whispered into the sudden quiet.

Wib knew. *The heart of his power. He can do what he likes here.*
Behind them came stealthy slitherings and rustlings and hisses as the
creatures crept nearer.

"Wh- who is that man?" Maura was trembling so hard she made
the whole triad shake. "Who are all those people?"

All around them, now, came sounds of crying and screaming,
voices from the walls. "Those are memories," Rebecca said faintly.
"The house remembers what happened here."

Owen lifted his head and listened, smiling. His eyes glowed a
deep hot red.

"This would be a good time for Dulcey to step in," Rebecca
murmured. "Or Aster. Or even Mrs. Doun."

"Maybe," Wib said. "I'm not so sure they'd be any help at all."

"But," Maura began.

"Who set up this scavenger hunt?"

"But you can't think—"

A thunderous banging and crashing drowned Maura out. Cracks
zigzagged down the wall beside the door behind Owen. He turned his
head to look back and barked a laugh.

"It's Henry!" Rebecca yelled. "Henry!"

"No!" Wib swatted away a many-legged crawler. "This is just
what he wants — to get Henry here."

"It's what I want too! Henry!"

"Who's Henry?" gasped Maura.

The banging and crashing didn't stop. Wib yelled: "No! Henry,
stay put! We're not in danger!"

"You think?" Rebecca swung her plank, connected with something, *splat!* then smashed another crawler on the backswing.

"These things aren't real. Like Mrs. Doun said, it's Owen making us see stuff that isn't there."

"They look awfully real," Maura gasped. Then she shrieked and kicked. "My leg!"

Something grey and worm-like had wound around her bare foot and fastened a sucking mouth on her ankle. Wib pulled it off, hating the slimy feel of it, and hurled it away. Maura's ankle was bleeding. *Real enough.* He looked around. A tumbling carpet of critters surrounded them. The ones at the front inched closer. Thin grey tongues flickered.

Owen shook with laughter as he watched. *Waiting to see them take us down.* Wib got a better grip on his plank. A crack ran along its length. One or two more smacks and he'd be left holding a six-inch stub.

The banging and cracking around the door redoubled. It shook but held firm. Then silence fell. A sigh seemed to blow through the room. *Maybe that's Henry giving up. He can't get free and he knows it.* Wib staggered.

Owen laughed softly. "Go on then, kiddies," and Wib realized he was talking to the critters. "Go get 'em!"

"Be ready," Wib growled over his shoulder.

"You betcha," Rebecca breathed. Maura just gasped. They gripped their frail bits of wood.

Then came a bang like a rifle shot. The door cracked from top to bottom. Stones burst free around its edges. Rays of white-gold daylight stabbed through the twilight gloom.

All around them the critters squealed and cowered away from the light. Some skittered behind the silken hangings, some faded to nothing, some vanished with a pop.

"Yes!" Rebecca yelled, and leaped and punched the air.

With a deafening crash, the door and the frame around it collapsed inward. Dirt showered, stones rolled and clattered. Wib and

Rebecca and Maura scrambled back.

Light flooded in. Through clouds of dust Wib saw that a section of brick, stone and timber at the base of the house wall had fallen inward along with the door. The staircase was buried under a landslide of debris.

"Where's Owen?" Rebecca spun, searching. There was no sign of him.

"It's just us three," Maura said. She suddenly sat down on the littered floor. "Oh! Wait till my mom—"

"Wait, look!" Wib pointed. A fourth figure staggered up from the heap of debris and shook grit from its hair. They froze, staring. Then Wib let out a laugh that was half a sob. "Henry?"

Chapter 44

"YES, ME. We can all get out now." Henry swatted dirt from his clothes, which were the same as what he'd been wearing when they met him in the mirror: flared pants, long-sleeved plaid shirt, knitted brown vest, lace-up leather shoes. "Come on, let's hurry!"

Rebecca picked her way over to him, stepping gingerly, barefoot. (Wib noticed that she'd lost her shoes somewhere, and so had Maura.) When she was close enough she lunged at Henry and hugged him. "What's the rush? You're free! We won!"

Henry laughed and hugged her back. Then he looked past her at Wib, who hadn't said anything because his throat was clogged up and he was afraid he'd make a spectacle of himself. Wib cleared his throat loudly, gave himself a shake and walked over. He held out his hand. Henry grabbed it.

"See, Wib?" Henry squeezed his hand, then dropped it. "I'm not your imaginary friend. I'm your real friend. Forever."

Wib looked Henry in the face. *Different, but the same.* He scowled, lunged at Henry and hugged him. Then pushed him away. *Friend. Forever.*

Henry looked at Maura, who blinked at him, shy and uncertain. "How's your ankle?" he asked.

"Hurts." She hung back, keeping her eyes on him. "You're the boy I saw watching us, the first day I came here."

"I guess I must be."

"So you're a, um, a ghost?"

"No! Not at all."

"Then, what..."

"It's hard to explain." He looked around nervously. "Can we get out of here? I hate this place. Even though I think... I *think*... it's harmless now. Or almost."

The swath of daylight from the broken door bounced from the walls and swept the shadows from the corners. Now it was just a big, grimy space littered with wreckage and hung with rags. Not as big as it looked before. Not mysterious. Not menacing.

The light glinted on something half-buried in dirt at the base of the stairs. "Look!" Rebecca pointed. "It's your medal, Wib!"

"Right. It must have dropped when Owen vanished." He didn't move to pick it up.

"Quest achieved!" She made a victory fist. "Aren't you going to take it?"

"Yeah, sure." But he had more than half a mind to leave it lying there. After seeing Owen wearing it, and knowing that monstrous black dog had carried it, he knew he'd feel uneasy about giving it to his mother.

"Well, go on!"

"Yeah, yeah." Mouth downturned, he went over and picked the medal up. Then yelped and shook it from his hand. Scraps flew: a dead leaf, a chunk of wood, bits of straw. They broke into fragments as they hit the ground.

"Whoa! A fake!" Rebecca nudged the bits with her bare toe. "So that's what you were chasing all this time? What was the point?"

"To lure him," Henry said. "To pull him around on a string. The dog never had the real medal."

They looked at each other. Wib turned up his palms. "Then where is it?"

THERE WAS NOTHING more to wait for. They held hands and started to scramble up the hill of dirt and stones and other debris, the two boys helping the barefoot girls over the broken bits, until suddenly Henry pulled back. "Wait. Listen!"

There were voices outside the jagged gap that used to be a door. "That's Dulcey," Rebecca said. "Don't worry, she's okay."

"I can't meet them, not yet." Henry retreated to the stone floor and led the way to the other end. Wib tried to tell him that door was probably locked, but at a touch of Henry's hand it swung open. Then there was a jostling rush out of the room with the jars, up the stairs, out the back door, and into the herb garden.

The sun struck down on their heads and filled the air with aromatic smells. Henry held up his arms and lifted his face, eyes closed against the direct rays, mouth open, drinking the hot golden light like syrup. His face shone. He breathed in, breathed out. "This — this tells me I'm really alive again." He dropped his arms and looked from Wib's face to Rebecca's and Maura's. "Being safe was never worth missing this. I missed so much, so long — and most of the time I never even knew. I just knew how confused and not-right I was."

"Then you won't go back in the house again." Wib was relieved. "I mean, *in* the house."

Henry laughed and spun on the grass, arms whirling. "No!" He whirled to a halt. "No, I'll never get trapped like that again!"

"We'd better find out what's going on," Rebecca said.

"Yes, we—" Maura looked down at herself. She clapped her hands to her cheeks. "Look what I've done to my clothes! And where are my sandals? My mom—" Her hands dropped and her eyes opened wider. "Wait. Did that really happen?"

"You mean, all that stuff in the cellar?" Wib shivered. "You bet it did."

"So we — we really did fight monsters?"

"Yeah, we did." He eyed her warily and braced himself for some kind of meltdown. "But it's okay now, we—"

"Oh!" She gazed from face to face. "We — I — really fought — Oh! That was *awesome*!"

Rebecca laughed and hugged her. "Totally awesome!"

Wib looked up at the sun again. "Uh-oh, what time is it?"

Henry whipped up his left wrist, stared, laughed with delight and held it out for all to see. "Look! It works! I'm back in time!" The hands of the watch pointed to half-past four. The second hand was creeping around in the proper direction. The word in the middle was TIMEX.

"Four-thirty! Is that all?" Rebecca said. "Feels like hours!"

Wib led the way around the house. They moved in single file, close to the wall, stopping behind the cover of a climbing rosebush when voices sounded near. Peering between the leaves they saw Aster and Dulcey in the meadow. They were standing close to the house wall and seemed to be looking it over. Aster sent a brief glance in their direction, but gave no sign that she'd seen them.

"I'll have to fix that," Henry said. "A big job. Probably take me all night."

"Fix it?" Rebecca frowned at him. "How?"

"Well, you know..." He held up his hands and wiggled his fingers. "Like that mirror I broke, remember?"

"I don't get it," Wib said. "You fixed the mirror from *inside*. You're not inside any more."

"Right, but I'm still sort of tuned into the house. I can feel it. That broken place hurts." He ran his gaze along the brick wall. "I bet I could get back in, if I wanted—"

Wib caught his arm. "Don't! You'll get stuck again!"

"Not to worry! Now, you three better show up or there'll be a search."

"And you too," Rebecca said.

Henry swept his hands crosswise. "Not me. I'm staying out of sight for now. See you later!" He turned and walked away. Wib watched him go. Henry stopped suddenly and touched a bright red tomato on its vine. He delicately, hesitantly broke it off. He ran his fingertips over the satiny skin, raised it to his nose and inhaled. Then he walked out of sight around the corner of the house with the tomato cupped in his palms like something precious.

As Wib, Rebecca and Maura walked toward the front of the house, under the trees, Dulcey looked around and gave them a calm nod. "The others have already gone home. There will be no club next week. That's just a precaution: there's no real danger." With a cheerful smile she added, "I'm glad to see you came out unscathed!"

She didn't mention the fact that the three of them were varying degrees of filthy and soggy, although she must have noticed, Wib thought.

"Maura got scathed," Rebecca said. "I think she needs antiseptic."

Dulcey beckoned Maura over. "Let's see." The ankle was still bleeding. "Mm, nasty. We'll get that cleaned and bandaged. Then I'll find you some footwear and walk you home."

"Oh, but you don't need to." Maura looked up. "I mean, I can walk home. It's just two blocks."

"Your mother will certainly want an accounting." Dulcey's smile was steely. "Never mind, I'll have a little chat with her."

"I..." Maura's mouth trembled; then firmed up. "I can tell her. After all, I just fought... I mean... "

Dulcey's smile softened. "Awesome. Let's tend to that bite."

They walked to the kitchen end of the house hand in hand, Maura with head held high.

Chapter 45

ASTER WATCHED them go, then shrugged and turned back to the gap in the wall near the southeast corner. "You two skedaddle," she said over her shoulder.

Wib's heart sank. "But I need to get in the house. There's something I've left in there."

"That medal? Plenty of time."

"No!" Wib shouted. Then wished he hadn't. Aster swung around and aimed her laser-bright, black-rimmed eyes at him. She looked ten feet tall. But there was no backing down now. "It's not just the medal," he said, not stammering at all. "I need to go in and find Henry."

"That's right." Rebecca stood shoulder-to-shoulder beside him. "We need to make sure he's okay. I mean, he just got out after being trapped for forty-five years, and the world's all different, and—"

"Who's Henry?"

"You know!" Wib clenched his hands to keep them from shaking.

"Whoever he is, he has his road, you have yours."

"But suppose," Rebecca put in, "just suppose, our roads are the same road for a while?"

Aster's eyes needled at her. "It does happen. Sometimes. But remember, we can't help."

Wib let out his tight-held breath. "We won't need any help. The black dog is gone."

"If you say so." Aster turned on one bare heel and sauntered around to the porch and in through the open front door.

"Come on," Wib said, and started after her.

Rebecca pulled him back. "Wait! People coming!"

Engines growled. Cars swung past the stub of wall and up the curving driveway. One car, then another. "Quick! Hide!" Rebecca yipped.

"Why?" Wib demanded, but he slipped after her around the trunk of the nearest tree, one of half a dozen thick-limbed chestnuts that stood along the south side of the house.

"My gran!" Rebecca whispered. "That's her car, the one in front. If she sees me she'll tell me to go home and help with dinner and step lively!"

"What's she doing here?" Wib peered around the curve of the trunk. That was Flora MacBeth, all right, stomping up to the front porch in her baggy khaki shorts and oversized T-shirt. A thin man with a briefcase had got out of the second car and was loping after her.

"That guy is the building safety inspector," Rebecca said. "Gran's the chair of the town council's Building and Properties Committee, and this house is the town's property, so they need to check on the damage. They got here fast! Somebody must have phoned them."

"We still need to get in and find Henry. Can we sneak around to the back without them seeing us?"

"No need," said a voice in the air above them. Rebecca squeaked and Wib jumped, and Henry laughed. "Come on up! Best seats in the house."

Rebecca touched the trunk hesitantly and searched the thick foliage with her eyes. "You haven't gone *in* the tree, have you?"

"I could, but I haven't."

A third car engine sounded on the street, and a dented white Mercury Cougar squealed in around the corner and up the drive. "Brendan Ryder?" Wib stared. "Why's he here?"

"Just come on!" Rebecca was already partway up the trunk, hands clasped around the first strong branch, bare feet scrabbling, hissing "Ouch!" In a moment she vanished into the surging sea of leaves.

Wib followed her up. He found Henry perched casually astride a massive limb, feet swinging. Rebecca sat at the base of the same branch, one arm tight around the trunk. Wib squeezed himself uncomfortably into the crotch of the branch just below.

"This is super!" Rebecca whispered. "We can see everything from up here. And nobody can see us." Her formerly white T-shirt and short pants were smeared grey, brown and green, speckled with grime and blotched with damp. That didn't seem to bother her.

Perched in this sun-dappled, wind-swayed eyrie, they looked down through gaps in the leaves to the patch of meadow near the broken wall. Aster had come out of the house and stood slouched, gazing off into the distance, hands in the back pockets of her tight jeans. Flora was talking, her hands jabbing out from time to time, poking the building inspector in the arm (So that's where Rebecca gets it, Wib thought.), waving toward the house, and flicking dismissively at Brendan Ryder, who was holding a small metal object toward her: a voice recorder, Wib guessed. A couple of other people were walking along the drive toward the house: neighbours, probably, attracted by the commotion.

"Huh!" Rebecca said. "The damage doesn't look as bad as I thought."

"That's my work." Henry ran his eyes over the wall. "Haven't done much yet, though. Just closed some of the cracks. It's hard to get anything done, with people around. Stones flying into place, timbers growing back together, that kind of thing could get noticed. And then there'd be a fuss." He turned his head, grinning. "And no, Wib, I

230

didn't go back *in* the house. I told you I'm tuned to it, right? I can change things from outside. It feels really neat. It's sort of like playing a musical instrument, a complicated one with lots of keys and knobs and things. A church organ, maybe."

"That's cool," Rebecca said. "But why are you hiding in this tree?"

"It's the Sisters. I'm not ready to meet them. I don't think I'll ever be ready. Honest, they scare the poop out of me!"

"Me too!"

Me too, Wib admitted silently. "What are they, do you know? And why are they here?"

"I can't even guess. I'm afraid what they'll do if they get hold of me. Because of what I did."

After a minute of silence Rebecca said, "Henry, we can't read your mind, you know?"

"What I did? I, I..." Henry ducked his head. "I," he murmured, in a voice so soft Wib could hardly catch it, "I killed my father."

Chapter 46

"NOW, WAIT," Rebecca said. "Mr. Ryder told us what happened to your father, and it wasn't your fault. It was a brick that fell from a chimney." A beat of silence. "Oh."

"Yeah, oh," Henry said dismally.

"That was you?" Wib said.

"Yeah. I know it now. Now that I'm free, my mind and my memory are sharper. I remember how I got stuck in the house, and how I killed Owen. Killed my own father." He swung his feet faster. "What will they do? Will they send me away from here forever? Or seal me up again? Or get the police to come and arrest me? I'd deserve it, whatever."

Rebecca tried to reach him with a hand. "But you didn't do it on purpose!"

"No, I don't think I did. I'm totally certain. Almost. I was just scared to death at the time." He swung his feet harder. Then scooted around on the limb, swinging his legs over — "Be careful!" Rebecca hissed. — to look them in the face.

"It was that night, after he was arrested," Henry said. "After he got out of jail. I felt him coming from a block away and I hid. I went to my secret space. Our secret space, Wib. Of course that was stupid, because he could feel where I was just like I could feel him. And the space has only one way in and out. Wib, you can picture it, right?"

"Yeah. Yeah, I can." Wib kept his eyes on Henry's face. Henry's eyes were black with remembered terror.

"He came into that space like a thunderstorm. There was moonlight shining through the little window, but he filled the place

232

with darkness. He screamed at me, he called me an ungrateful monster. He swore I would pay. I knew he would kill me. So then... well, I'd got really good at fading into the woodwork, remember. That was my talent. I closed my eyes, and hugged myself tight, and pressed my back against the slanted wall, and I went... away. And he couldn't come near me."

Wib and Rebecca were silent. Even the tree seemed to hold its breath and listen.

"But he knew. He felt the house trembling and he knew it was me. He shouted that he would burn the place down, and me with it. He backed out of the secret space and ran down to the kitchen to find matches. I felt every step, I knew exactly what he was doing. I heard him laughing. I felt him go out to the shed to find gasoline. I looked down from the cupola — by that time I was all over the place, I think I was as crazy as he was — and I saw him laughing up at me with the gas can in his hand."

He drew in a breath and held it so long, Wib was afraid he might pass out and fall and then he'd have to catch him, and he wasn't sure he could. Wib braced himself. Rebecca leaned sideways.

Henry breathed again. "Well, the commune members hadn't done much to keep the place in good shape. And I think the house got shaken up when I went into it. I was trembling so hard, bits were falling all over, shingles and eavestroughs and a window pane and nails, and.... And then a brick from one of the chimneys." He leaned his head against the trunk of the tree and closed his eyes. "I didn't mean to kill him!"

"So that's when Owen became a ghost," Rebecca murmured. "And stayed. Always trying to get at you, to punish you."

"Yes. And I felt him there and I stayed in hiding. I made myself small and invisible, like the dust. But then I found I couldn't get out again: I had no idea how. After that I slept a lot, except when new

233

people moved in. That always woke me up. Some of them, it was usually a young kid, could hear and see me, like Wib." He pushed away from the trunk and smiled at Wib. "But most people didn't know I was here. Or they did, and thought I was a ghost. One family held a secret exorcism."

Rebecca whistled. "How did that feel?"

"Like nothing, for me. Scared off a couple of low-level nasties, though, so that was good."

"Ooh! These nasties, what—" Rebecca began, then cut herself off. "Where are they going?"

The people below had turned away from the gap in the wall and were walking toward the back of the house. Henry swivelled around again on the limb and leaned over dangerously to get a look through the leaves. "Probably to see the damage from the inside." He sounded anxious. "I wish they'd give me some time! I could fix it if they'd just go away!"

And crawl back *in* the house and get stuck in there again, Wib thought. "Why not let the town fix it? Why does it have to be you?"

"Because it was me who busted that wall. It's up to me to fix it. Besides, I just know I'd do a better job."

Flora MacBeth and the building safety inspector and Aster and Brendan Ryder were all out of sight now. "Let's go," Wib said, and began the downward scramble. Rebecca clambered down after him, ouching at the roughness and making an exasperated noise when she ripped another pocket. Henry skittered down like a squirrel, clinging to the bark. At once he looked toward the house, but Wib said, "You're not staying there tonight all by yourself. You're coming to my place. You can share my room."

Henry looked at him, startled. Wib nudged him toward the street. "I mean, why hang around here? You're free now, right? You can go where you want!"

"Yes!" Rebecca danced along beside them on the grass. "Think! A whole new world! All yours!"

"But won't Wib's mom ask who I am?" Wib shuffled along in a scared-looking way. "Wouldn't she want to phone my parents and make sure it's okay? That's what my mom would do. And it's rude to just turn up."

"I'll think of something," Wib said. The important thing was to help Henry really get free of the Morphy house and its grounds. Until he did, there was always a chance that he would go back *in* the house, because it was familiar and he felt safe there, and the real world was new and scary. He caught Rebecca's eye and they exchanged nods.

They reached the end of the driveway. This was the first test. Henry stood on one side of the crack between the asphalt drive and the cement sidewalk as if he faced a glass wall. He wet his lips, took a deep breath, braced himself, lifted one foot; then settled back.

"I don't know if I can do this. After we came to stay here, Owen never let me past the gate unless I went with him."

"Well, Owen's gone and he can't stop you. See, you can do this!" Rebecca jogged back and forth across the line. "This is just like when you were in the mirror and we were outside and you pulled us in, remember?" She made a hop and landed with both bare feet on the sidewalk. Then held out a hand. "Come on, Henry."

He looked at her hand, smiled at her, took the hand. Took another breath. Lifted one foot, took a step. Moved the other foot. Crossed the line.

"There!" She swung his hand. "That wasn't so hard, was it?"

"N-no." He stood on the sidewalk and looked around. "Um... Now what?"

"Now we walk." Wib stepped out on the other side of Henry and started walking down the curve of Circle Road, slowly, because Henry and Rebecca were moving like snails. "My house is this way."

Henry was still tightly holding Rebecca's hand. "Wow, a sleep-over! You know what? The last time I was at a friend's house, it was for a sleepover. It was my friend Gary's house. There were four of us, all around eight years old." He shook his head in a wonderstruck way. "Gosh, Gary! I wonder if he'd remember me now."

"You could find out," Rebecca began, then let out a yip as a voice stabbed her from behind.

"Rowena!"

"Oh, no!" Rebecca tried to slip around to the other side of Henry, but it was too late. They'd been so wound up in easing Henry out into the real world that they hadn't heard the car rolling out of the drive-way and turning onto the road behind them.

"And where d'you think you're going?" Flora called across the passenger seat and through the open window. "It's nearly dinnertime! In you get, and be quick about it!"

"Phone me," Rebecca muttered at Wib. "Let me know how it goes."

"Rowena!"

"Okay, okay!"

"WHAT IN HEAVEN'S name have you been doing? Rolling in mud? Look at those clothes! And where are your shoes?"

"Um, well, there was a scavenger hunt, and um..."

"Now, don't tell me your shoes got scavenged!"

"Not exactly. "

"Never mind that for now." Flora stared at Wib and Henry as the car passed them, then again as she made a U-turn to drive back up the hill. "Who's that boy with Wib?"

"Oh, just a boy from the club."

"You said Wib was the only boy."

"He was. Now there's one more."

236

"What's his name?"

"Henry something. Maybe Herbert."

"Strange. He must be new in town. Never mind, plenty else to think about. I've called an emergency meeting of the Building and Properties Committee."

Rebecca put two or three things together and felt a chill. "What's the emergency?"

"That perishing house!" Flora wrenched the wheel around and turned the car into Park Circle. "We might have to rethink our decision not to demolish."

"Demolish! You can't!"

"Of course we can, child, it's our house!"

"But it's a heritage building, right?" Rebecca gripped her seat with both hands. "It— it's part of our history! You can't just—"

"And since when have you cared anything about heritage or history?"

"But there's people living there!"

"Oh, the tenants would have to move out first, of course. And we'd need council's approval — no problem there."

"But—"

"What's got into you? The house is evidently not safe, and we can't lease it in that condition. And even if we could get it repaired, which would be a terrible expense, it would be much more difficult to sell. Now, here we are! Out you get, I'm in a hurry. Go change! And wash!"

Chapter 47

HENRY KEPT LOOKING back over his shoulder as they walked down Circle Road. He only began to pay attention to where he was once the old Morphy house was out of sight. When they crossed the creek by the Hay Street bridge, he stopped in the middle of the span to lean on the stone parapet and smile down at the flowing water. "This hasn't changed at all!"

But as they explored the sun-baked streets around the centre of the lower town, he kept shaking his head. "There's so much that's different. All those shops are new. And there's a Vietnamese restaurant, look! I wonder what pho is. And what the heck are those things?"

They had stopped in front of a store called Wired Wilson. The window dazzlingly displayed dozens of iPods and Smartphones in a rainbow of colours. Wib started to explain, or tried to, until he saw the perplexed look on Henry's face. Then he tried to explain about the internet and wifi, and that made things worse.

They detoured a block to the east, to avoid the *Amstey Gazette* building on Albert Circle. "Mr. Ryder might be there by now, and he might recognize you. I don't know what we'd tell him."

"Nothing wrong with the truth," Henry said, looking around in a worried way.

"Except nobody'd believe it." Wib waved a hand at the glass-and-steel public school across the street. "That looks new. I guess it's a lot different from when you were here."

"Don't know. I never went to school here."

Wib stopped on the sidewalk. "But you were here what, a year?"

Henry stopped too. "About that. But I couldn't go to school. Owen wouldn't risk it." As always when talking about his father, Henry's voice flattened and lost colour. As if, Wib thought, he was making himself even *sound* invisible.

"I don't understand why you stayed with him. Mr. Ryder said he kidnapped you when you were eight. You waited until you were twelve to blow the whistle. How come?"

Henry plodded on along the street. Wib fell into step beside him. "I mean, you could've gone to the police any time, right?"

"That's just it, I couldn't! He said I'd go to jail, because I'd helped him steal stuff. And I couldn't just run away. Twice, in the first couple of years, I tried to, but he always knew exactly where to find me. After that I never got to go anywhere on my own."

"And there was one more thing. The most important thing." He stopped and faced Wib, his eyes dark and intense. "My mother."

"Um, yes?" Wib dreaded any talk of Henry's mother.

"After the second time I tried to run away, Owen said that if I tried again, or if I told anybody about him, or if I tried to reach my mom, then someday—" He took a breath. "Someday he would kill her. It might take years till he had the chance, but he would do it."

"And you believed him."

"Oh, yes. He promised. He broke most promises, but I knew he'd keep that one."

Wib waited, with knots in his stomach, for Henry to say it must be safe to go and find his mother now; but he didn't.

IT WAS NEARLY a quarter to six when they reached Fairview Avenue. Wib scouted and found his mother wasn't home yet, then he whisked Henry in by the side door and up the stairs.

"There." He closed the door of his room and let himself breathe normally. "If you're quiet and don't walk around much, she'll never

239

know you're here."

Henry nodded, and looked curiously around the room.

"Not much to see," Wib muttered as he yanked off his dirty T-shirt and pulled on a clean one.

He didn't like how this felt, hiding things from his mother. But he couldn't leave Henry alone in the Morphy house, and he couldn't let his mom know about him either, because of the questions she would ask that they wouldn't be able to answer.

"It's nice." Henry nodded admiringly at the narrow bed with its Spiderman coverlet, the small bookcase that was only half full, the desk with nothing on it except for a couple of plastic models, and the one wall that Wib had got around to repainting. It had been a dull brown; he'd painted it bright blue, then wished he hadn't.

"I'll go down and get you something to eat. Man, forty-five years without a meal! I bet you could eat a horse!"

"I ate that tomato." Henry's eyes sparkled. "It was amazing!"

"That won't last you. I won't be long. Till then, you could listen to music. I've got an MP3 player. Here, I'll show you how it works." He left Henry sitting on the bed with earbuds in and a fascinated expression on his face.

Ten minutes later Wib was up again. He dropped a rolled-up sleeping bag on the floor and set a bottle of orange juice on the bed-side table, as well as a cheese sandwich wrapped in waxed paper, an apple and three Oreo cookies. "There. I'll sleep on the sleeping bag and you can have the bed."

"Thanks." Henry had pulled out the earbuds. "Thanks a lot. But I can't do that to you."

"I'll be okay on the floor, don't worry!"

"No, I mean I won't need the bed. I'm going back to the house."

Wib's heart sank into his stomach. "But why?"

Henry got up and walked over to the desk. He picked up one of

240

Wib's plastic models. "What's this?"

"That's the Mars Rover *Curiosity*. It's a robot. I mean, the real one's a robot. The real Rovers are on Mars right this minute, rolling around, exploring, taking photos. Wow, there's so much for me to tell you!"

Henry set the model down. "Not yet." He walked over to the open window and looked out into the scruffy back yard. "Wib, I've been thinking. I know the world has changed. I know what year it is: there's a calendar in the kitchen. I know I'm really old, though I don't look it." He laughed, not happily. "Probably everybody I knew is either dead or old. Like Gary. He'd never know me now. And..."

Wib waited.

Henry turned around and looked at him. "My mother. She's dead, isn't she?"

Wib looked around the room, found no help anywhere, looked at Henry. "Yes."

"I thought so. I figured if she were alive you'd have said something." His voice was steady but his mouth was tight. "How do you know?"

"Mr. Ryder kept in touch with her. He told me. He, he said she never stopped looking for you. She always believed you were alive. She... she died three years ago."

"Just three years! If only I..." Henry put both hands to his head. "I have to think about that. And everything else. It's too much. I can't handle it all at once."

"So talk to me about it! Or stay here and I'll leave you alone, whatever you want."

"It's no good, Wib. Sorry. But I need to be back in the house. Just until I get my head around all this. And I should get to work on that broken place, too. I can feel it hurting from here."

Wib started to protest, then dropped his hands. There was an air

241

about Henry that told him there was no use arguing. Funny: at times he seemed just a kid, younger than Wib in some ways. Other times, he seemed grown up. Just now he was about as easy to talk to as a mountain with its head in the stars.

"I have to make supper for Mom and me," Wib said. "After, we'll go."

"You don't need to come with me."

"Yes, I do." He pointed at the bed. "Sit. Eat."

Henry smiled, finally. "Okay."

Chapter 48

WIB WAS IN the kitchen rolling a couple of frankfurters around in a pan and warming the rolls in the microwave when his mother came home. "What a day! Thank God it's Friday!" She went to the sink to wash her hands. Over the noise of running water she said, "Wib, I'm going out this evening. Just a couple of hours. You'll be okay by yourself for a while, won't you?"

"Sure!" He set an armful of jars and bottles on the kitchen table and they sat down and loaded up their hot dogs. His spirits rose. His mom out: that would make things easier. No need to sneak around. "Where you going?"

"Oh, just to meet Keith — Rebecca's dad — at Canadian Tire."

"Rebecca's dad? Why?" Wib lowered his hot dog.

"He emailed me at lunchtime. There's some repairs that need doing at his house and he has no idea where to start, poor man. So I said I'd help. Advice, mostly." She smiled to herself, took a bite, chewed and swallowed thoughtfully. "We might go for coffee afterwards. Tomorrow's Saturday, so if I sleep in it's no disaster."

Wib stared at her, while trying not to stare. She looked different. This was the end of a working day, and she wasn't all tense and tired. Instead she radiated energy and good cheer. Plainly it was good for her, making a new friend and going out. She never used to go out much after work, she was always too tired. So, yes, this was good.

But he wondered... "Is this a date?" he asked, before he could stop himself.

"A date!" She laughed and shook her head. Then thought about it. "Maybe, sort of." She put down her hot dog and looked at him.

"What d'you think about that?"

"Oh, nothing."

"Bother you?"

"Course not!"

Wib was washing the dishes and his mother was reading the hardware store ads when the phone rang. She grabbed the receiver from its cradle on the wall, listened, and said: "Sure, he's right here." She waved the receiver. "It's for you!"

"For me? Who would be calling me?" Wib crossed the floor to get it. "I don't know any... Oh, yeah."

REBECCA AND HER father ate dinner by themselves. Keith had started to make macaroni and cheese, but burned the sauce and let the pasta cook to a mush because he was thinking about other things, so Rebecca took over and made peanut butter and jam sandwiches and chicken noodle soup.

She had to do it mostly alone, and then organize the clean-up, because her father was distracted and kept drifting away. While he was drying dishes, he stopped three or four times to pencil a note on a foolscap pad that lay on the kitchen table. Rebecca rinsed out the sink, the way Wib did, and then went over to take a look.

"What's this? 'Kitchen cabinets — magnetic latches. TV stand — wobbly leg. Bathroom fan.'" She looked up. "What bathroom fan?"

"That metal grate in the bathroom ceiling?" Keith pointed upward. "There's actually a fan up there."

"You're kidding!"

"Well, it hasn't worked in years. Probably since before your time."

"Then why do we need it now?"

"No reason we can't have a ship-shape house, like civilized peo-

244

ple." He made another note and added, "These are all the little repair jobs I want to discuss with Sharon."

"You mean Wib's mom? Why?"

"Because she's going to teach me how to fix them. It's time I learned a few practical skills, don't you think?" He picked up the pad and stuck the pencil in his shirt pocket. "I'll be in the basement if you need me."

Rebecca finished cleaning up on her own, grumbling. Then she went upstairs to look out her window at the turret of the old Morphy house. Nothing to see there. She went into her closet and rifled through her collection of footwear, most of which was worn out or no longer fit her, finally settling for a pair of pink sneakers that did not totally shame her sparkly purple tee and bicycle shorts.

While in the closet she uncovered the jar of marinated mushrooms on the shelf in the back. They glowed faintly. Was there magic in them? Or poison? Who knew?

On an impulse she carried the jar downstairs and out to the back yard. She fetched a spade from the shed, dug a hole in the space between the lilac bush and the fence in the corner farthest from the house, opened the jar and buried the mushrooms. Then she put the jar in the recycling bin.

Did I do the right thing? She remembered a science fiction story she'd read in school. Come next spring, better keep an eye on that spot and whatever sprouted there.

Restless, unsettled, she flung herself on her bed and tried to read a magazine. Useless. She was too hot even with all the windows open, and there were too many things to worry about.

She went back downstairs. Her father was still clattering around in the basement. She went out the front door, fished out four hats from under the porch steps, beat the dirt and dead leaves off them, and tossed them through the open door into the hall. Then slumped

245

into a Muskoka chair on the verandah and watched the setting sun push golden spears through the trees of the little hilltop park and across the grass.

She thought about Henry. How was he going to get along in a brand new world, all on his own like that? It seemed exciting at first, but now she could only think of problems. He wouldn't be allowed to live on his own, or choose what he wanted to do, because in many ways he was still just a twelve-year-old kid. Somebody, probably Flora, would call Children's Services and Henry would be put in a foster home.

One place he wouldn't be: the old Morphy house. She wondered how he would feel if the house got demolished.

If it got demolished.... Rebecca sat up straight and wondered aloud: "He's still tuned in to it, or so he says. So...."

She jumped out of the chair and ran inside to the kitchen. Her father's cell phone lay on the table. Call Wib, yes, but how? What was his number? *Wait, maybe...* She touched a couple of keys and found a list of speed dial numbers. One of them was S. Willett. *Uh-huh.*

Once Wib was on the line she jumped right in. "Wib! Listen!" She told him what Flora had said about the house. "How will that be for Henry?"

"Might be the best thing for him."

"No way! Suppose he's still connected to it?"

"That may not be a problem." Wib sounded weird: stiff and stifled.

"Not a problem! Are you kidding? Won't it hurt him? Worse, if he goes *in* the house and he's in there when they knock it down — won't his molecules be all spread around? Wouldn't that kill him?"

"I doubt it."

Rebecca heard Sharon's voice in the background: "Oh, go ahead,

246

talk. Pretend I'm not here."

Wib covered the phone and said something, then uncovered it and said, "I'll see you in twenty minutes, okay?"

"Sure. At the Morphy house? With Henry?"

"Yup." He hung up.

Rebecca thumbed off the phone, then went to the top of the cellar stairs and called down, "Dad! I'm going out to meet Wib!"

"Wait!" Her dad trotted up the stairs, a can of machine oil dribbling over his fingers. "Don't stay out late. I'll be out too, but your gran should be back within an hour and you don't want her scouring the streets for you."

"Where you going?"

"Oh, just to the hardware store."

"Aha! To meet Wib's mom!"

"Well, yes, but there's no aha! about it. I've got my list of things that need repair and we're going to discuss supplies, tools and, I hope, techniques." His bony, ruddy face turned even ruddier than usual. Rebecca gave him a piercing look.

"Dad, admit it, you like her."

"Of course I do. She's quite likeable. Wonderful handyman, too."

"Handyman!" Rebecca would have liked to stay and pursue this topic, but she thought of Henry and ran out the door.

Chapter 49

WIB DECIDED not to tell Henry about the risk that the house might be demolished. Henry had enough to bother him now and he'd just get more bothered.

As they walked, he took a sidelong glance at Henry's face — inward-looking, anxious — and thought: Maybe it would be the best thing for the house to be destroyed. So long as Henry wasn't *in* it at the time, of course. That was what he'd wanted to tell Rebecca. If the house wasn't there any more, Henry would *have* to go free. He would have no choice: he wouldn't be able to hide himself away any more.

To lift Henry's spirits and keep him from worrying too much, Wib said: "I've been thinking. About my dad's medal."

"Oh!" Henry snapped back to the here and now. "You mean the one the black dog was *not* wearing."

"Right. That one was fake. So, where is the real one?"

"You have an idea?"

"Yeah. Here it is..."

THE SUN WAS nipping the tops of the trees in the west when they reached Number 3 Circle Road. The house was an angled black shape against the bright sky, except for the pale copper dome of the cupola, which caught the golden light around its edges.

Rebecca jumped up from where she'd been sitting, cross-legged on the grass under one of the big silver maples near the porch. "Henry! Did Wib tell you about what my gran—"

Wib cut her off. "We're going in to look for my dad's medal. Anybody inside?"

"Don't think so. There's nobody in the kitchen. And no lights on anywhere. Which is great, only all the doors are locked, even the one in back. I tried them."

"Let me try."

They followed him up to the front door and clustered around while he bent his head close to the panel and laid his hand softly on the brass lock plate. He closed his eyes and his expression went vague and distant. Wib heard the click and snap of a well-oiled lock. It took about three seconds, and they were in.

"Wow," Rebecca breathed. "If you can do that to any lock—"

"I can't. Just the ones in this house."

They decided it might be risky to turn on any lights, so Henry led them to the kitchen and lifted down two flashlights from the cupboard over the refrigerator. He handed one each to Wib and Rebecca.

"What about you?" Wib asked.

"Me? I don't need light."

As they climbed the back stairs, sliding the discs of light back and forth, Wib had the feeling that the house really, finally, was empty. It had that echoing feeling of a deserted house. The Sisters must have gone away. Maybe they'd only been waiting to see the finish: Owen gone, and Henry free. Maybe, Wib thought, that was why they'd come here in the first place.

This time, the secret panel at the base of the turret stairs was easy to find. As they crawled in, Wib in the lead, he said over his shoulder: "I remembered what Mrs. Doun said, 'He can change what you think you see.' And I thought, he could make us think the fake medal was real. So maybe, just maybe..."

He was afraid to look, in case he was wrong. They crowded together at the far end of the space and Wib and Rebecca ran their flashlight beams around and up and down, and...

Wib let out a gasp of relief and joy. The two beams zeroed in on a hand-sized blue bag nestling into the angle between floor and wall under the owl window. Its gold cord gleamed. There it lay, out in the open for all to see.

"It must've fallen out of the box with the other stuff and I didn't spot it."

"I didn't either," Rebecca said. "How could that be?"

"That shows the black dog had his claws into both your minds," Henry said. "He hid it from me, too."

Wib put out a wary hand. Suppose this was another illusion? But it wasn't: he knew that the moment he touched the soft velvet and felt the hard shape inside. He pulled open the gold cord and slid the medal out onto his palm. His heart gave a hard thump and he had to take an extra breath.

"There it is. There's the thing I stole."

They all studied the shining medal on its scarlet ribbon. After a moment Henry said, "It's cool. I get why you took it. Anyway, you were only six."

Rebecca bit her lower lip. "It's beautiful!" Then she giggled. "But I can see why it made your dad laugh."

"A bit too much?" Wib couldn't stop his smile this time.

She laughed again. "I think your mom has a great sense of humour. I like that."

"Quest achieved," Wib said quietly. "This time for real." The hard part was still to come, though: handing the medal to his mother and telling her what he'd done.

There was no reason to stay. They crawled out to the corridor. Wib stowed the blue velvet bag deep in a zippered pocket of his jeans, and zipped the zipper. No way he was going to risk losing it again.

Henry started down the back stairs, not waiting for a flashlight beam. "I'll have to find a place to sleep. Maybe the sofa in the north parlour, it looks comfy. Or — it's a warm night — maybe outside, under the stars. Y'know, its going to feel really weird, sleeping on an actual *thing*."

"What was it like before?" Wib asked. "Was it like floating?"

"No. It was like nothing. Like being nothing."

"I wonder if the Sisters ever sleep?" Rebecca said. "I guess we'll never get to figure out what they are. They seem to be gone now. That'll really fuss my gran, the tenants doing a runner in the night. Oh!" She whirled to a stop on the second-floor landing, her flashlight beam whirling with her. "That reminds me. Gran says..."

Wib opened his mouth, but there was no stopping her. Rebecca told what Flora had said about the house, how it might have to be destroyed if it was going to start falling to pieces. "See, if they aren't totally sure it's safe, they can't lease it out, and who'd want to buy it? And she said the repairs would be really expensive."

"Good thing you told me!" Henry started down the stairs again, full of purpose. "No sleep for me tonight!" Wib started to protest, but cut it off when Henry froze in mid-step. Rebecca aimed her flashlight down the stairs. The light caught two red eyes and a pitch-black shape that nearly filled the stairwell below them.

"But," Wib began. *I thought it was gone.*

"Back," Henry muttered, but there was no need, they were already stepping backward up the stairs, instinctively keeping their eyes on the thing below. On the landing they crowded out into the corridor, turned and raced toward the front of the house and the main stairs. Rebecca was in the lead, Henry in the rear, looking over his shoulder.

This time it was Rebecca who brought them to a halt, a stride short of the head of the main stairs. Wib craned over her shoulder and down the stairwell and glimpsed a dark shape that grew as it came.

"In here!" Rebecca yanked at Henry's arm. They ran into the

ballroom.

"The windows!" Wib hissed. "We can climb out to the porch roof!"

Someone laughed behind them. "You can try." Light burst around them.

They whipped around and stood shoulder to shoulder, Henry in the middle. The black dog wasn't there. A man stood in the centre of the room on the inlaid star under the chandelier, which hadn't worked in years but now shone like a galaxy of suns. A handsome, bronze-blond man, not big but radiant with power. A dark halo surrounded him: darkness visible, even in this dazzling light.

Chapter 50

OWEN SMILED and held out his hands, palms up. "So here we are at last! My son. My dear, dear boy. It's been too long!"

"Wib, Rebecca." Henry kept his eyes on Owen and tipped his head back at the doorway. "The way should be clear now. I can handle this. You get out."

"Like we would!" Rebecca said. Wib said nothing, just stayed. Movement in one of the mirror panels caught the corner of his eye, something white, but he didn't dare look.

"Owen, I'm sorry," Henry said, calm and quiet. "I'm sorry I had to turn you in. I'm sorry about that brick, too. That was an accident, it just fell. Because I was shaking so much."

"Shaking, right! What a rabbit you are!" Owen grinned. "No, less than that. A mouse! Come on, little mouse, come here. Oh, don't worry, I won't let the cat eat you. I want you all to myself." He held out his arms and crooked his fingers and stalked toward Henry, circling around to one side. He didn't look so handsome now. "Come here, little mousie. Come to Daddy."

Henry didn't move, just turned his head to follow. "You haven't changed. You're only more full of hate. But I have to warn you: I've changed."

"You! Warn me!" Owen threw back his head and howled with laughter.

"Wib. Rebecca. You've got to trust me now. Get away!"

"No way!" Rebecca gripped her flashlight like a club. Wib swept his light over Owen and saw that he cast a vague shadow. He was solid, almost. More solid than the dog. Owen laughed and sidled at

Henry, step by step, crouching, like a dog about to make a rush.

"Wib?" Henry turned his head to catch Wib's eyes. "Trust me?"

"Sure. But I'm not going anywhere." Movement flickered again in the mirror. This time Wib looked, and caught what might have been the end of a fluffy white tail whisking out of sight.

"Not to worry!" Owen laughed. "After I deal with you, my dear son, I'll deal with them. Then you'll all be mine, you and your chums. My own little team. Think of the possibilities!"

Henry went white. "You shouldn't have said that." His eyes closed tight, then opened. "I'm sorry for what has to happen now."

"Yesss," Owen hissed. "Oh, yes, little mouse, you will be very sorry. Very, very sorry."

Henry bowed his head meekly and stepped forward. Rebecca yelled "No!" and leaped to grab him. Wib darted after her, wrapped his arms around her and pulled her back. She fought like a fiend. "Whose side are you on?" she screamed.

"Henry said to trust him!"

"But he'll be killed. Or worse! We can't let him!"

She threw herself from side to side and nearly broke free. He shouted, "Listen to me! If you go and help him you'll be in the way!"

"But he—"

"He knows what he's doing!" Wib whispered in her ear. "Watch him!"

Rebecca grew quiet. Wib loosened his grip and she stayed put. Movement flickered again in the mirror and he looked and it was the white cat. It stared at Owen with shining green eyes. The tip of its tail flicked from side to side.

Henry took another step toward the centre of the room. "I know I don't look like much," he said humbly. "But I haven't been asleep all these years. I've watched and learned and thought about things. I know things now that you don't."

Owen growled in his throat. "Like what, little mouse?"

"Like why you're so miserable. It's the dog. You let the black dog in while you were still alive, and now it's eaten you up, nearly all of you, from the inside out."

"The black dog!" Owen howled with laughter. "You insect, I can be anything I want!"

"Anything except human. See, that's why I turned you in to the police. To stop you before it was too late. To give you another chance to choose being human." Henry took another slow step.

Owen laughed and laughed, and at last his laughter trailed off into head-shaking and chuckling. He fastened his smiling eyes on Henry.

"You chose wrong," Henry said softly.

They were face to face now. Wib stood so tense his whole body hurt. Rebecca grew still as stone beside him. She wrapped her hand around his and dug her fingers in.

Owen reached out both arms and Henry stepped into the embrace and slipped his arms around his father's neck. It looked like a loving hug. "I'm sorry," Henry said. "You need to show us what you really are."

Owen growled. Then stiffened and tried to pull away. Henry, unaccountably the stronger, held him close. "No more illusions." Owen lunged and snarled, but Henry held him.

And Owen changed. His chest thickened, head flattened and pushed out to a snout, ears pricked up, legs shortened and went crooked. Henry had his arms wrapped around a giant mastiff, a huge black dog. It howled and howled. Rebecca let go Wib's hand and clapped her hands to her ears. Wib felt sick.

Somewhere in the corners and heights of the room, or beyond the room, something was working away with a rhythmic clacking sound. It was very faint at first and Wib had no idea what it was.

"Is this what you really are now?" Henry looked straight into the mastiff's red eyes. Its fanged jaws slavered an inch from his face. It whined. "Or is there more? Or less?" He still looked like a twelve-year-old boy, but he didn't sound like one.

The black dog changed, but not back to Owen. It grew thinner and smaller, its snout and body lengthened, its legs shortened, and then it was a lizard the size of a cat. It slipped from Henry's arms and quivered on the floor.

The rhythmic clacking sound grew louder, and now Wib remembered where he'd heard it before.

"Dulcey's loom," Rebecca whispered.

The lizard shook itself and became a rat with long yellow teeth, humped back and naked tail. It scuttled away along the nearest wall. The white cat leaped from the mirror and snaked after it, belly to the ground.

Henry sagged. He looked as if he might fall down. Rebecca ran to him but stopped short and let her hands fall. She looked back at Wib with scared eyes.

"Is it safe to leave him... it... loose?" Wib asked hesitantly. Henry seemed a distant stranger.

"I don't think he can do any harm, not the way he is now." Henry hugged himself as if he was cold. "That's what he really is. He'll never be able to come back from that."

"Look," Rebecca whispered. "Over there."

The sound of the loom filled the ballroom. Shadowy figures moved at the end of the room, or beyond it, in a place untouched by the dazzle of the chandelier. Wib first recognized Aster, although her silver hair now flowed long and swung about her like a cloak. She pulled a thread from a rod wrapped in fleece and fed the thread to Dulcey. It was Dulcey who worked the loom, her braided hair a crown, and as she wove she sang.

Wib could see the fabric on the loom now. But it was so dark, its weave so distorted, that he could see no pattern. The sisters spun and wove and Dulcey sang, and the three who watched held tight to each other's hands.

The shadows stirred and Mrs. Doun took shape, as if she'd formed from shadow, all dark except for her death-grey face and hands. Aster and Dulcey faltered. The singing stopped. The loom fell silent. Dulcey rose and they stood with hands folded as if for a cere-mony. Mrs. Doun moved her ice-pale gaze over the fabric. Then turned it on her sisters.

"This web is finished," said the deep dark voice. Wib shivered.

Dulcey unfolded her hands. "Can we not correct it? There are flaws, but—"

"There can be no mending here. This one has made his choice." From the leather holster at her waist Mrs. Doun took a long pair of shears and cut the warp threads. Dulcey and Aster caught the web and unwound it from the loom. Most of it was discoloured and un-even, but here and there, close to the beginning, were a few bright patches. The first inch that had been woven, the last that was pulled from the loom, was a beautiful gold and sky-blue.

Dulcey and Aster folded the fabric between them. Now it looked very small, a thin dark square, with the bright newborn band almost lost in its darkness. Dulcey held the square against her heart for a moment. The Three Sisters stood still, facing each other, heads bowed. Then Dulcey held out the folded web on her palms and Mrs. Doun took it and the three walked away together into the darkness.

The light of the chandelier dimmed and went out.

"So," Henry said. "He's gone. It's over. Finally." He sounded coldly adult. Rebecca began to say something, and stopped herself.

"Henry," Wib said. "Are you okay?"

Henry sat down on the floor with a thump and burst into tears. He rocked back and forth, gasping and gulping, more like six years old than twelve. "Dad, I'm sorry," he sobbed, over and over. "I'm sorry. I'm so sorry."

Wib and Rebecca sat down on either side of him and held him until the storm was over. It took a long time.

Chapter 51

WIB KNEW he was in trouble the moment the police cruiser pulled in beside him on Victoria Avenue. It got worse, much worse, when the cops let him out in front of the house on Fairview Avenue and the front door burst open and his mother ran out and down the steps. The only good part was that his mother saved the blast for in private, disappointing the neighbours who'd come out to witness his humiliation.

The explosion started inside the front door and finished in the kitchen. "...nearly eleven o'clock, too young to be out this late, and what about Rebecca? I phoned Keith and she wasn't in either. He's worried sick!"

"She'll be home by now. She's fine. We're both fine."

"Is that all you have to say?" His mother dropped onto a chair, limp as a wrung-out rag. Wib's heart twisted.

"I'm sorry. I didn't mean to scare you."

"Where on earth were you?"

He took a breath. "We were in the Morphy house."

Her eyebrows pulled together. "That godforsaken place? At this hour of the night?"

"I was looking for something. I've been looking for it since we got to Amstey. And tonight I found it." He unzipped his pocket and pulled out the blue velvet bag. He held it out. She frowned at it. Then really looked at it, then at Wib. Then took the bag, loosened the gold cord and slid the medal out onto her palm.

"Oh, Wib..." Her face lit. He watched her eyes fill with wonder and amazement.

Worth it. Everything I've been through. Worth it.

"I thought it was stolen!"

"It was in the house all along. It got left behind when we moved away."

"But how did you find it?"

Now the hard part. "I had a good idea where to look. Because, um." He met her eyes. "It was me that stole it."

And he told her the story.

MIDWAY THROUGH Saturday morning and already sweating with the muggy heat, Rebecca met Wib at the end of the driveway at Number 3 Circle Road.

"Any trouble getting away?" he asked.

"Trouble! Dad and Gran were all for locking me in my room until I reach thirty!"

"So what did you tell them?"

"The truth. Part of it, anyway. Then as soon as my dad realized that I'd been helping you," she paused to poke Wib on the arm, "helping *you* find something that was important to your mother, he lightened up. Just a bit. Gave me a choice between being grounded for a week or losing my allowance for a month."

"And?"

"Well, I'm here, aren't I? Money I can live without, but I can't live without my freedom!" She made a fist and jabbed it into the air. She added: "How did your mom take it?"

"Not bad. Let's find Henry."

As they came close to the house they spotted a man in the meadow on the south side. "One of the neighbours," Rebecca said. "He was here yesterday." He was gazing open-mouthed at the house wall: at the place where the cellar door and the wall around it collapsed yesterday. They stood beside him and followed his gaze.

The man found his voice. "Can you beat that? This is impossible!

260

I have pictures! On my phone! It wasn't like this!"

"Somebody must've worked really hard to get this fixed so fast," Wib suggested, although not optimistic that the man would buy it.

"Fixed!" The man switched his glare to Wib's face. "Look at it!"

The door was back in place, its black paint shiny and unmarked. The timbers of the door frame and the stones of the foundation and the bricks on each side and above all looked — not as if they had been skilfully replaced or repaired, but as if they had never been damaged. Never been out of place. Even the mortar between the bricks looked old, though sound.

The man pulled out his cell phone, took a picture of the door, then punched in a number. *"Gazette*? Listen! I've got a story for you!"

Rebecca nudged Wib and tipped her head toward the house. They went in by the front door, which was still unlocked, and Wib shut it after them and turned the thumb latch. "Better lock all the doors," he said. The place'll be swarming soon."

"The Sisters will handle it, not to worry."

"If they're still here."

"Well, somebody's cooking. Smell it? Dulcey, any bets?"

It wasn't Dulcey. Henry turned and waved a spatula at them from where he stood at the kitchen stove in front of a large frying pan. "I'm rediscovering food!" he announced. "My mom taught me how to make pancakes a long time ago, and I never forgot. Took me a few tries to get them right, not soggy or burned, but I think I've nailed it now. Here, try some!"

He got three plates from the cupboard and slipped a pancake onto each of them. They were as big across as Wib's hand, soft yet firm, and the exact golden colour of a Jersey cow. Wib carried the plates to the table while Rebecca brought knives and forks, and Henry found the butter and maple syrup.

They dug in. Rebecca made greedy noises. "Henry, this is great! Fantastic!" He grinned, pleased. Wib looked him over and thought he looked tired, but happy. What happened last night might have left a shadow on him, but there was light there as well.

"Get any sleep?" Wib asked.

"Hour or so, near dawn. Looks good, eh? The door, I mean."

"Perfect!" Rebecca shovelled in another dripping forkful.

"Yeah, and that's a problem." Wib put down his fork. "There's going to be a fuss. No way anybody could rebuild that piece of the wall so fast, and make it look just like before. Not even with a lot of workers and machinery, and that's something the neighbours would've noticed. You're going to have Brendan Ryder knocking on the door any minute. What'll you tell him?"

Henry thought about that for a moment. "I always think it's best to stick to the truth."

"Which he won't believe."

"So I'll tell him to come up with a better story." Henry laughed. Then gave Wib a searching look. "But what about you? Did your mom.... How did that go?"

Wib filled his mouth with pancake, to give himself time. He felt shy about telling this. But at the same time he wanted to tell it. This was special and Henry should know it. Rebecca, too. Both of them got back to eating and didn't pester him, and that helped.

"First she chewed me out for giving her a scare," he said at last. "Then she forgave me for stealing the medal. She said she understood I did it because I missed my dad and I was too young to know better. Although I think I did know better."

Rebecca poised her fork. "And she's happy to have it back?"

"Yeah. Yeah, she is. She put it next to the big photo of my dad in the living room. And then she told me... See, I'd had it in my head all these years that I'd made her sad. But she told me that wasn't so." He didn't share the bit that came next. He kept that for himself.

Yes, Wib, the medal's precious to me. But my memory of Griffin doesn't depend on it. And another thing. I love Griffin and always will, but... well, I heard him say more than once: 'We need to remember the past, but not get stuck in it.' I've moved on with my life and you should too.

"So everything's all right now," Henry said.

"All right for Wib and me," Rebecca said, trying to capture the last drips of syrup on her knife. "But you've got a heck of a lot of things to think about. I mean, do you even have a change of underwear? Or money to buy food? And where are you going to live?" She waved her knife around at the kitchen. "You can't stay here, can you?"

"I'll think about that later. Time to wash up." Henry glanced at the kitchen window. People were moving around out there. "Then out I go to face the press."

NOBODY REALLY wanted to face the press. Rebecca had no trouble persuading Wib and Henry to detour to the cellar to see the starry river. The candle lantern wasn't on the landing, so Henry got one of the flashlights from the kitchen. In that strong white light, the cellar lost its air of mystery and danger. The room with the jars was just as before, but the next room was empty, the mushrooms cleared out and the shelves of flats gone. Mrs. Doun wasn't there, not that they'd expected to find her.

Rebecca hesitated before stepping over the threshold into the third room, fearing not what she might see, but what she might not see. And she was right. It was just a bare room with water gurgling under the flagstone floor.

In the centre of the floor was an iron grate about a foot square. The candle lantern, not lit, sat on the grate. Wib picked it up. "How did this get here? Rebecca, I guess you—"

"Not me. Somebody else."

She took it from his hand and lifted the chimney. The candle had burnt down to a half-inch stub. She thought of the warm yellow light that had shone, so brightly and so far, a homing beacon among the reflected stars.

Wib pulled up the grate and Henry shone the flashlight in. A dark stream rushed past beneath. There were no stars. Nothing glittered there except the reflection of the flashlight. Wib lowered the grate back into place.

Rebecca looked around sadly. "It *was* here. The woods, the river. The stars. You never saw such stars!"

"Another illusion." Henry turned to light their way out.

"I don't think so." Rebecca remembered floating in that river, letting it carry her, gazing up at those stars. She wouldn't forget, not ever. "I think that for a little while it was something else. Something more."

Chapter 52

THEY CAME OUT by way of the back door and walked along be-tween the house and the vegetable garden. Voices sounded at the front of the house, including one Wib recognized as Flora MacBeth's.

Rebecca stopped short. "Uh-oh. Never mind, Henry, we'll stick with you."

Henry led the way past the corner of the house, but he wasn't looking toward the front. He was gazing at the big silver maple with the limb that still threatened to crush the back wall of the garden. And he was looking, not at the tree, but at the three people in and near it.

Wib, Henry and Rebecca stopped in a cluster. "We thought you were gone!" Rebecca said.

Aster shrugged. She sat on the maple's lowest limb and swung her bare feet. "There's always a few loose ends to tie up. Like him." She pointed at Henry with her chin.

Wib looked toward the front of the house. People milled around in the meadow under the trees, waved their hands, pointed, talked, shook their heads. They appeared to be moving behind a barrier of thick glass. "Can they see us?" he asked.

"No. This is private." Dulcey stood in the bright sunshine outside the pool of tree-shadow. Her crown of braids shone like real gold. She wore the denim jumper that Wib remembered from the first day, or one just like it. She stood with sandalled feet firmly planted and hands in the big front pockets. He wondered....

"Sorry, I have no cookies for you today, Wib." Her smile was like the sun, rich and warm.

"No stars either," Rebecca muttered. The dark figure that stood

265

against the stone wall in the deepest, coolest shade stirred, but did not speak.

Henry walked forward, Wib and Rebecca flanking him, until they stood three paces from Dulcey. Her eyes stayed on Henry's face.

"I know why you're here," he said. "First I killed Owen and then I destroyed his ghost. I killed my father twice. Do what you have to do."

"You want us to judge you. To assign penance." Dulcey shook her head. "Judgment is not for us. That's your job, Henry."

"Owen wove his own destruction," Aster said.

Wib glanced sideways and caught Henry's expression, lost and confused. He wanted something sure to hold onto, even it was to be told how he'd be punished. "Then what's your job?" Wib demanded.

Aster jumped down from the limb. "None of your business!"

"No, Aster. They are all part of this." Dulcey looked at Henry again. "Our job is to help you follow the pattern of your life. Your proper road, if you like that better. Not to guide or even nudge, but to show you where to look for the ways and paths. What choices you make are your own."

"The scavenger hunt," Wib said stubbornly. "And those things that attacked us in the basement. That wasn't a nudge?"

"Right!" Rebecca snapped. "And Maura pushing me in the river!"

"Those things were not our doing. We only let them happen."

"But all that was to force Henry out, wasn't it?" Rebecca said. "If he hadn't bust out, we'd be dog food now!"

"Remember, Owen also wanted Henry out." Dulcey held out both hands, palms up, and turned over the left. "Owen's meddling wove a thread of darkness in Henry's web: a thread many years old." She turned over the right. "You two, with Maura, you wove a thread of brightness." She interlaced her fingers. "Making, together, a truly strange weaving!"

"You bet." Aster snapped up a blade of grass and nibbled it. "Beautiful, but weird. Totally."

"What will you do now, Henry?" Dulcey asked. "Will you go away from this house? Will you live as a normal boy?"

Yes, Wib urged him silently. Dulcey glanced at him and a smile lit her eyes.

"I don't know." Henry stuck his hands in his pants pockets and kicked at the grass. "I don't think I am normal. Maybe I can't ever be."

"But now you are free to choose."

"Am I? I'm free, but I'm still tied to this place. What kind of a life could I live?"

Dulcey looked straight up into the sun. When she looked back at Henry her eyes shone gold. "I can give you only this. Your mother would tell you to live in hope. Isn't that one of the things she used to say?"

Aster's icy eyes were serious. "Hope, yes, and more. To make life worth living, you need a quest. Find out what you're meant to do, and do that thing with all your heart and mind and strength."

Mrs. Doun moved forward, her cloak of shadow swaying. "Yet sleep on it." Her deep voice was unexpectedly gentle. "Night will bring dreams. And morning may bring more than one kind of light."

On the word *light* they turned inward, each reaching a hand to the others. They circled once and were gone. Where they had been the sunlight shimmered and faded.

Chapter 53

AFTER IT BECAME clear that the Three Sisters, whoever they really were, had decamped and were not to be found, Flora called a special meeting of the Town of Amstey Building and Properties Committee and proposed that in future the town should refuse all commercial leases for Number 3 Circle Road.

"It attracts oddities," she said. "From this point on we should engage normal, average families for long-term leases."

The Three Sisters sign came down and the A-frame club sign disappeared. The building safety inspector devoted the next week to examining the house. His report was glowing, but — if, like Rebecca, you read between the lines — puzzled. He had never seen a house of similar age in such good condition. And yet there was no indication of how the upkeep had been done. Certainly no local trades had had a hand in it.

Ten days after the Sisters vanished, Flora announced that a family, new to Amstey, had been found to lease the old Morphy house. By all accounts they were reliable, respectable and normal. They planned to move into the house at the end of August, in time for the children to start school.

Wib and Rebecca were told to stay away from the house, which in any case was locked up. A dozen or so paper bags had been found in the crafts room, each labelled with the name of a club member, containing objects and materials belonging to them.

Wib's bag contained his paper-making and fabric arts projects. He tore up the paper and dropped the pink knitting into a dumpster, except for the needles, which he gave to Maura.

Rebecca's paper bag contained the same things, plus her embroidered bag. She gave her hand-made paper to Flora. She gave the string/beads/feathers project to her father, claiming it was an art installation, and urging him to hang it in the living room.

The last thing that Henry said to Rebecca was, "Watch the cupola. I'll signal to you from there."

"Or you could phone."

"Can't. It's been cut off."

So Rebecca watched the cupola. Each day Wib asked if she'd seen Henry, but the answer was always no. Until the second-last day of August. That day, in the late afternoon, she looked out her bedroom window and spotted a figure waving at her from inside the dome's viewing slot.

She phoned Wib. Twenty minutes later they met at the Morphy house. Wib arrived panting, having run the whole way. He found Rebecca standing at the inner end of the driveway, under the silver maple closest to the porch, looking up at the house.

"But I don't see how we can get in," she said.

"If he wants us," Wib wheezed, "he'll unlock the door."

"Up here!" said a voice from the tree.

"Henry?" Rebecca looked up, half expecting to find him morphed into a twig. But no, there he was, sitting astride the third large limb from the bottom. When they climbed up to join him she saw that he still wore the same flare-bottomed pants, plaid shirt and brown wool vest, but they didn't look any dirtier than before. She wondered how he managed that.

"Are you okay?" Wib asked anxiously.

"Never better!" Henry beamed.

Wib studied him in a worried way, but Rebecca thought Henry was probably telling the simple truth. He looked like somebody who was regularly getting a sound night's sleep and eating a good breakfast, all bright-eyed and pink-cheeked.

"News?" she asked.

"Uh-huh. They came this morning to move some of their stuff into the house."

"Oh, the new family!"

"Right. I've made up my mind."

"About what?"

"I'm staying."

"But you can't!" Wib yelped. "Not with people here!"

"Why not? I did it before, years and years."

"Yes, but then you were stuck *in* the house. People didn't know you were here, not really. You couldn't do that again."

"Sure I could."

"But—"

"Look, I know you're worried. Don't be." Henry smiled at them both, calm and adult, very like Dulcey. "It cuts both ways, you see. I was part of the house, but the house also came to be part of me. Without me to take care of it, a few years from now it could be falling down. And without the house I'll be a turtle without its shell."

"But you're not a turtle!" Wib snapped. "You're human!"

"I'm not so sure. I think I may've become something different." Henry leaned back and gazed thoughtfully through the stirring leaves at the porch roof. "Besides, now I'm not stuck. I can move in and out of the house, no problem. I can go where I want, do what I want. Even go downtown, if I want. Cinnamon buns at Padgetts!"

"What'll you use for cash?" Rebecca asked. "You need a lend?"

"No problem! I helped a kid wash car windows and the drivers gave us money."

"What!" Wib nearly lost his grip on the tree. "You can't do that!"

"Why not?"

"You're too young. People will notice and the police will nab

270

you!"

"Not if I keep moving. Besides, I still have that talent for not being noticed." He smiled. "The point is, I'm free to come and go now. I'm not trapped. That makes all the difference."

"Well, okay, but... I mean, don't you want to get away from this place?"

"Yeah," Rebecca put in. "See the world! Learn stuff! Grow up!" She forgot where she was and flung her arms wide, embracing all the possibilities of life on Henry's behalf.

Next moment she lost her balance. Wib grabbed at her but missed; she shrieked and fell. The moment after that she was rising, floating up through the tree on the bending tips of a thousand leaves. She burst from the top like a swimmer breaking the surface of a pool and sprawled there on her back, bobbing on the leaf tops, blinking up at the bright sky. A moment later Wib burst up beside her, flailing and open-mouthed.

"No, this house is a good place," said the tree in a rushy voice. "And it will stay that way if I take care of it."

"But — what'll you do here?" Wib demanded. "What kind of life can you have?"

"Well..." The tree waved its branches back and forth, musingly. "I like the look of this new family. There are two kids, a boy your age and a girl a couple of years younger. And after they go away, other people will come to live here. Other kids. They'll need protecting."

"From what?" Rebecca made treading-water motions with her arms and legs, although she wasn't sure that was helping. "The black dog is gone, right?"

"Yes, but Owen wasn't the only ghost. The white cat's still around. And there are other things, good and bad. Other dangers." The leaves playfully bounced Wib and Rebecca like a trampoline, up in the air and down. "You'll come back, the two of you? I'll miss you if you don't."

"Of — course — we will!" Wib gasped.

"But Henry, what d'you mean, what other—" Rebecca shrieked again as the tree wrapped her in leaves and floated her down to the ground. She landed on the grass on her feet. Wib landed beside her, fell over, and scrambled up again.

"Henry!" they shouted. "Henry!"

The leaves whispered, but made no words. The tree was just a tree.

About the author

PATRICIA BOW lives in Kitchener, Ontario. She has written more than twenty books for young people. To find out more about Patricia and her work, visit http://www.execulink.com/~thebows/patricia.htm.

www.ingramcontent.com/pod-product-compliance
Lightning Source LLC
Chambersburg PA
CBHW060530260626
47161CB00003B/836